Dreaming of Oranges

An Unreliable Memoir

Dreaming of Oranges

An Unreliable Memoir

Marcelline Thomson

Bowerbird Books
284 Fifth Avenue, New York, New York 10001

ISBN: 1983666440
ISBN-13: 978-1983666445

First Edition 2018

Jacket Design by Nicole Parker King

For David

dreams become possible

Contents

—to go on passionately searching for

what I did not dare to find.

—Lawrence Durrell

Prologue

Part One: Out of Beirut in a Hurry 3

Part Two: Leaving Home 11

Part Three: Alex 51

Part Four: Aphrodite's Island: A Love Story 87

Part Five: Beirut 125

Part Six: Into the Desert 165

Part Seven: Another Stranger 217

Part Eight: Jean 255

Acknowledgments

Prologue

It seemed like such a good idea. Graduation looming, time to leave our little island of privilege, the sheltered college for women in Westchester north of New York City. But what next?

The expectation was marriage. Alien (almost) as joining a convent, another career choice available, one embraced by some of our classmates. We, pal Jean and I, wanted no part of home sweet home, baby makes three, life in the suburbs. This was not based on any deeply held conviction about the status of women and their inferior role in marriage and society. We wanted to escape, that was it. Jean had more serious reasons as I would come to find out, but this is what propelled us.

This and Lawrence Durrell's Alexandria Quartet, the final book published in 1960, the year before we graduated. There, in black and white, a blueprint for adventure. We could go to the places he described! Why not? Alexandria, of course, and Cairo. And how far can that be from Beirut, the Paris of the East? What about Damascus too—perhaps a conversion like Saul's? (Unlikely.) And Athens, the cradle of democracy. We both sought more. Neither of us could have explained what that might be although we spent many hours discussing it.

Now, today, I close my eyes and am instantly back.. If I let myself remember Andreas, the sun-drunk sea of Greece, that feeling of freedom, of being lifted out of myself, young, tearing into the wind, it all comes rushing back. Ecstasy. Knew it then. New then.

The scent of lemons, the trembling hand on my skin, the smoke of kebobs in the souk, a muezzin's cry, the clutch of dust and sand at my throat ...

PART ONE

Out of Beirut in a Hurry

January 1962

1

Jean, stop scrabbling around in your bag like a drunk squirrel! There's a checkpoint up ahead. Lots of uniforms and they don't look friendly."

Tearing along the bleak coast road in a banged-up taxi on the way to the airport, the same road we'd taken to La Gondola for lunch a few weeks back, past mounds of mud and sand littered with refuse, our last chance to get out of Beirut, a driver who spoke no English, or French for that matter, and so jumpy he might dump us anywhere and take off leaving us stranded.

"I can't find my passport!"

No passport. They would search us for sure. Carrying letters to King Hussein, so we were told, no idea what they said. Stuffed in our bras, hidden in lingerie in our luggage. No Arab would go there. And yet fingering our underwear hadn't bothered them in the slightest when they'd stormed in and arrested Asif. Pointing machine guns at the three of us. Days ago, yet in a way a lifetime.

"If I can't find it, you go on."

"Oh, sure. Think about what you're saying. Carrying messages we can't read to people we don't know …

The driver hit the brakes, cursing and calling on Allah at the same time. As we slid off the seat, I got a glimpse of the sea sparkling in the sun.

"Got it!" Jean yelled, holding her passport aloft.

"Ahlan wasahlan. Going somewhere?" The man peered

through the window at us sprawled on the floor. Rotting teeth, bits of gold filling flashing, comical more than menacing. Except for the gun.

"Airport?" Jean said.

We pulled ourselves up. More soldiers crowded the car. They yanked out the driver and shoved him in the direction of the makeshift command post in the middle of the road.

"Passports!" We handed them over.

They passed them around, a great show of examining and comparing photographs with our faces. Two marched off with them, while the others milled around or squatted, smoking and talking. Our driver had vanished. We checked our watches. If they kept this up it would be a close call making our flight.

"Do they think we've got all day to sit here admiring the scenery?"

"Why don't you march on up there and tell them we've got a plane to catch. Take Toothless with you." All this was her fault. Or was it mine for suggesting we come here in the first place?

"Was that supposed to be sarcastic?"

"A great weapon, sarcasm, when scared shitless. Which, quite frankly, I am."

"Okay, I know I've been a little cavalier … but … what do you think they're doing?"

I didn't want to hear any "but." What about that empty room at the hotel we just fled, the St. Georges? That odious General Osir coming down the hall? Afraid, then, for Asif. Now convinced he'd given us all the slip, even the wily Osir.

"What will they think we're doing?"

"Joyriding around out here, what else? What kind of stupid question is that?"

She kept at it. "What if we miss the flight? Can't be that many to Amman. And they said the airport was going to be shut down, we'll be stuck."

"Jean. Stifle the 'buts' and 'what ifs.' We can't let on we're nervous so let's talk about something else. God, it's hot."

The sun was high, nothing to shade us on the side of the road. Not a single car had passed. The soldiers came back, without our passports. One of them opened the door on Jean's side and motioned her to get out.

"No!" she said. "Why … why me?"

He motioned again, impassive. She squeezed my hand. Murmured something I didn't understand. When she climbed out of the taxi, she tried to take her handbag. He threw it back inside. They disappeared into the command post.

So this was it. They would question us, her first, then me, smack us around, take us back to Beirut to one of those jails the prince had described. Leave us there to rot, nobody to know or care what happened. Gone.

Fear rolled over me in waves, along with the heat, the nausea. I started to sweat. I lit a cigarette, hands shaking. I stuffed it out. What was I thinking? I could hardly breathe as it was. What were they doing in there? What doing to her? What should I do? Force back the tears to begin with, I would not give them that satisfaction.

Damn Asif. And damn our own stupidity. How could he do this to us? I knew he couldn't be trusted, had felt it from the very beginning. More and more as things didn't add up and Jean got more and more infatuated. The two of them always whispering, all so mysterious. They thought I didn't notice? I just didn't say anything and now look where we were.

That was a scream. Quickly muffled. No mistake, a woman's scream. I had to get in there. I gripped the handle of the door and struggled to get it open. A soldier jumped up and slammed it shut.

He didn't look at me. He went back to squat with the others, silent, smoking, working their worry beads.

For the first time in a long time I prayed. Not for the first time I wanted more than anything to go home.

Sensing movement, I opened my eyes. A merciful moment had taken me along the green strip of coast down towards Sidon and Tyre, crowded with orange and lemon orchards leaning against arched stone walls and rushing rivers and sleepy canals on a day in the sun, beautiful like Eden.

I looked around. Nothing much had changed, the checkpoint, the soldiers, still there, talking in low voices, the stifling heat of the taxi. No sign of Jean. How cowardly to just sit here and wait, numb, chasing my fears around in circles. What would they do if I just started yelling my head off?

A small delegation was coming towards me. My turn. And if they demanded the letters, what should I do? Give them up, of course. Take a deep breath, try to be brave.

The rabble of voices was sounding everywhere at once. A car came speeding in from the other direction, pennants waving brightly from the aerials. It skidded up to the checkpoint in a swirl of dust. The soldiers scrambled to their feet, brushing themselves off, stamping out cigarettes. The group on its way to me turned. They saluted the officer who got out of the car, pressed uniform, medals. He walked smartly into the shack.

In minutes the rabble was giving way for him to pass, Jean firmly in his grip looking shaken but defiant. He was hurrying her along. He opened the car door, "*Mademoiselles, merci.* You may go."

"*Maintenant*?" she asked.

What? Asking if he meant now? Did she want to hang around and discuss it?

"*Oui! Tout de suite.*" He handed over our passports and our tickets.

Affecting a composure I certainly didn't feel, I thanked him, terrified that there might be some mistake, that he might change his mind, desperate not to look too relieved and therefore guilty. Of something.

Our driver appeared from nowhere. In one motion he was in the taxi, got it started and roared off down the road.

"You lucky peoples!" he shouted when we'd gained some distance from the checkpoint. "You too lucky peoples!" He hunched over the wheel, mopping his face with an oily rag, leaving dark streaks.

"Not in my lifetime up till now …" He finished in a stream of Arabic and fell silent, one hand on the wheel, fingers of the other tearing through worry beads. I looked out the window, hardly daring to give voice to the question: What happened back there?

The driver started shouting again. "Army too crazy peoples!" He turned around to look at us. "You too crazy peoples."

"Save the speeches, Mister. Keep your eye on the road and get us to the damn airport." We'd escaped by the skin of our teeth to crack up with this lunatic?

He dropped us at the terminal, refusing to take any money, refusing even cigarettes. As if this would make him an accomplice in whatever we were up to. The Arab way, nothing at face value. A lesson I wish we had learned.

How had we gotten ourselves into this mess?

PART TWO

Leaving Home

2

She was the first girl I saw on campus that fall of 1959. I, a transfer student, feeling as foreign as an immigrant, trying fiercely not to give myself away. She, a vision out of *Vogue*, tall and slim in a swirly blue skirt and white silk shirt, walking towards me in a crowd, running a hand through her blonde hair and laughing. How I longed to be in that golden circle.

"Ever see so many penguins in one zoo in your life?" she called.

True, the place was crawling with nuns. In their black habits and white wimples, they did look like penguins.

"Just wait till you get a load of the rules they've got around here. *Merde!* We'll be seniors before we've memorized 'em. Should we survive that long. Welcome to Camp Lejeune!"

She'd nailed me, the newcomer. More laughter from the group. I stood there, slack-jawed.

"So where you from?"

"Minnesota."

"No kidding! Most everybody's from out here. Like me, I'm from the city. So boring."

The city. New York City, she meant. *Boring?*

"Whereabouts in Minnesota?"

"A little town near the Mississippi, south of Saint Paul. No place you've heard of." Plenty of people in Minnesota had never heard of it. "I spend a lot of time on the river," I added.

"How utterly fascinating," said one of the goldens, moving

pebbles on the path with her painted and sandaled toe.

"Just riveting. I'm on the edge of my seat," said another.

"Cut it out," said their leader. "I'll bet you've got one of those cute Midwest names like …"

"Sirrine. After my grandmother." Might as well hang out a sign saying *different*.

"Nice. Different! Mine's Jean." She made a face. "So ordinary. But I tell the nuns I was named for Jean Harlow. Horrifies them."

Catholics were supposed to be named for saints, not movie stars. And certainly not a sex bomb like Harlow.

"Sirrine doesn't sound Midwest."

"It's French."

"You do look … Mediterranean, I guess. I thought it was all Swedes and Norwegians out there where you're from. Speak French?"

"Some. And you?"

"*Mais oui*. Pounded into me in prep school. *Compris*?"

Yeah, I *compris*-ed. Understood all of it: New York, Park Avenue from the look of her, prep school, throwing *merde* around like she'd spoken French all her life. A girl who'd been around, and around was where I desperately wanted to be. But right now, let me out of here or at least think of something clever to say. By the time I could muster a sound, tell her my last name in case she wanted to look me up, it was lost in their wake. She had drifted away with the others.

Jean Hayes, a junior like me, English major like me, in the same classes almost every day. It didn't take long to realize how smart she was, that underneath the glib patter—the voice that could be low and slow or light and lilting—was someone who took life and the world seriously, an intensity coexisting with (camouflaged by?)

a breezy detachment. Nor did it take long to see that her beauty had a fragile quality. Even when she turned on her most dazzling smile, that Colgate smile declaring *I'm on top of the world and things couldn't be better up here*, a sadness lingered in her eyes, eyes that changed from blue to green depending on what she_wore. Mine were brown, no matter what I wore.

What most defined her was not her beauty or her sadness but a profound loneliness, never mind those glittering girls gathered around her. More than me, she didn't belong. Part of it was the Catholic institution we were in. If I refused to be pious, like so many in this setting, I accepted faith as a given. Jean challenged every bit of it, willing to pull the whole edifice down if that's what it took to get at the truth. This was what she was after, always. The truth. Bolder than anything I'd ever done, her unflinching questioning, at once shocking and thrilling. How could I know then how much more there was to it?

Consider this. A required course called Christian Marriage, talking about the relative influence of Augustine and Aquinas. I was sitting there wondering what any of this had to do with marriage when Jean said, "I don't buy it for a minute. Grown men discussing how many angels can dance on the head of a pin? What's the point of this nonsense?"

Father Mayhew sputtered, went silent. For some reason none of us could fathom, a Jesuit was brought in to teach this profound subject. Our penguins were their equal in scholarship any day of the week. And anyway, what about someone with a little experience?

Jean didn't let up. "Nietzsche had the right idea, forget about organized religion, ban it as a threat to civilization. *Thus Spake Zarathustra* and all that."

Nietzsche. I hadn't given a thought to him. Francoise Sagan was more my cup of tea. I told her how much I admired her audacity, her courage.

"We're going to be great pals," she said, fixing me in that gaze that defied anyone to turn away.

We were inseparable, smoking in our section of the Snack Bar, meeting in the dining hall, sneaking out of chapel, pushing the limits of curfew and covering for each other. I went home that summer feeling that I was in possession of a great prize, thrilled that someone so sophisticated had chosen me to be her friend.

Not even the absence of my favorite cousin, who had married and moved away, could put a dent in my happiness.

Have I given the impression that Jean and I were always serious? That would be wrong. We found humor in almost everything, a word, a look sending us sailing off on waves of laughter. Chances are you'll find yourself in some dicey situations if you consort with someone whose operating manual begins with "Can't we complicate it?" There are consequences. I should have thought about this.

Back at school, senior year, we went into Manhattan on a string of Saturdays to model for charity luncheons at the Plaza, the Waldorf, the Park Lane and other top-notch hotels where we paraded past tables of blue-haired ladies stuffing themselves on Crab Louis and Lobster Thermidor. Not a prayer they could squeeze into any of those little numbers from Bendel's, Bonwit's or Bergdorf's. But illusion was all. By December any illusion that this was fun was gone. We were bored.

Let's crash the cocktails! Berfield, who was in charge of the shows, was a good egg. She didn't say a word when we swanned past her sipping our Bloody Marys.

I clinked Jean's glass. "Here's mud in your eye, as my dad would say."

"What mine would say is unprintable. For this bunch,

anyway."

I looked around at the bunch in question. "Wouldn't that be most of the dictionary?"

"Hey, Pal, we're losing our touch," Jean said. We were doing another quick change behind the makeshift stage. "Let's see if we can liven up this joint."

Teetering on too-high heels, I was more worried about falling on my face than losing my touch.

She grinned. "I've got just the ticket, an experiment worthy of Edison. We'll kill the lights. See if the blue-hairs out there glow in the dark."

By God, they did! We fled before we were fired.

The Bloody Marys having been such a hit, we decided to head over to the Biltmore near Grand Central for another. No one there to flirt with, only a few barflies in a corner booth waiting for the train that left last week. This time, the drinks had the opposite effect. We were morose.

"I guess we loused that up, all right."

"It's not like they were paying us a king's ransom."

"But a great excuse to come into the city."

"To hang out with …"

"I know, I know. Blue-hairs, the old biddy brigade."

We decided to phone Berfield on Monday to make amends. I positioned myself in the booth at the end of the hall, turning my back on Jean who was making sad faces through the window, trying to get me to laugh. We hoped for a reprieve. Snickering on the phone would not be helpful.

Berfield doused that hope in a cold bath and quickly. "Hey, kiddo, you don't need to apologize to me," she said. "You've been good sports, you two, and your little caper was harmless, if you're asking. I went to bat with the powers that be, but no go. I'll say this, those old gals know when some spunk and sparkle comes into a room. They're going to miss you. Dammit, so am I."

"There's nothing we can do?"

"Nope." She sighed. "They always said they wanted the two of you, the blonde and the brunette. What a combo! Maybe this time one of you should have flown solo."

"Well, that's a prick in our little balloon," said Jean.

"With a fat glove of guilt laid on. Packs a wallop, our Berfield. As if we weren't feeling bad enough."

"Catholics. Jews. Guilt. The holy trinity. Guess we'll have to scare up some other mischief."

We did. I would have gone to the ends of the earth for her. And I did.

For a time she was the enemy.

The trouble started on a holiday weekend. Instead of the ski slopes of Vermont, we decided to stay at school with the bookworms. By Sunday morning snow was falling fast. In minutes we were on the phone calling for a taxi to the station. Marooned in Manhattan was better than being stuck on a deserted campus in Westchester. Maybe I'd have a chance to meet The Countess. That's what Jean called her mother.

As soon as we got in, I called Nick—Nicky, then, still on good terms—to meet for dinner. Now, a girl with any sense at all would have stayed miles away from this guy who had a line as long and well rehearsed as The Rockettes at Radio City Music Hall. He also had the brooding looks of Montgomery Clift and knew his way around the hip downtown scene, Chumley's and those dim jazz joints like the Five Spot that reeked of reefer and hinted at things I could only imagine.

Was I in love with him? I thought so, in that naïve way with the first one who pays attention. The seduction of being chosen. We were not intimate, oh, no, not with preserving virginity drummed into us every waking hour. We could sleepwalk through an entire semester and still not escape that lesson. Our bodies, temples of the Holy Ghost, would rise triumphant on the wedding day, miraculously freed from the stricture that we not be touched. Virginity defined everything: honor, duty, a clear complexion, stars staying fixed in their heavenly course depended on it. Sex unsanctioned by matrimony enslaved you like heroin, until you were ruined, groveling in the gutter with all the other addicts. A fallen woman.

There was never a question of dropping Jean from the dinner plan. We were still on drinks when she made a play for him. Which Nick, honorable character that he was, didn't exactly ignore.

"So what've you been doin' these days?" she asked. The drawl was a warning, I'd heard it before. It was both funny and sexy. I could see he was agreeing with the sexy part, definitely not laughing.

"Studying acting."

"Really? That is the one thing I'm dyin' to do."

First I'd heard of it. She started in on Stanislavsky and they were off. Actors Studio, Strasberg, Ionesco, he smiling at her like he'd found the one woman in the whole world capable of probing the depths of his *avant-garde* soul.

"Oh, I bet you're good, I bet you're *really* good." Leaning across the table under her halo of blonde. "Star material, that's what I'm bettin' on."

I looked at her in the flickering light of candles dripping over Chianti bottles, playing with her food, devouring him. That green-eyed gaze.

"Yeah, as a matter of fact I am good," he said, ever modest. "But I still have to do my time for Uncle Sam."

The expression on her face. As if he just said he had

seconds to live. "What a waste!"

He looked longingly at her. "Why not come downtown, watch me do a scene?"

What was *this*, if not a scene?

"Oh, I'd love to, I truly would." Gushing. Foaming at the mouth more like it.

Stunned, my face flushed with shame, I hated her as I had never hated anyone in my entire life. Actually it was a toss-up between the two of them. I couldn't wait to take my bodily temple and get out of there. And yet, the recklessness, the abandon—part of me had to admire it, even then. So *un-Catholic.* We told ourselves we were anarchists when it came to love—we could get pretty worked up over the idea. But they were the rebels, I realized. I was playacting and much too civilized to throw a tantrum. This is what happens to a small-town transplant: *Be civilized*, The Scold hisses in your ear, and no one will discover you're an imposter.

I was stuck with her. That's how permissions worked. *Sign out together, sign in together, no monkey business.* The refrain of the nuns on desk duty.

Interrupting the cozy twosome, I asked for the check. Nick offered, but I insisted on a three-way split, even more enraged that I had to pay for my misery. Snowstorm over, we went back to school. We could have spent the night at the Barclay, a quiet old hotel on Lexington and 49th Street sanctioned by the college, but I couldn't imagine sharing a room with her now and making this shambles of an evening even more expensive. I'd have to give up my chat with Jimmy, the hotel doorman, which I always looked forward to. No one else stopped to talk to him. I guess they were in a bigger hurry. Or maybe proving I had my own friendly doorman in Manhattan meant that I had truly arrived.

Tramping through deserted streets to Grand Central, we saw a couple gaily throwing snowballs, their shouts echoing off the darkened buildings. We rode in silence, forced to sit side by side in the crowded train, staring straight ahead, not even a pretense of looking out windows fogged over in the heated car. When I got to bed I cried and cried. I had lost them both.

For weeks we didn't speak, until she wrote a note attempting to explain. It was pretty theoretical, like French novels. She was good at that. "Sometimes you want pleasure for its own sake, without a reason. To escape what you are, if only for a moment."

Whatever that meant. There were more notes and pleas to forgive. I didn't relent for some time, I was too hurt, though I recognized that her betrayal had flushed out his. She had exposed the rat. To avoid her, I studied in the library instead of the Snack Bar, with marked improvement in my grades. I had to work harder than she did and I had slipped. In the end, I admit I was taken with the drama of it all—fighting, making up. Besides, we were studying existentialism.

At around this time, still atoning, she started to tell me about The Countess.

"Why Countess?" I had asked early on, fantasizing a Count, a manor house, croquet on the lawn under white parasols.

"My father called her that, said she carried herself like she was born with a tiara on her head." Both her parents were from the Deep South, one of those place names with a dozen syllables, moss growing on every one of them.

Gradually more details of the story came out. Her mother, born out of wedlock as it was quaintly put, a great beauty, much sought after, had just taken up a modeling career when she met Quinton Hayes, some years her senior. A prominent lawyer for one of the big railroad companies, he had argued before the Supreme Court, greatly impressing this daughter of a country lawyer. The marriage was a ticket out of poverty, a bid for stability, at least that was the impression Jean gave.

"I don't have a good example for how to relate to a man," she said in one of these conversations.

You might start by throwing out Dorothy Parker, I thought.

"Mine aren't exactly lovebirds either. But your father calls her Countess, I thought he admired her."

"Bitch more likely. Now."

"He says *that*? To her face?" I was deeply shocked.

"When he's been drinking. Gets pretty nasty. Says southern dames have brains the size of lima beans, their only talent is turning flirtation into high art. This is my mother he's talking about."

I didn't point out that she inherited the talent.

"He says she traps men like kudzu. But I'm not sure she even likes them. Men, I mean. She's charming and they admire her and want to be around her. He can't keep up, so he sulks. He told her she was a perfect stocking present, said it in front of their friends at Christmas dinner. Well, you get the picture."

"*Ouch*. What did she say?"

"Nothing. Left the table in tears."

"And you? What about you?"

"Made myself scarce. I never did have the guts to stand up for her. But I make it a point to go on calling her The Countess. It cured me of the holidays, that's for sure. Any more questions?"

No. But I wondered about it. I wondered about so many things she told me. How her father broke down when they lost a baby and couldn't have another one. How her mother went on spending sprees, ordering six Pauline Trigère outfits, all the same cut, all the same color, emerald green. How she came home from school one time to find dozens of sunglasses lined up on a table in the lobby, as if everybody in the whole apartment building was going on a cruise, all different colors like a display of captive butterflies.

Secret by secret, confidence by confidence, Jean won my trust. It was the coin of our complicity. I was stepping into knowledge of the kind of life I was sure no one at home could contemplate, let alone understand. My mother would never do anything like that. She was much too busy fretting over whether I was "running to extremes"—falling out of trees, flying off toboggans, smoking in the woodshed behind my grandmother's house with my cousin Kitty, sneaking into dance halls passing for eighteen, learning how to pick up boys—trying to ward off adolescent high jinks with incantations sounding like they issued forth from a cave: *Keep your voice down. Don't overdo it. We are but pilgrims to eternity*. That last was a real thigh slapper.

As far as I was concerned, she could join the rest of the women who sat waiting for it in their pews, hair under their kerchiefs as grey and dead as their dreams. I would not be one of them. That was my solemn vow.

3

Swarming through the corridors of the dorm on our way to the dining hall, a hundred pairs of heels chattering like cicadas, I heard Jean call my name. She caught up with me on the path, evening closing in, squeezing light from the sky like the quick smothering of a fire. I shivered.

"Several more months …" Her gesture took in the campus. I thought she was going to start grousing about having nothing to do for excitement. The outlook was grim. Jack Kennedy elected, no invitation to his inauguration no matter how hard we'd campaigned, weeks of thesis writing in the offing.

"So, here's where things stand," she said. "Pretty boy in the White House, the ingrate. In June we're liberated. Then what? I see no knights charging over yonder hill to carry us off. Not that we'd want any."

"T'would be a miracle, considering our track record."

"But you're out most weekends."

"Preppies all. Wind 'em up and they look and sound the same."

"That would make the heart sing."

She was right about the future. Without a man in your pocket it was a difficult question mark. Slinking back home with our new ideas was unthinkable. Home meant that lonesome town where you could see clear to the end of Main Street, out past the grotto where we marched in procession to the Blessed Virgin in May, carrying our lilacs and lilies of the valley, the fruits of our breasts (plums, pears, melons?) ripening beneath our white dresses. Out to where fields of corn and hay and clover stretched as far as the eye could see in an emptiness so vast nothing could fill it. No, not back there. "Love turns any old place into Eden for a while," my aunt once said. I never did believe it.

"I'd like a little adventure before I settle down," I said. "Travel, see the world."

"Where to?"

"I don't know, haven't gotten that far."

Her face lit up at this glimmer of a plan. "Let's skip the mess hall, get a burger in the Snack Bar and plot."

"We won't get out of there before midnight and I have a paper due." I glared at her. "Don't even think of deserting me."

"*Merde!*" We continued on in a gaggle of girls.

Shrieks shattered the buzz of conversation. The ultimate ritual of senior year. Our class president, a tall redhead, had kicked off her heels and climbed on a table, where she stood like Lady Liberty among plates of meatloaf, mashed potatoes and something resembling spinach. Nuns along the walls like guards in old prison movies.

"You know why I'm here," she teased. "Sue … Sue Maloney got a ring last night!" The grand prize we were groomed and sent away to school to win. Lady Liberty looked over at Sue's table, building suspense. Could the ring man be someone new?

"From Ted Reynolds!"

No mystery there, we had all seen *him* hanging around. A frenzy erupted anyway, even from those headed for the convent. Not from Jean and me. We weren't ready to join this assembly line, predictable marriage, beginner apartment.

"I'm going to gag," she said. "Let's beat it."

The Snack Bar was shrouded in smoke. We could just

make out the regulars: Peggy, collecting signatures on a petition for her boyfriend to come back after yet another quarrel; Mary Feeney (we had to use two names to tell all the Marys apart), clucking about the evil in the world; Clare, dawdling at the piano. She saw us and launched into a few bars of Jean's signature torch song, "Love for Sale," before starting on mine, "Cry Me a River," Jean vamping, me wailing, the rest cheering us on.

Still going strong when the warden—that's what nuns in charge of the dorms were called—closed the place down and chased us to bed.

"We can do this, you know." We were in our usual corner of the Snack Bar. I was reading the final book of Lawrence Durrell's *Alexandria Quartet* and interrupting her concentration on Hegel. Jean was a whiz at philosophy while the rest of us struggled, tempted to agree with Mary Murphy that it was cocktail chatter by a bunch of dead men.

"Do what?" She didn't look up.

"Go to Alexandria."

That got her attention. "We can?"

"We can!" It seemed so clear. *Alexandria.* The promise of finding all that we yearned for, the hushed voices of lovers in the city's velvet evenings and pale dawns. "Greece too," I said, appealing to her admiration of things Greek. "Beirut, even."

It was Mother O'Grady who started it all. She swept into class one morning, eyes full of mischief instead of the customary disdain inspired by our homework. "Girls!" I have just finished reading the most captivating books. Romantic too."

Romantic. We had been through half a semester of Modern Poetry without mention of the word. O'G, as we called her, had one of those huge intellects, the kind for whom romance is decidedly second rate. Or anything else that sniffs of being overwrought. "Such ripe sentiments, my dear," she had scrawled across the top of a paper on e.e. cummings. I cringed then, I do still. Jean's clear-eyed approach, or cynical, take your pick, was more to her liking. Fortunately, my romantic leanings didn't exclude me from charter membership in the Blithering Heights Club, our collective response to the excesses of Emily Brontë.

"I speak of *The Alexandria Quartet* by Lawrence Durrell. And, yes, he's Irish." She was quick to anticipate a charge of chauvinism, but who among us would bring it? Only a few in this class—in any class—were not Irish. "Listen to the music of the titles, *Justine*, *Balthazar*, *Mountolive, Clea.* And the city, what it conjures, a cosmopolitan stew of Muslims and Copts, Jews and Armenians, Greeks, French, Italians. A *tour de force*, girls!"

What had gotten into O'G? That weekend, we had scurried to Scribner's, that palace of a bookstore on Fifth Avenue. Enraptured, we scribbled in the margins, we read passages to each other and to anyone who wandered into the Snack Bar, caught up in the world Durrell describes, mysticism and the cabal, the intrigue of King Farouk's court, the British Foreign Office, layer on layer coiling in on itself like a cobra.

"Deliciously Byzantine," I said, trying out a word I hadn't found much use for until now.

"You're never sure what's going on, but you know something's at stake, they had something to believe in," said Jean. "The British hanging on in Egypt, Justine plotting in Palestine, the conflicting loyalties. Nothing here comes close, not in this cocoon."

"And bizarre characters. How about the aging *roué* traveling with his ideal woman, who turns out to be a rubber dummy named after his mother! Dresses her in evening clothes, escorts her to dinner!"

"Did he really see such things? Like the dwarf with the one, violet eye?"

I only have eye for yooooo, we crooned.

Jean turned serious. "That awful place of the child prostitutes, faces in shadow like they've been 'half-eaten by the rats one could hear scrambling among the rafters.' What an image."

"But also this, 'That last spring we walked together at full moon, overcome by the soft dazed air of the city, the quiet ablutions of water and moonlight that polished it like a great casket.' Isn't that beautiful?" Though I suspected some might say morbid.

"Who invented the human heart, I wonder?" Justine asks a lover. "Tell me, and then show me the place where he was hanged."

Those were the passages I underlined, longing to know that kind of love, neither sacrament nor sacrifice, the kind no one talked about. And no one, certainly no one we knew, lived it.

The ending of *Justine* put us both over the edge: *I no longer wish to coerce anyone, to make promises, to think of life in terms of compacts, resolutions, covenants. It will be up to Clea to interpret my silence according to her own needs and desires … Does not everything depend on our interpretation of the silence around us?*

What a passage to live by, smothered as we were in compacts and covenants, interpreting everything according to duty, never desire. Instructed to be passive in love, and in sex, pretend not to like it. Here was a man who left it to the woman to decide, to her interpretation of his silence.

It was indeed wonderful and our first glimpse into the heart of the woman who revealed it to us, a heart hidden in a nun's habit. It would be the first book to launch us on our journey.

* * *

"No, I guess Beirut isn't that far once you're in the neighborhood," Jean said, Hegel forgotten.

Outside the windows, maples and birches stood naked in the early spring chill. A year from now, sooner, we could be in a totally different landscape, as far from this as a desert.

"The world's flat here. Let's prove it's round again, find a life that isn't—oh, I don't know, so damned predictable. So *safe*."

"Self-satisfied, you mean." She lit a cigarette. "Like these comfortable folks in Westchester." We were surrounded by big estates, lawns perfect as putting greens.

"Exactly. You're Clea, I'm Justine! You fit the part, blonde, ethereal." Asexual too, I thought, sort of the way Durrell cast her. "And I look exotic, even if I'm not." I faked moody sometimes to seem more interesting, Jean didn't have to. I was good at reinventing myself. I figured she would be too. We could have used Vonnegut's warning: *We are what we pretend to be, so we must be careful about what we pretend to be.*

"And how do we pay for this little escapade?"

"What about that money your father set aside for you?" Laughingly referred to as her dowry. "And I'll have what I didn't spend on that summer abroad my parents were pushing, the Continental hit parade of cities."

"Do you think they'll let us?"

Looking at her delicate beauty, I wondered if I wanted to go anywhere with her. Skin so pale it was see-through, the sadness behind the laughter. I pushed those qualms aside. "We'll talk them into it. Or we'll lie. Won't cost much. We can hitchhike, stay in youth hostels."

"Hitchhike? Over there?" She looked like I'd suggested we seek haven in a harem.

"Why not? They've got gobs of oil, they must have cars." I was cheerleading myself too. "But you might have to give up being a blonde."

She ignored that. "Are we crazy to even think of going there alone?"

"Probably. But what an adventure!"

"Yeah," she said uncertainly, "what an adventure."

The Snack Bar crowd was not enthusiastic.

"*Beirut*! Where the hell is that?"

"Can we find it on a map?"

"Don't forget Saint Ursula, wandering around with her band of virgins. Murdered, every last one. Huns got 'em."

"A *dowry*! How quaint."

"If there's a dowry, can sex be far behind?"

"*Sex?* Now that's what I'd call quaint. Around here anyhow."

"My mother can get you those old lady underpants she made me wear in Italy to ward off germs. Hang down to your knees so you have to walk like this." Lucy, slightly bowlegged already, mimicked to howls of laughter. "One look at the underwear we were packing and you could tell we weren't headed to Sweden."

The 'germ' turned out to be an old man exposing himself one morning after church, sending her mother shrieking across the piazza, leaving Lucy to gape at it hanging in front of her, cluster of bruised grapes. When they got home her mother wrote the Pope telling him they wouldn't consider going back until he had those heathens with their nasty henrys locked up.

"All kidding aside, if this can happen in Rome, what do you think goes on in a place like Alexandria?"

We were not deterred. We continued to plot and dream. I

can't explain it, really, the sheer audacity. For as long as I can remember, the sound of a train whistle, far over the fields but clear as next door in the night's stillness, made me long to be on it, even an old freight going a few miles up the line.

People have all sorts of reasons to hit the road. I learned this early on. I learned that people already in the heart of somewhere, like Jean in Manhattan, could have the same longing. The promise of our adventure embraced us with a fervor not felt for anyone or anything before.

4

Graduation day upon us, Jean getting honors, I getting by (with occasional bright moments) and eagerly looking forward, finally, to meeting The Countess. As we filed from the chapel in our black caps and gowns, I saw my fellow conspirator waving her arms over the sea of us posing for snapshots. I made my way through the throng.

She put her arm around my shoulders, propelling me forward. "Come on, The Countess is dying to see you."

"She is?" I was suddenly shy. No photograph could have prepared me. Our mothers were attractive in their way, approaching middle age and looking it. Not her. No wonder The Countess didn't think much of marriage, or so Jean said. How could anyone so lovely sort out the confusing claims on her? How begin to choose?

"I … I see why Jean calls you The Countess. But you look more like her sister than her mother." Large grey-green eyes smiled at me, astonishing eyes under a broad-brimmed hat, green like the sheath she wore emphasizing how slender she was—one of the Trigères? Pale skin like her daughter's, pale as moonlight.

"Sirrine, how pretty you are, pretty as your name." Her voice falling like rose petals, a memory of Alabama in the soft drawl. "I'm so happy to lay these tired eyes on you after all Jean has told me."

She put her hands on my shoulders, drawing me under her spell. "You two chums will be the best traveling companions.

Thick as thieves, I reckon. Oh, how I long to go with you, how I long to go anywhere at all! You must promise to make her write to me every day, the little vixen. She's all I have." Again the voice. Enough cream to drown a bowl of peaches. I would have promised her the earth and the stars.

Jean's father beside me then, large, rumpled, greying hair, thick glasses. He did not look like a man who would be cruel to his wife. More than anything he looked preoccupied, as Jean had also described him, so it was surprising when he brought up our plans for the trip. We had only told our parents we were sailing to Europe in the fall and maybe going as far as Athens. Greece was an unusual destination at the time but not alarming.

"I'm not sure I approve of this idea, going off on your own," her father said. "Seems unnecessarily risky."

"But I haven't had a chance to tell you, we've got others signing on." Jean gave me a kick in the shin. "Safety in numbers, right Sirrine?"

The Countess made a peculiar sound, not quite laughter. "*Risk*? If only you would risk something, just once in your life."

The crowd on the great lawn seemed to pause and take in its breath. Her father reached a hand to her, but she recoiled like a frightened bird. What little color there was left her face, all expression too—Lot's wife turning to salt. But what had The Countess turned back to see? What regret leaving behind?

She came out of it abruptly. "Don't touch me!" she said. She brushed her hand across her forehead, sending her hat to the ground, and walked away. Her husband stooped awkwardly to retrieve it and followed her.

A man standing near me let out a low whistle. "That's one swell-looking dame. Who? Rita Hayworth or somebody?"

I ignored him and went in search of my parents, hoping they hadn't witnessed any part of that episode. I searched for Jean too. She had disappeared.

What had she been hiding from me? I could not put out of my mind what she had told me about her parents, could not stop thinking about The Countess, that sudden fear, those small hollows at her temples, like the imprints of a thumb. The whiteness of her skin, that dreadful whiteness you could see right through to the blue rivers of veins throbbing beneath.

We kept up a steady correspondence that summer, Jean and I, seldom splurging on phone calls. But there was one that came in the night. My father woke me. He was stern, alarmed, irritated by being disturbed at that hour. A call in the middle of the night definitely fell into the category of "running to extremes."

"I know I must have seemed peculiar lately." Her voice crackled along the line, a storm somewhere, over Lake Michigan probably. "Not sounding off about our trip and all."

"That had occurred to me but not in my sleep. You woke everybody up."

"I need to come out there right away."

"What? It's after midnight, unless you've already traveled to another set of time zones."

"I'm not kidding, I need to get out of here, Sirry. My mother, she's … well, she's gone into something strange. Wanders from room to room, tearful, saying nothing. Yesterday, to give her something to do, I asked her to make a grocery list. She sat there, pencil in her hand, got up, walked to the refrigerator, opened a few cupboards, sat down again, didn't write a thing."

The Countess struck me as the kind of woman who on her best day would have trouble with a grocery list. "What do you think is wrong?"

"I don't know. People when they get like this … she's said it to me, she's said she doesn't want to live." Jean started to cry.

Her mother saying such a thing, the sin of despair, the one that damned you forever. I couldn't think of a single word to comfort her. All I could think of was my father picking up the other phone and hearing her talk about getting on a bus in the middle of the night and people not wanting to live.

"Sirry, are you there?"

"Yeah. I'm here, I'm listening."

"I've never been so frightened in my life. I'm almost mad with worry. If there *is* a God, why would He take someone so devoted and destroy her like this? Or is it to destroy me who's never had much use for Him?"

"I don't know." All of a sudden I knew very little. "God can't be that punishing, can He?" But hadn't I been taught all my life that indeed He could?

"When I hear her turn over in bed at night, I'm on my feet. That's why I'm up now. We total about four hours sleep between us."

"What can I do?"

"Nothing. But we can't go, I can't go. Not the way things are."

I twisted the phone cord, clinging to it like a lifeline. "No, of course not. Your father … what about him?"

"He's away—some big case he's working on. He doesn't confide in us, I assure you. Useless anyway, he just wants to know why she can't shape up and sort herself out. He seems to think a person is either raving mad or posing." She was silent a moment. "I think I hear her roaming around, I'd better hang up."

"Okay."

"Sirry ..."

"Yeah."

"It can't get worse than this, can it?"

* * *

My parents were sitting at the kitchen table in their bathrobes, waiting for me to tell them what happened. Did this mean she had cracked up? The mother of the person I'd been planning to spend a year of my life with mad as a hatter? Mental illness was a terrible stigma, unknown and awful to contemplate. The question now would be, why *aren't* you going? I had no time to make up a decent lie.

"That was Jean. The Countess, her mother, I mean, she's sick. We're not going."

"What on earth's wrong with her?"

"Don't know exactly. TB or something."

"*TB?*" My father's voice sounded the alarm. I'd forgotten about Doc Olson's son next door who had TB, an invalid all his life, dead before he got to thirty. When they let him come home from the sanitarium, he would stand on the upstairs porch in his burgundy robe, the kind with grey piping around the edges, looking out over the fields, sad as Chekhov.

"No, guess it can't be that," I hastened to correct.

My mother was getting cross. "What, then? Don't you have any respect for your father and me, talking such poppycock?"

"Look, I wasn't really awake. This is a pretty big surprise for me too, you know. *Merde!*"

"Is this the kind of language they taught in that school?"

"You will apologize to your mother and cease and desist from using that word." My father, the lawyer.

I was tempted to recite my full repertoire, most of it learned from a classmate who had four brothers. She was my role model, she swore like a trooper. I apologized, ready to howl with disappointment. "I'll call her back, find out exactly what it is," I offered, anxious to leave the room.

"Might as well, now everybody's up," my father said evenly. "After all, you youngsters have your whole future in front of you." To him, we'd be youngsters at sixty-five, cashing our Social Security checks. I charged upstairs to the other phone, hoping Jean would pick up and I wouldn't get their answering service. Our number was three digits and on a party line, conversation kept to a minimum unless you wanted to broadcast all over the county. This one would be a bonanza. (There were stories, of course, eavesdroppers forgetting themselves: *Speak up, can't hear ya*!)

"Jean, it's me. What are we going to say she's got?"

"Why are you whispering like some third-rate Mata Hari?"

"Jean, there's something you should know. Not much happens out here, we watch corn grow, squirrels in the yard are entertainment, so a phone call in the night? It's an event. They're asking what's wrong, they're concerned. I don't think I should tell them it's—*mental*. They'd worry a lot more about that than going to the Middle East. If they ever found out."

If they'd let me go anywhere with her, tainted like this. We came up with something serious enough to postpone our trip but nothing really bad, nothing lurking in the genes. Pneumonia. Not exactly common in summer, about as likely as leprosy.

Beyond the crushing disappointment, I was frightened. The only "evil" I'd ever faced was sin I myself committed, easily gotten rid of in confession. But how do you ask forgiveness for a nervous breakdown? Yet somebody has to be guilty, that's the whole point of original sin, isn't it? Having somebody to blame? Despite all the talk of the devil I'd grown up with, I never really considered evil a force that could invade at will, convinced that if I was good, so would the universe be. Hitler and Stalin somehow didn't enter into it.

As much as I cared about Jean, I was beginning to realize

that my feeling for her might not matter one way or the other, might not make a particle of difference in what happened to her. That sadness that made her so intriguing, did it signal something more serious? And wasn't I, her closest friend, a mirror of her in some way? If she could break, what about me? "Please, God, don't let this happen to Jean too," I begged on my knees.

Thinking about The Countess and how her beauty couldn't save her, let alone her faith, I went back to bed, afraid to wake up and discover escape to be a dream after all, nothing to look forward to but the drive to the country club once a week for dinner with my parents, the two of them bickering in the front seat.

5

Shock treatments. Afterwards, a stillness came over Jean's mother. A temporary loss of memory. "I have read about how wonderful these treatments are but when it comes to putting your own mother through them, you have to just hope they know what they're doing."

That was all she would say about her. I kept seeing her in the eye of my mind, walking down a forest path strewn with pinecones, dressed in a white gown, sometimes in chains. When she turned to look back, the chains became flames that consumed her, even her face. She screamed but no sound came. I'd wake up dry-mouthed, as if I were the one trying to make the sound. I never told Jean about those nightmares.

In our town, we knew everything that happened to people, the good and the bad. Like Dwayne Petersen, who fell off a tractor and got his leg ground up in a combine. Accidents were natural in their way, not like somebody being strapped to a table and nearly electrocuted. What was it they killed? Did they kill what made her go out and buy six green outfits, all exactly the same? I thought of her father, heavy in his chair, drinking, Jean darting between them, trying to protect her mother and failing.

This is one way she wrote about it: *Tonight it is very hot, it is very still, no air or movement anywhere but my typewriter. I feel as though I am just hitting, the only one hitting, and it doesn't matter because nothing else will move. Only ghosts here. I wish I could enclose myself in this letter because there is so much I want to say to you.*

Six weeks later she called again, this time her voice full of excitement. "Guess what, we're going!"

"Wait a second …"

"No, I've figured it all out. I've found another ship, exact same money, sailing October 18. So we're going. *Compris?*"

"No, I don't *compris,* not one bit. *Rien.* What happened to change anything?"

"I had a nice little chat with the doctor. Who says she's manipulating—to keep me from forsaking her. Her word."

"You mean from the beginning? All of it?"

"No, now—not getting better. Refusing to, in a way."

"You're sounding like your father. Saying all she has to do is shape up. I don't get it, how is that something she controls?"

"Beats me. But Doc says I need to start thinking about myself. Everything here is decay. All I can think about is clearing out of this country and beginning a life."

"Look, are you sure? Really really sure?"

"Yes."

"Thus spake Z?"

"You bet."

When I first left home to go east to school, my grandmother said something that has stayed with me ever since. "Growing up near the river turns your mind to wandering and when those dreaming thoughts take hold they never let you go."

Here we were again saying goodbye. I found her, ornery bird in his cage at her shoulder, on her sun porch where she could do a running commentary on cars passing, all three of them, happy as if she had the traffic of Broadway outside her window. "There goes Earl, lickety-split, late for lunch, anxious to get home to his lady love."

I reminded her of her oracle. She added a postscript. "You'll come back," she said. "The river pulls you away but it will always bring you home."

That afternoon my pal Sam and I had taken his boat out to the sandbar to swim. Starting back after dark, we lost power and stalled in the path of a barge bearing down on us, fixing us in its lights, like bugs bobbing on a leaf on the wide Mississippi. Frantically Sam tried to restart the engine. It caught finally and he gunned it to free us from that terrifying beam of light. We imagined the bargemen watching our panic.

"I hope they would've prayed over us at least."

"If they could quit laughing long enough."

"Sam, would we really have been finished?"

"No way they could stop in time."

In the safety of the boathouse, I wondered why I couldn't be content like my grandmother, constructing a world around someone passing by her window. Sam knew what I was thinking. "Why do you have to go?"

"Because my mother read me stories about Ling-ling instead of Winnie-the-Pooh?"

"Be serious."

"I am. I've been so intent on our differences I refused to see how much she's given me, how much she longs for too."

"Your mother's lonely."

"I never understood why she couldn't make the best of things."

"Meaning?"

"Meaning we're similar, I guess. That I don't have to dislike her in order not to become her."

"And you'll come back?"

"Why? To be miserable like her?"

"Maybe it's not where you live that dictates happiness."

"There's nothing for me here, Sam, you know that."

"No, spose not." His face was lost in the dark and the fog.

Leaves fluttered and danced along the platform at the foot of Grandad's Bluff, where the *Zephyr* came through La Crosse on its way north along the river to St. Paul or south to Dubuque and over the prairie to Chicago. The chill in the air meant a fall afternoon perfect for football and bonfires.

My father, courtly in his country lawyer way, wore a suit and hat to drive me to the train. My mother, pleading a headache, did not come along. Too painful to watch me go off and do what she could only dream about?

The enormity of our deceit was killing me. Any moment now I might blurt it out, tell him what I was up to, but how could I even begin? He had that reserve so common among Midwesterners, and I was the child still, our bond the banter that shielded us against my mother's moods.

"You have your passport? Tickets? Traveler's checks?" A similar litany every time I left home. "You've got my credit card number? And don't forget to call when you get down to Chicago. Plenty of time between trains, if you make it snappy."

"I won't forget."

"There won't be a hitch now, with Jean?"

"Dad, don't worry. This is why I'm taking the train, easier for her to meet me. I've managed before, all the time I was in school, remember?"

All the leaving I'd done, when he had stood on this platform, my rock to come back to, me wanting to get away, thrilled to get away, even from him. Part of me wanting to turn around and go back home with him. But it was exactly that certainty, unchanging as the prairies, asking only that I stay and at the same time telling me not to, pushing me to go as fast as I could.

"I have to do this. If I don't go, I never will." I hugged him and started for the stairs. I turned and saw tears in his eyes.

"Mind your p's and q's," he called. "Don't forget what your grandfather used to say. *A thoroughbred never jumps the fence*." I smiled at the familiar injunction. "And write to the girls in the office, they'll get a kick out of it." Half the town got postcards whenever he went away. Even Slippery Elm, who didn't have an address, didn't have a real name, just Slippery Elm because no one could tell where he'd turn up next, and if you saw him, say, down by the lumber yard, by the time you got uptown he'd be sipping water from the fountain on the corner as if he hadn't been anywhere but there the whole day long. Could sleep standing up, people said, swore that's what he did most nights.

"It'll be all right, Dad, really it will." He handed my bags to the porter, and I climbed up after. The whistle blew. As the train pulled out, gathering speed as we cleared the end of the platform, I saw him waving his hat in the air, leaves swirling at his feet.

Two days later, I was on a West Side pier with Jean. The *Saturnia,* towering above us, straining at the ropes, white, gleaming and rising in tiers like a gigantic wedding cake. Landfall Lisbon, last stop Trieste. We would make our way to Greece and east from there. First and cabin class passengers in front, waiting to board. We were back with the cheap fares, *tourista* class, most dressed in black, going home to the old country. Nobody in trench coats, nobody our age.

"I'm getting dizzy looking up at that thing." That made two of us.

"I have a thumping headache. Where's your pharmacy?" I wondered if she'd actually packed all that stuff I'd seen spread out on her bed the night before—Merthiolate, milk of magnesia, Alka-Seltzer, aspirin, Anacin too, Ben-Gay and Vicks VapoRub, essence of Grandma shining in its little blue jar like a vigil light. Plus an ointment her uncle in the South concocted to cure everything from hives to herpes. As if we really were going off to boot camp. Something of a hypochondriac, our Jean. With all the shots we got, each one notated on our yellow inoculation cards, we couldn't catch a cold.

I stole a glance at her, not used to the new look. She had met the train wearing boots and jeans—jeans had never stalked our campus—and a tweed cap, the kind Irish men wore. When she doffed it with a flourish, dull brown hair fell to her shoulders. *What have you done!* I checked myself before blurting it. But why so drastic a change?

"You were worried about hitching with a blonde, so I went for the mousy look. 'Bout as tempting as a bowl of cold grits, right?" She was laughing, then we both were.

"You're still awfully pretty, even if we don't get half the attention." We walked out of Grand Central, arm in arm. Something else was different, I sensed it almost immediately, but I couldn't quite put my finger on it. In the taxi uptown, we talked about everything but The Countess until I could no longer contain my curiosity.

"She's upset I'm going." Jean rolled down the window and lit a cigarette.

"She won't be happy to see me, then."

"Don't worry, sleeps most of the time, seldom leaves her room. You won't run into my father either. He's out of town, per usual."

"But it's the weekend."

"No such thing as weekend for a big-shot lawyer."

It was one of those grand pre-war apartment buildings I always associated with New York, tucked away on a leafy side street in the East 80s, rooms with a past, vestiges of other people's lives. Lights dim, furniture dark, big kitchen with glass-front cabinets all the way to the ceiling. Jean took me down a hall to a room that was at once spartan, plain covers on twin beds, and frilly, cabbage roses on upholstered chairs. Stuffed dolls, tossed any which way, were climbing out of one of them. Like the rest of the place, it smelled of furniture polish and radiator heat.

"I'll leave you alone for an hour or so. I have to finish packing."

"Wait a minute, packing's been going on for weeks!"

"Let's just say I got sidetracked." There was more to it and I told her so.

"Okay, I pack. By morning I'm unpacked."

"Your mother?"

"Bingo!"

"Does it in her sleep, I suppose. Oh, Jean." I was beginning to understand what this was costing her.

I must have dozed, for when I opened my eyes, I was startled by the figure at the foot of the bed. The Countess, white bathrobe, even whiter face spectral in the gathering dusk. She was moving her mouth, as if trying to muster enough saliva to swallow. The heat was coming up in the radiator, steam hissing and banging in the pipes the way it does in those old buildings.

"So the witch awakes. She's stealing my little girl, but we're not going to let her do that, are we. We're not going to let anyone do that." The voice was a monotone. When it stopped she kept working her mouth in that agitated way.

I slid off the bed and made a dash into the hall. Unsure where to go in the twilight gloom, I headed towards the kitchen, colliding with Jean as she came around the corner.

"Hey, slow down. I've lost The Countess."

"You'll find her in my room."

"What's she doing there?"

"Scaring the hell out of me, that's what."

"Nah, she's harmless. It's the time of day, that's all, something about evening coming on unsettles her."

When they came back down the hall, Jean guiding her gently, The Countess was still talking in that monotone, tying and untying the sash of her robe.

I slipped back to my room, checking to see if I could lock it—couldn't—when Jean showed up with a bottle of scotch.

"She's quiet, but maybe we ought to stay in. We can order something from the coffee shop. Jerry's a pal, he gives me extra helpings, so there'll be plenty. Even for you." I ate like a trencherman. Jean no slouch in that department either.

"Sure, whatever you think best."

"Don't go 'way." She returned with glasses, a bowl of ice and cashews. "Help yourself to the nuts. There's no shortage around here."

I left that alone. "Is this how it's been—since the hospital? I thought you said she'd become very still."

She shrugged and handed me a drink. "You get used to it." She had that look, the one that signaled *stop*, closing in on forbidden territory, change the subject. She put on a record, Philly Joe Jones, her latest jazz crush. We no longer had time for the hip-swiveling antics of Elvis.

"How anxious are we about this little venture? Truthfully."

"Truthfully? Mail flying in and out of here for weeks with visas to places any child knows aren't Europe? Lucky no one was paying attention."

"I used my grandmother's address. She didn't pay attention either. At least she didn't let on."

"They'll be pretty steamed when they find out."

"We'll be back safe and sound by then, so what the hell."

"Yeah, what the hell." She lit a cigarette. "Still, I wish we could come clean. In case something happens to The Countess."

"I didn't think of that."

"I did. Confession, my godmother Thayer knows."

"Shouldn't you have asked me first? You swore this Thayer person to secrecy?"

"Of course. But think about it, we say almost nothing between hello and goodbye around here anyway, so our secret is safe."

"What does she do, this godmother of yours?"

"What she likes, pretty much. She's a journalist, freelance, hard-boiled type with her own stash of dough. Had a lover once, but he dumped her and went off to Spain for the greater love of the fight against Franco. Oh, and she's a devoted atheist."

"You're kidding. Atheist as godmother, now that is admirable."

"A perfect example of my mother's ironic view of things, despite her faith. Or maybe because of it. Entitled to have her little joke since she felt so close to Him." It was her turn to change the subject. "What will be our favorite sight?"

"You'll be swooning over the Acropolis, I'm pretty sure of that."

"And you'll be swooning over some Adonis, I'm absolutely sure of that."

"Well, I might sneak a peek or two."

She looked at me sternly. "We stick together come what may, right? You got me into this. You're not waltzing off with some guy and leaving me in the lurch."

"*Some guy* is nowhere on my list of tourist attractions."

"Promise? Like at school, we sign out together, we sign in together."

"I wouldn't want you running off either."

"Not a chance."

"Jean, what is it you're afraid of?"

"I don't think I'd be much good at it, frankly. Another way for people to destroy each other, isn't it?"

"I don't think it has to be like that."

"Anyhow, against the rules, isn't it? For good little Catholics?"

I ignored the jibe. "No longer convinced they apply. Love—passion—a sin? With all the real evil in the world?"

"Hey, you're catching on."

Sex was okay, it seemed, so long as it was coupled with rebellion. She went into the hall, listening until satisfied all was quiet. "What I really want is to find a way to live that's normal. Wait, cancel that, not normal exactly. If there's no risk, what is there? Sound like my mother, right?" Her face brightened. "But suppose we really complicate it, leave all this behind. Suppose we not only pretend to be somebody else but …"

"You have to come back, you know." Feeling the drinks, my mind rambled to when my cousin Kitty and I got it into our heads to walk all the way to La Crosse, that starved for something to do. We walked out past the root beer stand and the island of trees at the edge of town and on out to Highway 44 in our shorts and sneakers and kept going, La Crosse twenty-three miles away, Kitty making wreaths from the grass growing along the highway. Hot, that August heat that can turn everything the same color, which is no color at all. We got up to the ridge three miles outside town, no cars passing, out of breath, leaking sweat. That's when she told me about Diane. Who had wanted to be a nurse but was pregnant and getting married instead. "She'll be doing plenty of nursing now," Kitty said. "Won't even have to go to school for it." She tossed the wreaths into the cornfield. Without another word we turned around and trudged home.

Jean got up to freshen our drinks. "You're lost in thought.

What about?"

"How I've always been on the road out of town, one way or another."

"But it sounds so appealing, your little town, summer days on the river with Sam, Granny spinning her soap operas on the sun porch."

"You'd say that, growing up in New York? That's what I would call appealing."

"Consider who with. I'd rather your setup."

The run-in with the spook at the end of the bed did give me pause. I lit a cigarette and tossed her the pack. "So, what are we gonna do when we can no longer traipse around the world postponing the rest of our lives?"

"A question I dread. How do you create the right kind of life for yourself?"

"Sooner or later it's a matter of putting one foot in front of the other, isn't it?"

"Not so easy when you're a cripple."

"Oh, Jean, cut the drama crap, it's not that difficult."

"Not when you can fall on your knees. I really need to find out, what's the point?"

"I only agreed to this trip with you. I didn't sign up for the meaning of life."

She thought better of it too and reached for my hand. "Hey, thanks for waiting for me. You'll never know how much it means."

"It didn't occur to me not to. Whatever happens we see this through. Nothing is more important. Promise."

"You're right. Nothing is more important. Solemn promise."

We proceeded to get sloshed and never got around to calling Jerry for food.

* * *

A loud blast from the ship's horn cut short my reverie. It sent us leaping into each other's arms. Our fellow passengers, amused, looked on.

"So much for sophistication."

"They'll just have to take us as we come."

Thus spake.

PART THREE

Alex

6

Back at the checkpoint I said Jean was to blame for the fix we were in. In fact, there was plenty of blame to go around, even before we were cast out of Beirut like a couple of criminals and beginning on the ship that carried us to Alexandria.

Sailing from Piraeus I watched the shore fall away and begin to blur, like a camera out of focus, taking with it all that I thought of as familiar. After a month in Greece and the islands, we were finally on our way to the city we dreamed of and yet for the first time I felt uneasy. I found our cabin, crawled into the lower bunk and took a nap.

What Jean had told her father about others joining us wasn't a total lie. A friend studying French that summer in Paris was all set to come along but by the time she arrived in Athens she got cold feet. She missed her boyfriend, her cat, something, and flew home, giving us a book, *A Room in Moscow*, inscribed by the author and belonging to Graham Griggs of the Beirut bureau of *Time*. He had been called back before she could return it. We should ask for him at the St. Georges Hotel.

"Nice intro," said Jean. "A guy on the inside track might come in handy in a place like Beirut."

The book was by Sally Belfrage. She had lived in Moscow and crossed Siberia by train. Obtaining permission to do that was unheard of, it was the Cold War and anyone who had anything to do with the Soviet Union was suspect, Communists could be lurking under every bed. We were impressed. "If she got out of there in one piece, we can survive the Middle East," I said. "Those sinister-looking guys we saw in newsreels, purged and sent to Siberia to freeze to death?" Even if innocent, they still looked scary as hell.

"Staring at the camera through those round wire-rimmed glasses, bug-eyed, like they were drugged. Probably were, come to think of it."

"And tortured. How else did they get them to incriminate themselves? Or anyone else they wanted to get rid of. Tortured priests, too, didn't they?" That last nuance provided by the nuns.

We stopped at American Express on Syntagma for a last mail pick-up before going back to our little hotel on Kolokotroni Street. We were pleased with ourselves. We had hitchhiked all over the mainland, mostly with truck drivers, to Delphi and the Temple of Apollo, to Mycenae and Argos, reciting the doom-filled stories of Aeschylus and Euripides. We made our way around the islands, surviving near shipwreck on the *Andros* out of Crete, limping into Rhodes greeted by cheering crowds and realizing what a close call it had been. It was there that we encountered Turkish toilets, so-called because they were remnants from the Ottoman era? This luxury was a hole in the ground, flanked by ridged blocks meant to resemble feet, once white but now covered with crud the origins of which it was best not to contemplate, and, if well equipped, a rusty nail with strips of newspaper for toilet paper, unsteadily attached to a cinder block and invariably just out of reach. The stench was epic.

On Crete, Jean had her first declaration of love, a young man who came up to her and shouted: *You are my destiny, you are my street*! And an affirmation at the grave of the great Kazantzakis, who wrote *Zorba the Greek,* in his epitaph: *I hope for nothing, I fear nothing, I am free*.

"My kind of guy," she said.

This last night in Athens, we would stay up composing letters for the night man to post to our parents, doling them out while we were on the lam in the Middle East. Our bribe would keep him in ouzo till Easter.

Who could have guessed that *A Room in Moscow* would also launch an adventure?

I went looking for Jean. How long had I been napping? She was on the upper deck, standing along the rail, smoking. Not alone. A man was leaning in to her, his elbows on the railing, his back to me, hair as dark as the waves curling up from below. Jean once again a blonde, the ugly rinse finally washed away, the second bottle buried at sea off Mykonos along with her prized British walking shoes that she couldn't move in without breaking her neck.

She was listening to what he was saying. Intently. Obviously I'd missed out on something.

"Hello!" I called. He turned. I gaped, all composure lost. He was beautiful—the only word for it, a statue, a *kouros*, like the ones we'd been staring at in the museums of Greece, come alive. Not tall, taller than Jean beside him, perfect features except for a thickening on the bridge of his nose. It made him look rugged.

"You woke up finally. This is Andreas."

"I'm Sirrine." I did not look away. Nor did he. He smiled.

"Sirrine. Sounds almost Greek."

"What? Uh ... yes ... everyone said so when we were there. In Greece, I mean."

Jean's voice seemed to travel from a great distance. "Andreas is studying art and writing for the theater in Athens. He's on his way home for Christmas, a town called Famagusta, in Cyprus." She knew all about him, then. Already.

"We've been talking about Alexandria. He doesn't think we should get off there. He's invited us to come with him instead."

Invited *her*. Plans get changed, just like that, because of some man. The Adonis I was supposed to be swooning over.

"Why not Alexandria? It's the whole point, isn't it? From the very beginning. Or have you forgotten?"

"I am not sure it will be safe for you," he said. "The Arabs are … well, different. They're not accustomed to seeing women traveling alone."

What kind of attitude was this? But hadn't I been apprehensive too, an hour or two ago pulling away from shore?

"Oh, come on, you make them sound … scary. Greeks lived in Alexandria, you know. Still do, probably." I assumed he was Greek.

"Yes, before Nasser came to power. They were welcome under Farouk, whatever else you might say about *him*. But now? They have left. You will find it changed from the city you read about. It's not what it once was."

"Hey, look, we don't have to decide this right away, do we?" Jean said brightly. "We've got a couple days to think about it."

"I hope you will think about it," he said, looking from one to the other of us. "See you at dinner?"

We watched him move easily with the sway of the ship. "Jean, this is the last time I will ever get caught napping. He's beautiful. I think he's the most beautiful man I've ever laid eyes on in my whole entire life."

"I wasn't thinking of him that way."

Who was she kidding?

"We were talking about his writing, and the war or uprising or whatever it was. On Cyprus. He was in it, Sirrine, a guerilla fighter. I'm not sure that's what they called themselves but it's what it sounded like."

"He fought the British? He can't be much older than we

are!"

"Not only that, he was captured. Ask him, though you might not get very far. I don't think he likes to talk about it."

"How did you find out?"

"I asked what he was up to before he started university. Prison. That was the answer. Hasn't been out long either, a year maybe. Only eighteen when they caught him."

"My God."

"Jean tells me you fought the British."

The three of us were at a table by ourselves in the overheated dining room below decks. The cheap seats.

"Yes." The frown made the ridge on his nose more pronounced.

"And?"

"And."

"Tell us what it was like." We were pushing spaghetti drowning in tomato sauce around on our plates.

"That's not so easy for me."

"Try. We want to understand."

"It isn't a romantic story, if that's what you think." Exactly what I did think. "What it was like? Tedious at times, dangerous at times, hard going mostly. The British—they made things difficult for us."

"How did you get caught?" Jean was looking at him with that gaze of hers, eyes the color of grass when the dew is on it.

He hesitated. He took a cigarette from the box of Craven A's beside him and lit it. His fingers were long and slender. I imagined myself under them.

"An operation near Tseri, village not far from Nicosia," he began, exhaling slowly. "We were in a grove of trees, an orchard left untended, so there was cover enough. Waiting for a patrol to get out of the area. It was a little after midnight. We were discovered, betrayed, I'm sure. Most got away, I was unlucky."

"What did they do?"

"You must have been terrified," Jean said.

"I have said the British made things difficult."

"But what happened *to you*?" I pressed.

"They knocked me around. I was young, they thought they could make me talk. Maybe I would have but I knew nothing." He laughed. "So they wasted their time. That's how I got this beautiful nose." He rubbed it lightly, where the bump was. "I was sent to Wormwood Scrubs, in North London."

"Right out of Dickens, that name," Jean said.

His face turned hard. "IRA boys were locked up in there, not much older than me, in with criminals and murderers, all of us, all treated the same. For us it was war, treat us like prisoners of war. They laughed. They opened the doors of our cells, taunting us to come out, and slammed them shut again. Until I die I will never be finished with that sound." I looked at him, eyes brimming.

"The sentence was life. Fortunately for me, the fighting ended in my country. The others? They're still in there, in there waiting to die."

We were constant companions after that, the three of us, reading or walking on deck buckled into our trench coats against the wind off the Mediterranean, smoking, drinking countless cups of coffee and talking, talking, talking, ideas like knots we were struggling to untangle. Life. Death. Art. God knows what. God too, of course. They were not, as Andreas put it, on good terms. "Why this suffering? To make sure we have need of Him? As if my friend Doctor Thanos would make people sick to prove his worth. This is what I will ask if ever I see Him, I will ask how He can bear to see our pain, how in the face of it He dares to be God? But He doesn't dare, He doesn't exist." Jean hadn't gone this far.

"He does exist, Andreas. This is what gives meaning to the suffering," I protested. Never having experienced any, I wasn't much good at the argument.

He could turn playful, doing imitations of Orson Welles or James Cagney, puffing up his cheeks for a profile like Hitchcock, swaggering like John Wayne. *Do Americans wear jeans for cowboy courage? Where can I find some? Do you eat hotdogs for breakfast? Go on the road like Kerouac, baring your breasts for truck drivers?*

He laughs, dimpled, deep-throated laughter against which there is no defense. Alone, he and I have a game. *You're looking at me. No, I'm not.* He gives in. *Okay, you noticed, what else have you noticed?* He studies me. *The way you tilt your head, like this* ... he imitates that too. *A voice like yours, beautiful as the rain. Hair like yours, see how it catches the light. Long legs like yours, do all American girls have such long legs? What would you think, Sirrine ...?* His voice trails off, allowing me to think just about anything. And I do.

He does not play with Jean. They talk about Sartre. He notices how high-strung she is—have I not noticed this, he asks? He tells her so, says she's stretching her nerves like antennae, better to make them of steel and accept. I do notice how she looks at him, almost demanding that he tell her more, tell her how to be in her own skin. She doesn't get it, I think, intellectualizing everything. I like that she doesn't get it. What I get is impatient. Inhibited for so long I yearn to feel free. Like a reckless gambler, if there's a game, let's play it.

One evening he was unusually quiet. We weren't prepared for the question. How would we choose between fighting for an ideal, for freedom, say, and harming someone, even killing, in pursuit of it? Was this a confession? I shivered, though the evening was balmy approaching North Africa. Caught between fear that he might actually have done such a thing and fear that if I knew that he had, I would respond to him even more. We told him we'd never given the question thought, never had to. Well, maybe in an ethics class discussing something like whether ends justify means.

"This is the tension that creates tragedy."

How I wanted him. Drunk on words and the sound of his voice, I was intent on having him, driven by the thrill of competition and that exquisite frisson of doubt at the outcome. And if I won? What then? I won't pretend this had nothing to do with Jean. The truth is I didn't want her to have him, my jealousy as disturbing as my desire. I was sure he desired me too, but he said nothing directly.

We weren't far from Alexandria, not much time for something to happen. I was ahead of Jean, leaving our cabin for dinner, and he was there, in the passageway. Waiting for us? For me? I almost tripped over him. He took my hand and led me up on deck. No mistaking this now. Lurching with the ship, I went, my heart thumping so absurdly he must hear it. Feeling his eyes on me, I stared at the horizon watching dusk begin. When he spoke, I found the courage to look at him, sure that he could read everything in my face.

"You know, don't you," his voice soft as the evening air.

"Yes. I also know I feel guilty being here with you."

"But why?"

"She found you first."

"So that's how you American girls decide these things. Finders keepers—that's the saying, isn't it? When something is lost?"

His finger traced the line of my cheek, a trail of fire. "I was not lost, Sirrine."

"It will be hard, she'll think you've made a choice." I

turned back to the horizon. Stars were coming, wands of little fairies.

"Is that what *you* would think?" Had he seen through me or was he teasing? "We have so little say in these things. Fate laughs and makes fools of us when we presume we do. No matter what we do, fate laughs. Even your God steps aside."

"Are you always so … so fatalistic?"

"We can live with honor, still. What matters is that we are truthful, take responsibility for everything we do. Look at me, Sirrine. This I know to be true. I don't feel towards her the way I do with you. Is this wrong?"

"I almost wish you didn't."

"But why?" Surprise gave way to hurt.

"Because I … I'm afraid all of a sudden." I touched his cheek, awkward, not gentle the way he was. "I'd better go, she'll be looking for me."

"We can't ignore what's happening, can we?"

"Andreas …" I didn't know how to go on. I made myself walk away from him.

He didn't come to dinner. My thoughts were a jumble. Much too infatuated to mean what I said about wishing he didn't feel the way he did, far too relieved that he did feel it, that it was out in the open, between us anyway. I wanted to tell Jean. But what if she wanted him too? I would never trust that pretense of indifference.

When she asked if I knew where he was, I snapped at her. "Is there some existential meaning attached to whether or not he comes in to dinner? Maybe he's tired, maybe it's just that simple. Tired, not hungry, doesn't fucking feel like it." I didn't believe a word I was saying. What if I never saw him again?

"You don't have to take my head off. What's going on?"

"Nothing. Nothing's going on."

"Sure."

We didn't say much the rest of the evening. I didn't sleep, either. Restless, tossing, wanting the night to be over, remembering his fingers on my face, wondering what would happen next. The Scold coming along to spoil it. *A shipboard romance, the kind people laugh at, the ultimate cliché and you're falling for it like a silly schoolgirl. All he wants ...*

I fought back. *Skip the propaganda about all he wants. Go back to the convent and let me have some fun. Scram!*

The argument raged. By morning I was exhausted. I skipped breakfast. It was warm, I could wear something that showed a little skin. *Take that, Scold.* By the time I got up on deck he was there, Jean too, talking to someone else. He came towards me, the look in his eyes so urgent it startled me, didn't even notice the sundress I was wearing, could have been the same dirty old trench coat.

The Scold was stalking, echoing a line we had made fun of once, my romance loving grandmother and me, in a story she was reading. *His dark eyes penetrated her.* And here they were, *his* eyes. Maybe I was making a fool of myself but with him all caution fled.

"Sirrine, where have you been? I didn't sleep, not the entire night."

"Me either."

"Tomorrow we land at Alexandria. What are we going to do?"

"I don't know." I wanted him to decide, for us both.

"We have to find time alone." He wove his fingers through mine. All the little boats bobbing in my stomach capsized at once. "After dinner, same place."

"Yes, same place." No idea how I would manage it.

7

An air of excitement comes over a ship the night before making landfall, a sudden animation as if everyone has shaken off the spell that being at sea has cast. We all felt it, mixing freely before dinner, piling into the bar after, people chattering about what they would do in port, the onward journey. It was easier to slip away.

The sky was filled with stars, so close it seemed I could reach up and pluck them one by one. No sign of him but The Scold was there. *I told you so.*

Of course he'll come. Why not? If it's a fling, what difference does it make, tomorrow I'll be gone. So get lost.

My eyes accustomed to the dark, I could make out his hands on the rail. He sensed I was near. I knew it the way I seemed to know everything in an especially alert way. He turned to reach for me, checked himself.

"You did come. I was losing hope."

"Not so easy to slip away," I lied, wanting him to think I'd taken a risk for his sake. "You missed the farewell party."

"I've been thinking about our situation."

"And what is that?" I teased, running my fingers through my hair, a gesture I assumed made me irresistible.

"Don't get off in Alexandria, stay with me. Cyprus is beautiful."

"Like you."

He laughed. "Will you? Say yes." He lifted a strand of hair, curling it around his finger before tucking it carefully behind my ear. Concentrating completely in that way he had, as if nothing in the whole world existed outside that moment.

No more fooling around now. I reined myself in, willing him to understand. “Andreas, I can’t. Alexandria’s the reason we’re here. I’m not sure we understand it ourselves, what we’re after, but we read this book by Lawrence Durrell and we knew we had to come.”

“It doesn’t exist, this Alexandria of yours. You’ll only be disappointed.”

“Maybe, but I’ve got to find out. Otherwise I’ll break all kinds of promises to myself—and her. We made a pact.”

“You would put your faith in what some British colonial has to say!”

“Please understand, I have to do this. It’s not just Alexandria. I want to have my adventure, I want to be Odysseus too. You must feel this way about what you do, your art, your writing?”

“I don’t give a damn about any of it, not when I’m with you.”

“I know you don’t mean that.”

“What I mean is I want you with me. My dreams are filled with you now.”

He pulled me closer to him. His scent was clean, like lemons. I longed for him in a way I never imagined, a painful longing.

“I want that too.” But did I? Did I really want this exquisite tension to end? Or did I want to stay just as we were, suspended, desire fixed forever like a star? What I’d told him was true, I was afraid. How would I find the strength to say yes? Or to resist? I moved my fingers gently, oh so gently, over the ridge where the blow had fallen. I was tearful.

"It's all right. It didn't hurt that much."

He took my face in his hands, searching for an answer to how much I wanted him. Kissed me. Riding a Ferris wheel, up up into the sky, everything below falling away, smaller and smaller, floating in clouds. In each other's arms, kissing throats, lips, eyes, me calling his name, he murmuring mine. Smashing the barriers that separated us.

Before we pulled away from each other, I gave my word that Jean and I would stop in Cyprus on our way to Beirut. And why not? Ships called there anyway, what was another week or two? It's why we had no set itinerary, to take advantage of whatever came along, and staying with his family wouldn't cost anything. I convinced him not to talk to Jean, I would do it. On the face of it, she wouldn't mind the idea. But when she understood the reason? That part was delicate. What if she refused? At the bottom of the stairs I composed myself. She was coming out of the bar.

"There you are. I turned around and you'd disappeared." She looked at me curiously.

"I needed some air."

"Bedtime for me. I'm tired."

"Me too. Must be all the noise and confusion." I couldn't wait to be alone in the dark, to go over every word, every touch, to make it last through the night and all the nights ahead.

The stairway was narrow. We had to push past a group of women who did not want to step aside. I'd noticed them before, always together, Arabs, I'd guessed. In colorful silks and makeup, eyes heavily lined with kohl, they looked like fortune-tellers at the county fair. The tall one spoke first.

You must not go to Egypt!

Nasser no good!

No good for Christians. They torture them!

We were born there. We will never go back.

"What is this?" I said to Jean under my breath. "They sound like Andreas."

"Like a Greek chorus, you mean."

"A chorus of witches. Let's get out of here."

Jean decided on a farewell speech first. "Madames, it has been a long evening and we must pack."

Madames. I suppressed a giggle. Their prophecies of doom followed us down the passageway.

Think on what it is you do.

You will die in that place.

Yellaaaa! Yella emshee! Hone! Hone! Hone! Allah rahim, Allah rahim!

Harsh cries coming from the dock below. Taxi drivers hanging out half-open doors, honking and shaking their fists, cutting off flatbeds sinking under the weight of oil drums and donkey carts piled high with sugarcane, melons and baskets of dates, black-robed vendors making their way through the throng, carrying steaming glasses of tea and heaping trays of pastries high above their heads, dirty-faced urchins nipping at their heels. Passengers fighting to get off, others fighting to get on. Porters in long *dishdashas*, like nightshirts, crawling up ropes and swarming over the ship, hurling luggage willy-nilly over the side, shouts mingling with the screech of horns, the high-pitched blessings of beggars, the monotonous wail of Arab music.

From the safety of the upper deck the women from the night before stood and watched.

It had looked like such a peaceful scene, drifting in past the breakwater. The low white town hugging the shore, golden in the setting sun's embrace, minarets pointing slender fingers to the sky, the dreamy chant of a muezzin calling the faithful to prayers floating across the water.

"Welcome to Alexandria!" said Jean, as we cowered against the rail. "Quiet little spot, isn't it? On second thought, maybe we should have stayed home and taken up typing."

"Try typing us off this bucket. What the hell do we do?"

"Find Andreas, tell him we've reconsidered?" She looked around dubiously. "I don't mean it, at least I don't think so."

"We'd better move before they throw us over the side too! Where is Andreas anyway?" I'd looked everywhere for him to say goodbye.

Jean plunged into the crowd, me beside her, both of us clutching our suitcases. "Somehow, I don't think Justine or Clea ever had to deal with a mob like this," I said.

We almost knocked over a young Egyptian who was struggling to organize a line of porters. They filed past carrying huge cardboard cases bound with twine, an evergreen tree and, bringing up the rear, a refrigerator! Like the British who traveled to outposts with grand pianos and trunks full of morning coats. He laughed at our bewilderment. "Follow me!" He delivered us safely onto the pier. "English? No," looking us over, answering his own question. "Thinking America, Kennedy!"

Same thing as in Greece, America invariably meant President Kennedy.

"I am Ahmed, *studeten.* Coming from German. Excuse me, my speaking not good, am coming from *Allemagne*." How many eons since Napoleon occupied Egypt and still using the French word for Germany. The long memory of the Middle East.

"Where going?" he asked.

We showed him the address of a youth hostel. "*Nein, nein*, this ..." He searched for words. "This too bad place. With custom people helping, to uncle going."

He guided Jean into the customs shed to get the forms, I

staying behind to guard the goods. Surrounded by our luggage, his boxes, the tree propped against the refrigerator, I attracted more than a few stares. I felt a pull on my sleeve. “For you, Meessus.” A boy in a dirty *dishdasha* held out a folded piece of paper.

“*Shoukran*.” Thank you, one of the Arabic words we’d learned. I pretended not to notice the hand kept extended, sure that he’d already been tipped. “*Shoukran*,” I repeated.

He put on a pitiful face. “Please, Eengleesh. *Baksheesh*?”

Searching my pockets I found only drachmas. Greek coins wouldn’t do him any good. Finding a pack of cigarettes, I shook some into his hands. Maybe he could sell them. I unfolded the note. Under the drawing of a whimsical bird Andreas had written, “You are taking my heart, be careful with it.”

Looking up, I found him standing near the chorus of women. I raised my hand to wave goodbye. He gave no sign in return.

8

Alexandria—Alex to the locals, Durrell's "great winepress of love." Customs a nightmare. Bored officials rifling through papers, tossing them aside to wander off scratching themselves and yawning. People shoving for position in lines that went nowhere. A few bulbs hung listlessly from the ceiling. Under their pale circles of light we were figures in a Rembrandt. New officials appeared. The crowd rolled in their direction. Had they come to open another line? No. We rolled back again, Jello in a bowl.

When our turn finally came, they didn't raise an eyebrow over all the stuff Ahmed was bringing in, while we were made to declare every drachma, dollar and traveler's check because of the currency black market. Without him wheedling, no doubt bribing us through, we would have been stuck for hours.

Ahmed was not more than twenty, stocky—all that schnitzel and beer?—skin the color of caramel, with a gentleness common among many Egyptians we met. He had the gift of tongues, a curious mix of Arabic, German, English, some French, all of it exhausting to follow. As we straggled out of customs, the family fell upon him like a returning hero, kissing him, holding on to his sleeves as if he might evaporate if they let go. When they turned their attention to us, his uncle was adamant that we spend the night with them. By the time they had rounded up transport for all the goods, it was going on midnight. In their apartment, his aunt served a delicious supper of eggs, sausages, sardines and round breads with marmalade.

Before bed, Ahmed told us his uncle had urged him to take us along to his family in Cairo. The dire warnings of the women and the chaos at the port were sharp in our memory. When we got what seemed like a better—and safer—offer we took it. This time, at least, we were (mostly) right. Alex could wait, it wasn't going anywhere, and when we came back to get the ship for Cyprus we would be more comfortable on our own. Driving along the Corniche, turning in through the darkened streets, we had begun to suspect that Andreas might be right, perhaps it was not what it once was. Without that halo of sun, it looked to be a shabby old town, buildings faded and crumbling, only vestiges of the world Durrell described. One was the blue hand painted on doors to ward off evil.

It was settled, we would leave in the morning. But first the business of getting the refrigerator and the tree strapped to the roof of the taxi hired to take us to Cairo. As soon as it pulled up, faces appeared at doors and windows. Women and children crowded onto balconies, men roused from sleep came running, suit coats and vests thrown over *dishdashas* and pajamas. They poked at the tree, then the fridge, stroking their chins, looking wise. They circled the taxi, the driver, Ahmed, us.

Eengleesh? *Americani*? *Allemagne*?

Where finding such womans? Ahmed shrugged, as if to say I have no idea how I got saddled with these two.

This not Cairo tree.

This Allemagne tree.

What costing this tree?

How long making bargain in souk?

"*Souk*, in Allemagne?" Ahmed threw up his hands.

The evergreen exhausted, they moved on to the refrigerator. *Where putting? What costing? Why having?* A murderous look came over Ahmed's face. He would happily throw the lot of them inside and bar the door.

"What do you think why having? For freezing my *schnitzels*, this is why having!" He seemed to intend something rude, the embarrassed flush that came over his face confirmed it. He appealed to us. "Please explaining, I finished. Finished!"

They'd beaten him and they knew it. Stubs of cigarettes were produced. They lit them carefully, waving them in our direction.

Cigarra Americani?

Leeky Streek?

We faced a sea of grins and shook our heads. No Leeky Streeks. Grins faded. We offered Greek cigarettes. They turned up their noses but when we started to put them away they changed their minds.

Ahmed and the driver began to lift the tree and were stampeded by the oncoming surge. Seizing it with a roar, the crowd tossed it in the direction of the taxi. Somehow it landed on the roof. Milling around to admire a job well done they jostled the car, sending the tree to the ground in an explosion of dust. Guffaws from the balconies. Raised fists from below put an end to that. Up with the tree once more, the driver scrambling after it this time to secure it with rope. Backslapping, thanks to Allah, time out for another smoke. Someone went in search of a tea vendor. The sun was beating down.

"It's the show of the year, they ought to be selling tickets!" Jean was gleeful. I was impatient to get on the road.

Refreshed from their tea break, it was time to tackle the refrigerator. Whatever doubts they'd harbored about Ahmed's sanity in bringing this thing all the way from Germany, they knew they couldn't let this ricochet off the roof. Each had an opinion on how to proceed conveyed with much shouting and gesticulating leading to further discussion leading to operatic argument. Time again for a smoke. Jean was still enjoying herself immensely. "I take it back, it's the show of the century, and you can bet they're going to keep it running as long as they can."

"Don't they have something better to do?" I groused. Like Ahmed, I wanted to throttle them. And her. Time away from Andreas was beginning to seem like time wasted.

It must have been 90 degrees in the shade, what little of it there was, but nobody defected, not on the ground, not in the balconies. After several attempts to hoist the refrigerator up beside the tree, Ahmed conceded defeat and went in search of a larger taxi. An hour later, both strapped to the roof, we set out to a resounding cheer.

It was midafternoon.

9

Two roads to Cairo. One crosses the desert. The other skirts the delta formed by the spreading fingers of the Nile in the shape of the ankh, the ancient symbol of life.

We took the delta road, through rice paddies, cotton plantations and palm groves. Women in black robes, balancing water jars on their heads with the same proud bearing as camels, walked along canals lined with eucalyptus, leaves cloaked in dust. Oxen, blindfolded to keep them from getting dizzy, plodded round and round turning water wheels. Children, barefoot, chased down village paths, past mud huts brightened by carpets airing on the roofs. Over all a brooding, eternal silence.

Until Cairo. More jarring even than the dock at Alexandria. Masses of people thronged the boulevards and clung to the backs of speeding buses, the white robes they wore billowing like sails on the feluccas of the Nile. Some had eyes soft and cloudy with disease, magnets to flies. The very existence of these multitudes was an attack on every comfortable belief. The notion of the individual soul, each held in the mind of God (each beloved by Him!) in the face of this? Fate laughs, even your God steps aside, Andreas had said.

Ahmed, his good mood restored, was babbling nonstop. He directed the driver to his neighborhood, al-Faggalah, not far from the train station. Turning into the spidery streets of the old quarter was like closing the door on the sudden quiet of a church. He gestured in another direction. "Too big mosque, El-Hakim. He too much …" Ahmed made spinning motions over his head.

"Crazy?" We asked.

"Yes, crazy too much! Killing all dogs in Cairo, not liking sound." Apparently this Hakim character killed his concubines too, ordered them drowned as they bathed. History did not record the offending sounds they made.

Ahmed's family lived on the upper floor of a narrow house. His mother lowered a basket from the balcony every morning for breakfast, bringing up bread and a bean paste called *fu'l* from a vendor in his donkey cart below. This was virtually her only contact with the outside world. She spent her days in the kitchen or on a prayer rug outside the sitting room, reciting suras from the Koran, bowing towards Mecca. Never in doubt which way was east in this part of the world. Contrary to the prophecies of the women on the ship, the only danger we faced apart from the smell of buffalo fat she was rendering one morning, a smell so nauseating it sent us reeling to the balcony for air, was the vigilance of Ahmed and his brothers. We could not leave the house without one, usually all four, tagging along. The pyramids, the Sphinx, the museum, the mosques, we saw it all with the brothers in tow. We tried to slip out, only to turn and discover them behind us, waving cheerfully. Even in Khan Khalili, the vast labyrinthine bazaar, we couldn't lose them. Giving up, we joined them for kebobs in a café, cats crawling over our feet.

Jean, the blonde, was the one they worried about. She was the exotic pet in this zoo. I looked like the rest of them, locals stopped me to ask directions.

"We're back with the penguins," I said to her. "Actually, they're more vigilant than the nuns ever were."

"How can we ditch them?"

"By getting out of town. Let's go to Luxor." We asked Ali, the eldest, the one whose English was best, to break the news to the family.

"But you must not go," he said. "Nasreem will have a visitor, Mr. Hoseibi. Stay one day more, she will like it too much. He has asked my father for her."

Nasreem, the sister, not yet fifteen. Jean was horrified.

"She does not have to accept him," said Ali. "She can refuse."

"Sure, with the whole family conspiring against her? Dirty old lecher!"

"What means this, lecher?"

"Compliment, really," I said, glaring at Jean.

Morning found us hidden behind a screen with Nasreem and the other household females to get a glimpse of the prospect. All of them giggly and coy, especially her mother. The whispering started as soon as he arrived. He walked the length of the sitting room to where the men, all in dark suits, solemnly waited. Eventually, Ali came to us. More huddled whispering. Nasreem, blushing, looking at us with a mix of fear and pride.

"How can she tell anything about him?" Jean asked.

He did look so much older that I couldn't help chiming in. "How do they know if they have anything in common, if …?"

Ali knew exactly what I was driving at. "If she has no experience of men, she will be satisfied with the first."

Ah, that simple. He left us to go deliver the verdict and shake Mr. Hoseibi's hand. I wondered how long before Nasreem showed her satisfaction and kicked his *schnitzels* out of her bed.

Upper Egypt. Squeezed together on wooden benches, choking on dust drifting through the open windows of the slow-moving train. It settled over us until we looked like we'd been shaken in flour, chickens ready for frying. Luxor, by contrast, was as refreshing as a sultan's garden, trees green, not yellow and struggling for breath like in Cairo, the boulevards lined with flowers. We clopped along the Corniche in a horse-drawn carriage to the Savoy overlooking the Nile. The old hotel, high white ceilings and wooden fans, was almost empty, only a group of Coptic Christians there to celebrate Christmas. We'd almost forgotten about it—Jean was cured of the holidays anyway, she'd once declared.

The group took us under their wing to cross the Nile to the tombs of the Valley of the Kings. We struck up a particular friendship with Najih, round and jolly, and Sayid, tall and serious, a Mutt and Jeff duo. They offered to show us around when we got back to Cairo, said they would give us a view of the city quite different from our humble Faggalah, offered to drive us to Alexandria too, where they had the use of a flat—two bedrooms, they added. They seemed honorable. We didn't think twice about accepting.

One afternoon they hired camels and we rode into the desert. The dunes rising and falling to the horizon looked like reclining nudes, a feminine landscape, the sighs of sand and wind, its ever-changing surface. Dangerous too, light when you most need cover, quicksand that could suck in a man unwary, leaving not a trace, not even a bone. Jean loved it. "Beyond anything I ever imagined," she said, gazing into the distance, beautiful eyes glittering. She took off at a gallop. "Come on! We can do anything out here," she shouted. "It's all wiped clean in the wind."

How she got that sluggish camel to move, I don't know. Mine stood there coughing and passing gas. "Don't go so far from us!" I yelled after her. I tried to follow, but my gallant ship of the desert refused to set sail. Where were the men? Sayid reached me first, not amused. "Bloody foolish thing to do!"

I started apologizing for her. "Never mind that now, stay with Najih." He galloped off. Jolly Najih could think of nothing to say while we waited, the excursion in ruins. But it wasn't ruined, not for the runaways. When they came sauntering back, there was a look of pure exaltation on her face. And on his! *He must like being led on a merry chase*, I thought. Or was it a promise of things to come? Riding back, we all marveled at the beauty of the dunes, rose red in the late afternoon sun.

Our old lives were slipping away. On Christmas Eve, we would smoke hashish.

What is it they say? *Smoke hashish and your dreams come true. Smoke hashish and if your dreams don't come true you will forget to care.*

How much time since the pipe made its rounds? Loud ticking sound, Laila's clock. Big Ben in the corner. Big Brother watching.

Hickory dickory dock
Nasser's run up the clock ...

His face was everywhere, staring down from photographs in the shops and from billboards in lurid colors, like those advertising the cinema. Rouged cheeks, scarlet lips, blue tint around the eyes, he looked like a creature from the crypt. Human likeness was supposed to be forbidden in Islamic art, yet there he was, patron saint of the city. I leaned against the cushions and stopped thinking about him, stopped thinking about the police who were surely on their way to arrest us.

A hickory full of hicks ...
A dickory full of dicks ...

Sayid talking. Or was that Najih. A steady drone from the other side of the room, speaking through cotton it seemed. Hashish. The Voice saying something about hashish. I tried to focus. It flitted away, wisps of fog, couldn't hang on to it, couldn't keep my eyes open. Fell back against the pillows.

The clock struck one

Nasser fell down ...

Giggling, unable to stop. Was that Laila giggling too? Somebody was.

The whole thing had been our idea, the journey wouldn't be complete without trying hashish, a destination right up there with Alexandria. But first the final getaway from the family in Faggalah. We concocted a doozy of a story about going on a tour of Biblical sites, banking on no questions asked where piety was concerned.

"I hope we'll be forgiven for lying to them." I had a few qualms.

"Wasn't it the platform Jesus ran on, battling oppression?"

What neither of us banked on was how difficult the parting would be, even from the exasperating bodyguard of brothers, knowing we would never see any of them again. We were all weeping and clutching hands, making us feel worse about our deception.

Mutt and Jeff picked us up in front of the museum in a sleek Mercedes. It certainly was a different Cairo they showed us—Shepheard's, where we wandered into a tea dance—the original hotel had burned in the riots leading to King Farouk's overthrow; chic shops and cafés of Qasr al-Nil; the Sports Club where the Brits had played polo; Roda and Gezira islands. Then Laila, the belly dancer who lived in Zamalek, a smart address at the tip of Gezira. Our friends didn't look the type to consort with belly dancers, but she had what we wanted, hashish.

Laila came to the door in a brocaded caftan, dark almond eyes lined with kohl, long lashes thick with mascara. She invited us into her sitting room, heavy Victorian furniture pushed against the walls, thick folds of maroon velvet drapery at the windows. How oppressive it must be in the heat of summer.

"Najih has told me you wish to smoke hashish," she said in a husky, nightclub voice. "It will be a new experience for you, no?" She looked at us, amused. *What a pair of naifs I've got on my hands.*

"Oh, yes," we said in chorus. Pretending sophistication about drugs, even if we could get away with it, didn't seem smart.

"You take a chance, no? They have explained, no?"

"No."

She frowned.

"Come now, there's little danger of being discovered here." This from Sayid.

"But you should have told them."

"Suppose *you* tell us, then, just for the record," said Jean. What happened to *If there's no risk, there's nothing*?

"Our dear General Nasser has outlawed hashish, that is all." Sayid was dismissive. "Another of his reforms."

"So if we're caught?" I thought about the women on the ship, their warnings.

Laila laughed. "We all go to jail!" So why go along with this? Or was she mocking us? "Anyway, it would go easier with you, the innocent victims."

I wasn't anxious to test the theory. I didn't quite picture our parents bailing us out of a Cairo jail. Who would be so angry, they might just leave us there. Laila shrugged and pulled shut the heavy draperies. Dust motes rose from the folds like moths. Suddenly it was night. "Safer this way," she said. *Safer?* Closed curtains at midday were a dead giveaway. Didn't they have special cops assigned to checking curtains?

Laila began the ritual, bringing out the pipe, the hookah or hubbly-bubbly, reverently placing a coal of hashish on the small pan and lighting it. Like incense. She waited until water bubbled in the bulb before showing us how to draw the smoke slowly in and hold it. I sputtered and coughed and handed it to Jean who gave me a scornful look. "Wait till you try, it's not that easy to get the hang of it," I muttered.

By the third round we were puffing like pros.

I turned to Jean, lost in the pillows, Big Ben in the corner getting louder. I had the notion we should ask Laila to talk about her life as a belly dancer, but she showed little interest in conversation. Wasn't that how she managed to get hashish, through clubs she worked in? Lovers too, I bet, fat ones in fezzes—those little pillboxes on their heads, tassels dangling alongside their noses, bobbing in time to her dancing. Formed the question but no sound came. Tried again. *Do you get hashish in those places you dance?* No answer. I found Jean. Her head was moving, Mutt and Jeff's too, heads floating, bigger as they came nearer to me, lips opening and closing like fish in an aquarium, then gone, whoosh! No sound, only the ticking of the clock, the belching of the pipe. Burrrp. Burrrp.

"Hashish performed a useful function in Egypt." The Voice again, Sayid's voice. Serious expressions all around. "Useful, that is, beyond the obvious benefits of escaping care, easing a life of labor, the tedium of the everyday round ..."

The music goes round and round, ho, ho, ho, ho, ho, ho, and it comes out here. Was that me singing? Nobody took any notice. I started giggling again.

"It was a fairly common practice, clitorectomies." *What?* That woke me up. I'd never heard the word said aloud, but I had a clear idea what it meant.

"Hashish helps the man prolong lovemaking, so he can bring satisfaction to the woman, so he can wait and pleasure her." What an astonishing idea! A culture devoted to the sexual satisfaction of women. Maybe Nasreem would be okay after all.

"Grounds for divorce, you see, if the woman was not satisfied." How did they judge? Did they use a scale like Richter, measuring seismic orgasm? But wait, must be a lot of frustration around since Nasser put a stop to it. Only then did my fried brain register the horror, the mutilation that made it necessary.

What was Jean thinking? She looked at me and winked, nothing to disturb her mellow mood. The sight of her sobered me up. Wasn't this talk a little out of line? All the soul-searching we'd done with Andreas, we never got into anything like this.

Then it struck me. A setup, the two of them conspiring with her in our seduction? Would Laila betray her own sex? Why not, what were we to her, especially if there was money in it. I tried to think it through. We had become expert in sizing up men, or so we thought, take Ahmed and his brothers, all-time pick of the year for any pair of virgins. And these two had behaved perfectly. Yet we'd be spending the night in the same apartment in Alex. How stupid a plan was that?

Smoke hashish and you will forget to care … Better leave the pipe alone.

Laila was serving tea. Hours had gone by, maybe days? Sayid had been lecturing about something—what was it? I sat up, struggling to recall. Hashish. *Orgasm.* I looked at my watch, after five. I nudged Jean. "Drink tea," I whispered. "We've got to straighten up fast or there'll be no virgins walking out of here this night. *Compris?*" Unless Nasser nabbed us first.

Najih was asking Laila to dance for us. "Do it for me, then," he coaxed. I coaxed too, any activity that would move things along, get us up and out of here and on the road. We should have started for Alex by now. She left the room and came back wearing a gauzy yellow skirt gathered in a band round her hips, just below her belly button, a beaded bra top, breasts exposed to the dark beginnings of her nipples. Her feet were bare. I'd never thought about how erotic bare feet can be. Holding a record between her hands, priestess with an offering, she placed it on the turntable and began to dance, slowly, like palm leaves swaying in a gentle breeze. Languid movements, each gesture suggesting a caress, not giving in to it, prolonging desire. Her slender hands arched over her body, hovering here, now there, teasing with the expectation of that touch, knowing what it would do when it came. Steadily, she picked up the pace, the very air aroused by her movements. Faster and faster, hips pulsating, building to a frenzy that kept pace with the rise of the singer's lament and the urgent whine of the lutes and mandolins.

She was in front of me, inviting, the scent of her perfume mixed with sweat as intoxicating as the drug. *I possess all the secrets your flesh can know*. I wanted those secrets, I wanted her, I wanted Andreas with all my soul.

She moved on. I looked at the men, impassive, as if defying her to excite them. A harem could wander in and they wouldn't stir. Hashish was doing its job. They could wait. And wait. They might as well be watching traffic on the river below. And Jean? Still nodding. I poked her. "Are you pretending or are you really bored by this?"

"Leave me out of it," she said drowsily.

We saw belly dancing after that, raucous affairs in nightclubs usually, men leering and cheering, stuffing bills between dancers' breasts, throwing coins at their feet. We never again saw anything like Laila's dance that day in the darkened flat in Cairo.

We took the desert road this time, a straight ribbon of macadam through the sand, bright in the headlights of the car and the rising moon. Sayid was driving, fast, no traffic. Jean dozing beside me, not a worry in the world, abandoning me to fend them off. I would attempt to be invisible, draw no attention to us. Najih, in front, kept up a steady stream of conversation in Arabic. At a rest stop midway near Wadi Natrun, ravenous again, we bought candy. Before leaving Laila's, Najih had gone down to a street vendor for kebabs, so tough they made our jaws ache. We didn't care, we would have eaten our shoes. It was the drug.

It had rained in Alex. Oily puddles lit by neon transformed into shards of stained glass. We pulled up at a restaurant, a parking spot right in front of the door. Jean still dazed, her limbs loose as the *Wizard of Oz* straw man. "Take aspirin," I told her. I couldn't think of anything else. "And for Christ's sake act like nothing is wrong."

She took a few steps and faltered. I suggested they go on in, she needed air. As soon as they were out of sight, I propped her against the car and slapped her, hard, on each cheek. They resounded like thunderclaps in the deserted street.

"Jean, come out of this." No response. "Where are you?" Mumbling some gibberish. "C'mon, tell me where you are."

"Here." Her purse fell, a lipstick rolled into the gutter.

"Where's here?" She looked at me blankly. "What city are we in?"

"Alex."

I took her face in my hands. "We've got to sober up. Eat something. We're staying with these guys we don't really know, probably the dumbest thing we've ever done but it's too late now." Her eyes blinking stupidly, like plastic eyes on a doll.

"Jean, you're scaring the shit out of me." I peered into the darkness. We were not alone. Someone was there, in the shadows. "Shit. We've gotta go!"

"Go," she said.

"Move. Keep talking."

"S'all numb, tongue too."

"C'mon, move! Say what you know by heart, say prayers, nursery rhymes, they'll think we're having a conversation." I looked over my shoulder. Someone still lurking. "*Now I lay me down to sleep.* No, let's scratch that one. Recite *Ring around the Rosie."* Once inside we ordered Cokes. By the time food arrived, we had knocked Humpty Dumpty off his wall. A singer wailing about love and treachery covered our mumbled prayers and rhymes.

It was Sayid's idea to swing by the port to check the schedule. The *Media* bound for Beirut, stopping at Cyprus, was to sail in two days. We waited as he questioned the watchman. "This bloody fool says you sail in the morning, 0700. I'm so sorry," he said when he came back. "We should have made allowances, I suppose."

He suggested we search for the captain or a crew member to make sure. We saw no one. What we did see as we headed back to the car was Ahmed, of all people, coming right at us with Omar, the youngest of the brothers. No place to hide, the dock flat and wide open as a football field. *Busted.* This far from Cairo and al-Faggalah and we still couldn't shake them.

Caught red-handed, or as they would see it caught with our pants down. What they had been so determined every waking hour to protect us from. Excuses and explanations rushed to our lips, but what was the use? They stared at us, expressions as inscrutable as their Sphinx. What would they go through life thinking of us? Sentenced, helpless to set it right, we watched as they turned their backs and walked away.

Regret about letting the city slip through our fingers vanished. We couldn't leave fast enough. I don't know whether Jean realized it but if we waited for the next ship we would miss Andreas, he would have gone back to Athens. To me the choice was clear. Our Alexandria would have to be the scenes at the dock and the farce featuring a taxi, an evergreen tree and refrigerator, and a bunch of local busybodies.

The apartment was in a concrete block near the port. Sayid and Najih said goodnight at the door of our room. We listened for their footsteps in the hall and the sound of another door closing. Several hours later they woke us for the drive to the port. Perfect gentlemen, just as we'd pegged them. The minute their backs were turned and we could salvage a scrap of humor, we decided they had to be eunuchs. Not a pass, not once, not even in Alexandria, fabled city of lovers in shuttered rooms, embracing under slowly turning fans.

Durrell's great winepress of love.

PART FOUR

Aphrodite's Island: A Love Story

10

This time it was Jean who slept as soon as we boarded the *Media*, on the way to Cyprus, and I who stood watch at the rail. In Egypt I tried to tell her how things stood. I couldn't do it, something she'd say, something in her eyes, and I'd stop, afraid to hurt her, afraid to disrupt the pact we had made. That counted more than anything.

Before pushing off from Alexandria, I watched dawn break and heard the call for prayer rising from minarets, one after the other, joined in holy relay. Now we were churning through a strong sea, sun bright in the southern sky, sailors shouting to one another as they cleaned the deck below. But for them I was alone with my thoughts, my mind churning too, the nagging questions, not all of them from my other companion, The Scold. What would his family think of me? What would I think of him? Had I invented someone whose reality would only be a letdown?

Look at a map and you will see that Cyprus stands alone on the sea, pointing an accusing finger—or beckoning one?—at Lebanon. By the time we docked at the little port of Limassol, the sun had disappeared and it was misting steadily. I saw him right away in the crowd huddled together in the wind, his collar turned up against the cold, waving, happy to see us, hugging us both, lingering with me longer, exactly as I remembered him, the chiseled features, the smile that cleared the brooding intensity so often shadowing his face. I read the question in his eyes, *Does she know*? I shook my head. He frowned but said nothing, only a whispered “I thought you’d never get here!” We climbed into the car of his friend Nikos for the drive to Famagusta.

The house of Andreas was on the corner of Alexandrou Street, old-fashioned rooms on the second floor that reminded me of my grandmother’s. Homesickness rushed over me. Gone almost three months, sagging beds at the mercy of bedbugs on land, dodging mice and snails crawling loose from crates or worse on smelly ships at sea. The feeling didn’t last, I wouldn’t start counting the days, not yet. With his family, we felt an instant familiarity. Imprint of the British? Cyprus had been administered by them for years. Andreas wouldn’t like it if he knew this was the reason we felt so much at home. Another reason was the absence of veils, though not all women in Egypt shrouded themselves and when they did, it was perversely provocative to lock eyes in faces otherwise hidden. If eyes were mirror of the soul, then everything was revealed. It seemed a contradiction.

Andreas’ father clasped our hands in his. “You are welcome in my house.” His mother said over and over, “You are welcome, my son never stops talking about you,” then hurried into the kitchen where she’d been for two days, Andreas laughingly told us. Affection so unconditional all we had to do to earn it was breathe. It was the legendary hospitality of the Greeks but something more, something that must have come from living at the edge of loss as they had done. It showed in the way they were kind to each other. I resolved to try to be more like them, to act only out of genuine feeling.

Down a road away from the house, strewn with rocks and swept by sand was the sea wall, and across that sea, less than a day’s sail, Beirut. Cyprus was like Greece in the sun and Ireland in the rain. Narrow roads and stone walls, intense green of grass, greyness in the hills and lonely stretches. Jokes and laughter they had in common too, and that foreboding sense of tragedy, the dark stain beneath the surface that excites poets.

When we came in from our walk, dinner guests had gathered. Doctor Thanos, a foot taller than everyone else, Uncle George (Yiorgos) as stout as Uncle Yannos was gaunt, others crowding around, greeting and gossiping. The table was soon loud with politics. Cyprus had been ruled for centuries—by the Republic of Venice, Othello an actual overseer at one point, by the Ottoman Turks, most recently by the British. The recent conflict, the bloody struggle Andreas had been caught up in, came with rebellion against British occupation, many Greek Cypriots demanding *enosis* or union with Greece, an outcome unthinkable to the minority Turkish Cypriots. It ended with Makarios, an Orthodox archbishop, becoming president of an independent Cyprus.

Bitterness between the two sides continued to breed treachery. The night before there had been an incident, impossible to know how serious with all the words and opinions hurled at it. Andreas' father turned to us, sighing, "It's a pretend peace we have," his wife chiding him for worrying us with his dire predictions. "For all our suffering only a pretend peace. We will never trust each other. Never."

"Might as well ask a lemon to grow on an olive tree," said Dr. Thanos. Heads nodded as they pondered this thing that could never be.

"Let us leave this subject," said Uncle George, flushed with wine, wisps of mustache curling out like spines on a lobster. "Our guests grow tired with our weeping and gashing of teeth."

"Gnashing," Dr. Thanos corrected.

"Gashing, ganashing, whatever it is, let us leave this sorrow. Begin the toasts!"

Andreas laughed. "Watch out, my uncle makes a game of this, winds us all up."

"Yes, let us begin," said Uncle Yannos. "Let us toast our archbishop, Makarios."

"*President* Makarios," George amended. "At least he is worth something, that priest, not like those other windbags who fill our heads with their rubbish."

Yannos crossed himself. "Those are holy men you speak of!"

"You see my brother, how he lives in a fog of incense and ignorance?"

"Our guests," Andreas' father reminded but George was rolling now. "Father Demetrios, fat wife waddling behind him like a duck, so full of gas he could keep us farting for a week. Even the Turks!"

"George!"

"Not even Dr. Thanos can find a cure. Oh, how our wives moan in their beds. We take heart, thinking how much we have satisfied them, but it's only the gas!" George pounded the table until the plates jumped. "See how these priests control us? We don't know if it's children we are making or air!"

"What nonsense." Laughter swallowed the comment from Andreas' father.

"Shame," said Uncle Yanos.

"I speak truth." George subsided, took a sip of wine and was off again. "How is it you sit here like old women dozing in the sun. Loosen those tongues. What about Marilyn? Let's drink to Marilyn Monroe!" If he thought she would scandalize anybody, he was mistaken. Similar tributes followed.

"To Melina!"

"Melina." The man rose from his chair. "I will tell you about Melina Mercouri." Someone pushed him back into it.

"To Ireni!"

"Eleni!"

"Ah, Eleni, breasts as white as goat's milk."

"Is that you, Michaelis?" said Uncle George. "The gods are singing tonight."

"To Aphrodite and her blessed island," said Dr. Thanos.

"Yes, to *Kypros*." The Greek word for Cyprus called forth a litany of uprisings, their leaders and cohorts.

"'55 and Grivas!"

"'21 and Byron!"

"Capo d'Istria!"

"Capo d'Istria," mused Andreas' father, "How could a man with such a name escape destiny? Capo must become head of something, so the Greeks put him in charge of the country."

"Americans make presidents for better reasons?" said George. "Lincoln and slavery? Yes, I know our democracy had slaves, but this was two thousand years before! Anyway, both of them wiped out." He pointed a finger to his head. "Capo kaput!"

"To all the dead heroes!"

"To freedom!"

"To President Kennedy."

"Back to serious? Come, we'll drink to my mother-in-law's beard."

Andreas' mother had had enough. "George, what foolishness you talk, Freni has no such thing."

"Since when have you been nuzzling her old cheeks? But not even God speaks in straight lines. How can He when He must keep up with us who are so crooked?" George did not pursue toasting the beard. He looked at us slyly, "Watch this, this is certain to send our brother straight down into hell, guaranteed, no return ticket." He tapped his glass for attention.

"What now, Yiorgos, oh, excuse me, *General* Yiorgos, a bulletin from the front?"

This from Matsis, laughing so hard his belly shook beneath

the napkin draped over it. His neighbor took the opportunity to pluck a pack of cigarettes from his pocket and pass it down the table.

"No bulletin, my friends," said George. "Only a poor tribute to that uncommon liberator of common people, Karl Marx."

"That … that … unbeliever!" Yannos was on his feet. "I will never drink to him, not under torture. What? Mao next, then the devil himself." He made the sign of the cross several times in rapid succession.

George bowed in his direction and raised his glass. "My dear Yannos, why did I not think of it? To Chairman Mao!"

"Blasphemy!" yelled Yannos, punching the air. "That Communist! That murderer! That … that Long Marcher!"

George was helpless with laughter. Andreas too. All of us, except his mother. "A lollapalooza," George spluttered. "I've been waiting to use this word since I first heard it in the cinema. I didn't mean it, Yannos, not when we know what those Communist bastards did after the war, it's just that …" He was laughing too hard to continue. Even Yannos was finding it hard to resist. "You looked exactly like a chicken who knows its neck is about to be twisted. By all the saints I couldn't help giving it one more spin!"

Yannos' smile vanished. Andreas' father raised his hand. "Enough! Isn't there something more important to tell our guests this night?"

"To our American friends!"

"For they are jolly good fellows. *Yasas!*"

"*Yasas!*"

Yannos sighed. "May they remember us with a few crumbs of dignity."

"*Dignity*?" George shouted. "Explain, please, what use is dignity? Does she sing to me when the moon is full, my soul spilling over in terror at the silence of God? Does she rub my feet when I stink of wine? Fetch the doctor when I howl with pain? The priest when I howl no longer?"

"Stop!" Andreas' father covered his ears. "We are grown dizzy with this man."

George, grown pale with the exertions of his speech, did stop but not for long. His voice was subdued. "When the Christ hung naked on the cross, where was dignity? When Andreas was in that filthy prison, where was dignity?" Tears were coursing down his cheeks. "You and I watching while our young men slipped away to fight for freedom and to die. Forgive me, my brother, your dignity is a whore."

He got up from the table and was gone. Dr. Thanos rushed after him. The others resumed talking and smoking as if nothing at all unusual had happened.

11

A knock on our bedroom door, Sunday morning, Andreas' father inviting us to church. His mother stood behind him in the narrow hallway. "Can't you leave them to rest?"

"But we'd love to go, wouldn't we, Jean?" I thought he might talk to us about the evening before, that wild ride from wordplay to toasts to tears. Along the way he pointed out the café where old-timers in overcoats were already playing backgammon under a spreading plane tree. The bakery, display windows shuttered. The school, whose headmaster was English. "How we admired them, how grateful we were when they came to defend us against the Germans. And in the end? Our tender feelings could not save us. They would not grant independence without a fight."

During the service, enough incense was lofted over the pews to fell a herd of elephants. Afterward, he proudly introduced us to the priests and anyone else he could collar. Walking back, we stopped at a tidy little house and followed him into the garden as he lifted a vine here, checked a window there. "My friend who lived here went to fight the Germans. I told him war is not for greybeards. I was right, he died before he could kill even one. One day, I hope, the family will return." He searched the sky, as if to puzzle out a meaning there. "There seems so little use for this loss."

"We've never done anything worth a tinker's damn, have we," Jean said that night getting ready for bed. "Nothing real or important." It was New Year's Eve. We had spent it at home with the family—no noisemakers, no confetti, no Guy Lombardo. Just enough wine passed around to fit into a thimble.

"No, I guess we haven't." I attached little significance to what she said. I was too busy thinking about how Andreas looked at me when we touched thimbles at midnight.

Roaming the island by day, haunting the cafés by night, more talking, soul grinding we called it, sometimes until morning like on the ship. A magical time. We had joined a mad band of poets and singers and storytellers, the Pied Pipers we called them—Ko-Ko and Costas, Pandelis, Antonio, Nikos and Vias who took a shine to Jean—free as pagans in a place where the word *freedom* itself was more powerful than any drug. It was a magical time for me. Not for Jean. She ignored any overture from Vias. When I asked she dismissed him. She began to withdraw in a way that was different from the world-weary attitude she sometimes assumed. She went off by herself to smoke, took solitary walks. Before, when something struck us as funny, one glance and we were convulsed. Nothing was funny now. We always talked over the day's happenings before diving into our journals, now she went straight to her scribbling. Maybe I should have looked there for clues. Picking at her food she seemed to grow thinner before my eyes, while I felt myself rounding at the corners, blooming under the eyes of Andreas. When I asked what was going on, she wouldn't, or couldn't, say.

"Well, send a letter if you decide to talk about it." That's how far away she seemed. I felt pity at first. What a sly perversion is pity, the superiority of it, but that was only part. I was soaring outside myself. One afternoon on the sea wall, looking out over the water, I felt so completely at one with the universe, so naturally a part of it, that had I died in that moment I would have been perfectly happy. I've never felt anything like it since. The moment passed. Her sadness remained. Pity turned to fear.

Dr. Thanos' clinic was not far. I thought about consulting him but it felt like a betrayal. I managed to push aside any thought that I was living a bigger betrayal. On our way out one evening, I went ahead to let him know where to meet us and found a waiting room full of people, most of them women, most of them in pain. They didn't go to a doctor, it seemed, until they were *in extremis*. When he came out of the examining room, he looked like he was too. "I will be delayed, if I can join you at all."

"How can I help?" Stories of heroic deeds made me want to do one good one. A large woman, tearful, was rocking herself near the window, closed against the damp night air, the chair crying too under her weight. She was dressed in black, even her kerchief. They all were, the widow's uniform. I went over and soothed her like a child. To my surprise, she grew calm.

"That's as effective as anything I can do. But, no, it presumes too much, you young people have your evenings ahead of you."

"I can and I will help, as long as we're here!"

"I cannot accept this from you, Sirrine. It's your holiday, you didn't come here to watch over sick people." Holiday. How frivolous it sounded then, in that room.

"But you said I was useful." He was doubtful still. "It's a chance to spend time with you," I added.

"Well, put that way, I am grateful." He frowned. "If you are sure."

After that I stopped by whenever I could. The more involved I got, the more morose Jean seemed. "Come along," I urged, convinced it would bring her out of herself.

"So I can play Lady Bountiful too?"

We all felt the gloom, even the Pied Pipers. I was sure her black mood had nothing to do with Andreas and me. We'd been discreet, he letting me know with a slight word, a touch, that we were lovers on hold. I decided to make certain.

"You've got to tell me what's wrong," I said one morning. We were brushing crumbs off the long table in the dining room. "You're not talking to anyone."

"Words die." She was staring absently at an old photograph on the sideboard, a dour couple, his face a nest of whiskers. "I don't trust life."

Good Grief! I checked myself, I put my arm around her. "Can't you stop questioning everything, just for a little while? Let go, have some fun?" *Am I on this journey alone?* That's what I was really asking.

"I don't know how."

"It doesn't have to be so damned complicated!"

Couldn't she snap out of it? I was beginning to understand how her father could say this to The Countess.

"But if we don't find meaning ..."

"Jean, what is this? My life according to Sartre?"

"Answer me, what is there if we don't find meaning?"

"Look around you! The sea, the beauty of this island, the family who loves us, Thanos and his poetry. Is it so bad? All along we've heard about this vale of tears and woe on woe and set your sights on eternity. Is there no pleasure at all, no happiness to reach for? Now? When we're young?"

She looked up from the photograph. "Maybe for you."

I was drowning too. Each night when the lights went out and I was in bed in the room I shared with Jean, intense longing came over me. I knew it was only a question of when. And how. Most of all, I wondered how.

A day came with an early promise of spring. Our little band made plans to drive to some temple ruins. We wrapped up a picnic of bread, olives and cheese, a few hard-boiled eggs, stuffing it all into a string bag, and went into the countryside. Even the air smelled of spring, that fresh smell that signals winter's end. At home it was the drip drip of snow melting and gutters turning into rivers and kids jumping on membranes of ice, daring them to break, squealing when they did and soaking our boots. Here the sun was shimmering in young orchards and old olive groves alike, in the vineyards linked arm in arm down the rows, in the myrtle tangled in embrace. Even the rocks seemed eager to bloom.

We stopped to explore a small chapel, so lost in the undergrowth we had trouble finding the door. We struggled to part the vines, pricking our fingers on thorns, stumbling back on each other and laughing when they gave way. Curious birds circled, rebuking us for disturbing the peace. When we got the heavy door open, light shot through like an arrow, transfixing us in the eye of a saint in a fresco high up behind the altar, the somber Byzantine face silencing us.

We found a place for our picnic, chasing off a goat who watched angrily from a distance until he lost interest and wandered off. We scattered in the meadow that marched to the edge of the stream and the far-off hills rising in a green haze on the other side, clouds skidding recklessly overhead. Andreas caught up with me. He put his hands on my shoulders, forcing me to stand still and look at him. "We've had enough of this now, enough waiting. What do you think?" His expression grave, like that saint back there. *At last! That's what I think.* Surprised, finding ourselves alone, we had no more words. He pulled me to him. His finger traced my face as if drawing it before he kissed me, pressing for responses that came without ceasing. Until we heard someone call.

He pulled away, words tumbling out. "I have respected this time for us, finding out who we are, not wanting to rush you, to hurry anything, but we know now, don't we? Enough anyway to begin! I can't stand it, you in my house, so close to me, sleeping alone." He raised his eyes to the heavens. "What do you want from me? Am I a saint? No, I am not a saint. Only a man, a man who wants you, Sirry, now, here, these bloody people shouting around us, don't answer them! I think of nothing but you, my head is filled with it, my nights are filled with it. All I dream about is running to you, down all the rivers and all the streams into the sea of you. If you will take me."

"I will take you."

He lifted me into the air. Whirling like demented dervishes, joy and madness together. "Oh, God! It is your God, isn't it? Was my uncle wrong? Is He talking in straight lines at last?"

"Andreas, put me down. You're crazy!"

"I am crazy! Because of you, Sirrine, it's you, it's you!" We fell to the ground clutching each other, rolling in the grass until I was lying under him, and we were still.

"Where have you been?" He was a shadow above us, face as dark as the trees, Nikos. "We've been calling and calling, didn't you hear?"

"Right here the whole time. Sirry tripped—a rock or something. I was trying to help her up, then I fell too." For some reason that set off laughter again.

Nikos, awkward, not sure what was so funny, turned and shouted, "Over here, I've found them."

We got up and brushed ourselves off. When the others walked up, I met Jean's eyes. She knew.

"Come in, my child." Dr. Thanos was in his office, from which he had banished any sign or smell of medicine, only his books, piles of them. The waiting room was empty. "I saw you coming down the road. I lit a fire to take off the chill now that the sun's gone. Here, give me your coat."

I was shivering, but not from the cold. Andreas, my words to him, I will take you. That look on Jean's face when the knife of recognition went through her. I needed to talk. "Are you really here alone?"

"My dear, I'm never alone. I have my poets."

"And patients?"

"All of them cured. A tribute to my skills and your soothing hands." He lifted his fine head and laughed, not something he often did.

"So which of your poets is keeping you company today?"

"One of our own, Cavafy. Ever hear of him?"

"No—wait—maybe in a book I read. Wasn't he born in Alexandria?"

"Yes, but he's Greek and his poems are in Greek. About love and longing, the ravages of time, how fleeting it is. About the world he comes from."

"A world that doesn't exist anymore, I guess. Not as he knew it."

"Perhaps it never did. Perhaps it's only in our hearts that Alexandrias exist, must exist, to help us bear the rest."

"Just as well we didn't see it then. It will be the way we imagined, always."

"Would you like to hear something of his?"

Settling into the worn leather chair, I listened to his voice over the crackling of the fire. I thought of O'G the day she came to class raving about Lawrence Durrell. Had she read Cavafy? "The words sound beautiful. What do they say?"

"An old man in a café recalling his golden youth and how he did not seize it in time. Now too late, it's gone."

He closed the book, his finger marking the page. "Regret, my dear, the gift of memory, a poison sure as hemlock. Not swift but just as sure."

He continued to read, this time in English:

how he always believed—what madness—
that cheat who said, "Tomorrow. You have plenty of time."
He remembers impulses bridled, the joy
he sacrificed. Every chance he lost
now mocks his senseless caution.

"I begin to feel this, Sirrine."

"But you're not old."

"Not young either."

Half past twelve. How the time has gone by.
Half past twelve. How the years have gone by.

"But tell me, how was your excursion today?" He looked up, moon brows rising over the rim of his glasses, eyes blue as a sailor's at sea.

"All right."

"Just all right? Something is bothering you, it seems." What was it about these people, boring into your psyche day and night, an army of little drills! Yet I was the one who came here wanting to talk. It was the opening I needed, but I didn't take it.

His voice broke into my reverie. "Hmmm … lost somewhere, I see. And who's with you, I wonder?" He lit the pipe he'd been filling from an old pouch on the desk. It smelled of apples and cloves, like my grandfather's used to.

"We had a perfectly fine day exploring your beautiful island. Perfect weather too. That's all I was thinking about."

"And you're a perfect little liar!" he shot back. "You're not fooling the doctor."

"What do you mean?"

"My child, what I mean is that you are in love."

"I am?"

"Perfectly obvious, again using your word. About this you

cannot lie. Nor he."

"*He*."

"We both know who," he said gently. "Why pretend? He lies no better than you."

"Then everybody knows?"

"My dear, I don't know about everybody. This is not my concern. My concern is why you want to hide it. Feelings this strong must have their freedom, will have their freedom, no matter what we do." That word again, the word they loved so much. Fate must be coming next.

"Your Andreas is a talented young man, Sirrine. Idealistic, ready to sacrifice everything for his country. Some were not so willing …" His voice broke. "Well, you know what we think of him, you heard George the other night. Difficult to understand his emotion, if you never had to face anything like this. I myself, well, I am not proud of how I responded." He leaned forward. "I should tell you this since we have grown close. Yes, there should be no illusions …" He didn't speak for so long that I was certain he had decided against taking me into his confidence after all. He put down his pipe, went back to studying the glasses in his hands, pressing the bows against his lips.

"Well, then, it was late, I was closing up here. The telephone rang, someone shot, could I come straightaway? I had heard nothing, no sirens, no disturbance in the streets. I suspected a trap and hung up. This is what I told myself. In truth, I was afraid. The most dangerous man is the man who cannot trust himself. I came to my senses soon enough. Do not think me a hero or anything like it. I recollected my sacred oath, that's all. I rang the number I'd scribbled down. The accent was Turkish. He gave instructions. I hurried out through the dark streets. Close to my destination I was grabbed from behind. There were two of them. We turned into the Turkish quarter where my bag was taken from me, my face covered. For my protection, they said.

"A trap. So I had been right all along. I made a move, but they tightened their grip and we wound through the narrow passages, turning this way and that. It was well after midnight. Still in the Turkish quarter, spices lingering from the evening's cooking, sweet perfume hanging in the mist like cobwebs. I tell you I was terrified. Not of death. I know a bit of that, after all, so what if it comes sooner? No, it was fear of what might lie in wait between me and that old adversary. What choice? What betrayal?

"We walked on until I heard the scrape of an iron gate. Then we were inside a room where they allowed me to see. Lying on a mat on the floor, a young man not much older than Andreas, no obvious distress, a wound that was not bad. Imagine my relief. Imagine too my surprise at discovering the chap to be Greek. But what was he doing in this part of town, sheltered from by these people? It went hard for anyone caught giving aid to so-called terrorists and Turks were not sympathetic to the cause, although there were some. Two women, one squatting beside, cooling him with a cloth she refreshed from a basin, the other weeping. Was it compassion or was this young man her lover? Uncommon, perhaps, she being Turkish, but not impossible. One of my guardians spoke harshly to her. Fearing the noise would raise suspicion? Or in opposition to such a liaison? How this boy came to be there, I did not ask. Best not to know too much. I set about patching him up, and they guided me away. So late even the whores were asleep. Two days later his body was dumped by the side of the road."

The whole time he had been talking, he looked at his hands. I waited for him to go on, listening to the ticking of the clock.

"How often have I searched this out in my mind? I held myself to blame, surely I overlooked something. To this day I cannot be certain. To this day there are those who would accuse me of bungling the job. Or worse. Impossible to say what happened, this being a time when no one knew who was friend, who was enemy, when overnight anyone could become a traitor and many were quick to become fanatics. Did those men decide to kill him? Did the boy decide on a rash act? Or did something go tragically wrong, something I should have foreseen? On the hinge of this question swings my hope and my despair."

"But what you did took courage beyond what most people would ever dream of!"

He shook his head. "Why make so much of this, you may ask. Island life is a very particular idea. Self-reliant, we look inward, while at the same time we know we are far more dependent on one another than in most communities man inhabits. Yet here, on this beautiful island, we are at war with each other and so we are at war with ourselves. We distrust each other, so we distrust ourselves. And we hate.

"In any event, I was never called upon again, by either side. You see now what my good works are made of. The poor are in no position to question my skills."

"I think you're a saint!"

"Oh, not by a long chalk," he said, smiling at my outburst.

"But so many people are hypocrites, obeying commandments to the letter, never getting tested. Not tolerant or forgiving. All those rules, very little kindness. Even my own family sometimes, if it isn't too awful for me to say so."

"Yes, I too know people like this." He got up to switch on another light against the gathering gloom. "But we were speaking of Andreas, weren't we? I'm not certain we can hold him here."

"But where would he go? He couldn't breathe anywhere else! The world he paints, the colors, so much a part of him. I can't imagine … well, Athens maybe, he's happy there, he says he is."

He looked at me sharply. "And you? Could you be happy

there? Greece is very poor, recovering from the war, still, and the civil war that came after. Tell me, how many hours for you to reach your own country—nine, ten? What cost to book a ticket each time you feel homesick? I am sure you would miss your family, even if they are not perfect." Was he mocking me?

"Yes, I would miss them. I haven't thought that far ahead."

"Of course not," he said more kindly. "You are young."

"Do you think we have a certain fate, Dr. Thanos? Each of us, an indelible imprint when we're born like the stain of original sin they say is on our souls? Or does it change, depending on the choices we make, the people we meet, where we go or don't go? Like moving chess pieces of our lives."

"To know that, my dear, I would have to be far wiser than I am."

"Did you ever think there's one person for each of us to love, one special person sent by God? Or fate? And if we don't recognize him, don't follow …"

"Yes. I have thought so."

"What about you, then?"

"I let him go." He turned his face from me. "He's very sensitive, Sirrine."

I was still absorbing that word, *him.* What it might have meant to turn his back on this love. My tears were sudden, stinging. "I don't want to hurt Andreas! Believe me. I don't want to hurt myself."

He knocked the ashes from his pipe, stood and put his arm around me. "Well, then, you must love him. And if you love him enough, no one has to be hurt. If you have courage. No one is given freedom as a gift. No one. There is always a price. To live in the way that we would live, to feel passionately about anything …"

We heard the bell and footsteps in the hall. He dabbed at my cheeks with his handkerchief. "I hope you will find that courage and if you do, then perhaps all of it is possible. Now, my little Nightingale, let's see what we've got here. Let's see if this, at least, is something we can cure."

12

Dr. Thanos had given his blessing, it seemed. And if it was time for us to begin, as Andreas said, it was obviously way past time to talk to Jean. This filled me with dread. We were at home with the family, Andreas' little sister, Ismene, curled up beside me, her head in my lap, humming softly. It was raining. I could see it falling in sheets in the light of the lamp on the corner.

"Very English, this weather, wouldn't you say?" Andreas had more than a touch of irony in his voice.

"Yes, it's given me a headache," Jean said.

"I'll brush your hair, it will make you feel better!" Ismene jumped up.

"No thank you," Jean said sharply. "If you'll excuse me." She went around the room kissing everyone goodnight. *A prima donna,* I thought, thwarted in my plan to sit up with her after everyone had gone to bed. Andreas knew my intention. He glanced at me as if to say, *It will have to wait. Again.*

Ismene brushed my hair instead, singing to me in her high, sweet voice. I felt Andreas watching us, what a pretty picture we made. I too said goodnight and went to check on Jean, hoping to find her reading, hoping she'd only pretended about the headache so she could be alone, but the light was out and she was lying on her side, facing the wall. I got into bed without undressing, listening to the rain and her steady breathing. The house fell silent and I made up my mind. Tiptoeing out, I found my way to him on the floor below. I wouldn't take back anything that happened between us that night, not even now. I meant to stay an hour, not more, to lie in his arms and make love with words and we did that, all talk finally down to just the two of us. I wanted him to know everything I was or knew or could name, the way new lovers do, nothing too trivial. He seemed to understand everything, except a Minnesota winter.

"How cold? This is a joke, right?"

"No joke. You can almost hear the air, climb on snowdrifts that crunch under your feet like toast but don't break, everything the color of steel, like the sea under a cloudy sky, beautiful in an eerie way. So still it's as if you've fallen through to the bottom of the world."

"What does it *feel* like?"

I curled up closer, hearing the rain beat against the windows. "When you come back inside, your body is so grateful, a sense of well-being floods through you like … like pleasure."

"How did you escape with a heart that's still warm?"

"Who says I did?"

"Ah, maybe a long summer can thaw it out."

"A Cyprus summer."

"Will you?"

"Maybe we should see how this goes first." Brazen and I didn't care.

His lips brushed my ear. "Are you that hard to please?" He leaned over me, his eyes darker than I'd ever seen them. The answering throb, the dance of desire.

"Don't," I whispered when he moved to shut off the light. "I want to see you, to remember everything."

He undressed me carefully. Not practiced but not fumbling either, no, definitely not, and when he uncovered all that he'd imagined, he gasped. Or was that my sound? His hand curved over my breasts, tracing the circles of my nipples rising to my defense, tracing the larger circle below, then down, on down to the dance. I arched under his touch like a cat. "You're so beautiful," he murmured.

"Tell me."

"More beautiful than anything I ever dreamed of holding in my hands." He left me, letting his clothes fall where he stood, never taking his eyes from me. His body was tanned still, the color of the desert when the sun goes low in the sky.

He asked if I was afraid and pressed me against him, letting me get used to the feel of him. He knew I was at the far end of my experience.

I confessed that yes, I was, a little, but startled more like it, seeing him naked in front of me, wondering what I was doing there, trying to shut out The Scold, who'd returned with a vengeance putting in her two cents, starting the ping-pong game. *If I do this, will I ever be able to leave him? If I don't, will I ever have this chance again?* Until the voice stilled and I began to do with my hands what he had done, riding over the sharp planes of his hips and into the warm hollow of his stomach, hearing him catch his breath when I got to that part of him that was harder still. Pleasure and triumph, his mouth moving over me, following where his fingers had been. Desire in waves. *So this is how it's supposed to be.* I kissed his fingers one by one.

"You taste of sweet lemons," I murmured.

"Come to me now," I heard him say, and when I opened to him his eyes were even darker than before, smiling down at me, all will, all sense of otherness gone. He was gentle, as I expected he would be, telling me again how much he wanted me, talking me through it, holding back for me, whispering encouragement.

Whispering, too, a word that sounded in my ears like a song. "*Agapimou*," my love, the "g" soft as it caught in his throat. He covered my mouth with his when I cried out.

13

I was dressed to go, forcing myself to go, wanting to stay, when she stormed in, trench coat over her pajamas. Came straight for me.

"Jean, no!" Andreas started towards her but something stopped him, made him understand she wasn't going to hit me. With a little training, slim Jean from Manhattan looked like she could throw a pretty good right hook.

Her eyes welled with tears. "I'm loved in this house too."

"Yes." He reached for her but she pushed him away.

"Why did you do this? Behind my back?"

"We meant to tell you—I meant to, Andreas would have, a long time ago, he wanted to tell you himself. I said no, I would do it but I was afraid."

"You couldn't tell me?"

"I didn't want a rift between us. You never seem to understand …"

"Sex!" She spit it out, the deadly asp.

"Yes," Andreas confirmed. "And more than that."

"She always has to have a man."

"Jean, please. Don't do this."

She was riding a bull and couldn't let go. "I thought you and I were after something else, finding another way to live—wasn't that it? Or was it this?" She gave a cynical laugh. "Why didn't you stay home, have one of those boys lined up to get at you?" One more punch.

"What is it that's so terrible you just want to destroy?"

"We have a song, Andreas, one of her favorites, 'Love for Sale.'"

"Stop! You're the person I'm closest to in the whole world."

"I guess you should have thought about that before. Both of you."

Lights in the hall were on. Someone up, wakened by slamming doors and our voices. His mother on the stairs. When she saw us she retreated. No idea where Jean went. I turned to the window to see the first streaks of dawn, rosy-fingered of course. I wished a horse with wings would come charging through and sweep me into the sky like a page out of myth. Andreas put his hands on my shoulders. "I'm sorry," he said.

"What do I do now?" I pressed my forehead against the cold pane, hoping he'd find something to say to heal us. "I hate her for what she's done. She's taken it, she's made it dirty and small. I won't be part of that, I refuse that shame."

He took his hands away. "We hurt her, more than we realized. We betrayed her trust, something I vowed never to do since it was done to me. That was our crime."

Crime. That was a bit much. How did he get to be so pure, so concerned about how it's our fault, my fault? I had hoped for words to heal us. *What about me?* I wanted to shout. *I'm the one you were making love to, or have you forgotten already?* I said nothing. I no longer belonged in his room. I no longer belonged in the room I shared with her either.

Morning comes that puts an end to battle. So said Homer.

Morning comes that puts an end to the whole shebang, so said I and The Scold, in agreement for a change. Only Ismene chattered away, unquestioning. The parents, not comprehending the heavy atmosphere that had settled over the house, avoided us. They usually spoke English when we were around. Now, it was only Greek. I wondered what Andreas was telling them.

Seeking refuge on the sea wall, I tried to sort things out and be rational, above all to hold on to the tenderness of the night before. Like trying to hold on to a dream that's slipping through the margins of memory and is gone, only a vague sense that it might have been important. Taken aback by what I'd done, but I didn't have time for that. Thrilled by what I'd done, but Jean had ruined it. Could I forgive her? At the same time I wanted us to be the same as before. We'd invested so much in this journey, all the cherished ideas of ourselves and what we might become, all of it lost if we didn't continue on. A terrible defeat.

What a *merde*, what a mess. I certainly couldn't follow Andreas to Athens, much as my jumbled emotions might cause me to waver. Besides, he hadn't suggested it. He was distant now, all that talk about betraying her and not a word to me since. Maybe he believed her accusations. I didn't dwell on that. I stayed away from the house until dinner. This time, the table loud with silence. *Pass the potatoes* was about it.

Afterwards, Jean, in a strained voice, suggested we three go for a walk. Wrapped in our own thoughts we were as far away from each other as from the stars. When we reached the strip along the beach where the tavernas were, boarded up for the season, we stopped to sit on a terrace under a thin canopy of vines. She spoke first, nervous. "I believe—well, I know I behaved badly. Very badly."

"Jean, you—"

"Wait! Give me a chance, Sirrine."

Andreas helped her light a cigarette, shielding her from the wind off the sea. I heard her inhale deeply. "The truth is, I wanted to hurt you. On the way to Alexandria and again here, all those hours together, grinding away, souls hanging out one minute, dancing in the streets the next …"

She cleared her throat. Too dark to see her face, but when she spoke again I could hear the better-buck-up tone in her voice.

"Where were we, dancing in the streets when last seen, right? I'd look at the two of you and you had this … glow. Everybody did, but you especially. You were happy, so easily a part of everything and I wasn't. I was alone." The sobs came in little bursts. I hardened myself against them. "I can't do it the way you do. I hear the empty little sounds I make and see the little blue words I write and all that's ever nourished me in my whole life is Spam. One of the Spam people lined up on the shelf in a can. Then I want to scream."

I have no idea how long we sat there. No one said a word, not even Andreas for a change. I saw him take her hand, I think she let him hold it. I didn't mind. I just wanted us to find a way out of this and go on. I assumed that's what she wanted too. How to resolve my feelings towards her after that was anyone's guess. When we were too chilled to stay longer, we got up and walked home.

The house was dark, everyone gone to bed, one light at the top of the stairs. Jean went to our room. I started to follow but Andreas pulled me back, circling me with his arms. He turned me around to face him, hoping to see some friendly sign. I turned away.

"Come with me for a little while. Please. I won't touch you, if you don't want."

"I need some time." *And another ritual of courtship*, I thought. From them both.

"Sirrine, don't hold this against me. I regretted my silence, that's all, leaving you to tell her. We were wrong, we made her feel cut off from us."

"You took her side. You called it a crime."

"Too much time behind bars, I suppose." Trying to tease me out of it.

"I have enough guilt, Andreas. Enough for the two of us and this whole island and all the islands of Greece. I was brought up on it, it was my pablum. So don't heap any more on me or I'll fall under the weight of it."

"Fall, I'll catch you," he said, drawing me back to him. "We can get over this, all of us, even Jean, trapped as she is in her sadness. But you will be gone soon and every moment until then should be ours, must be ours." He ran his fingers through my hair, bent to kiss me behind my ear, his lips moving down my neck. He knew by now what this would do.

"Guerilla warfare," I said, barely breathing.

"I want to change your mind. That moon up there that doesn't give a damn about anything will see more of you than I will." He smiled, a wan little smile. "Are we to abandon this gift we have given each other? You have your dream and you will go. I can't stop you. But tonight come with me and let us make dreams of our own."

Towards morning I said, unable to stop myself, plunging in, "If we're going to … be serious, I mean … we have to talk."

How could I leave him without something to hang on to? No more an option than jumping into the sea and swimming to Beirut. What happened to seizing life and taking what comes, having the courage to do that, the freedom from compacts and covenants, like the passage in Durrell we admired so much? Here I was, clinging shamelessly, seeking any compact or covenant I could get my hands on. Where do I sign? Babbling like an idiot about the future, worse, uttering the fatal, the forbidden word, *marriage*. Certainly not a word that passed his lips. Babbling about religion too. Where was The Scold? Missing in action, the one time that voice might have been useful.

He was instantly awake. "We've talked about this. Religion that says even to ask a question is wrong? Asking questions *is* my religion. Yours too, I thought. If not, we'd better tell each other now, because I don't accept it. I can't. Faith is supposed to save us. Yours tells us only that we're doomed. I'm not saying I don't accept rules, I was brought up on them, I respect them. But it's not the rules of a priest in Rome we will break. It's our faith in each other and in ourselves, if we fail each other. I don't look beyond that."

I didn't sleep. Quite apart from worrying about why he wasn't on his knees for my hand, did he never get relief from being so rigorous, so uncompromising?

How will you ever live in the world? I whispered into his shoulder. He was a lot like Jean. Yes, in many respects just like her. Thinking of him in this way, and only of him, I failed to reflect on what any of this revealed about me.

14

Our days in Cyprus were at an end. Andreas gloomy, I miserable, Jean only too eager to be gone. My feelings towards her wavering between anger and sympathy. Dr. Thanos came by with a book of poems. The Pied Pipers put on a skit, a hilarious mash-up of Ride 'em cowboy and Hey, pardner with ten gallon hats made of cardboard, Chicago gangland Stick 'em ups and Hollywood pin-ups, with our mannerisms and expressions which they had down to a T.

At home, Ismene waited, inconsolable, and for the first time we were allowed into the kitchen to help, his mother wanting us near. That's where we were when his father called, "*Ella, ella.*" Come, come. He was listening to the radio.

Andreas darkened as if a storm were passing over where he stood. "What is it, what's wrong?" I asked.

"Trouble in Lebanon, an attempted coup."

"Oh-oh."

"What are they saying, exactly?" Jean demanded.

"We know what a coup means, over there especially. They have enough of them."

"Yes, Andreas, I see, Arabs at it again."

"Please, just tell us what they say," I suggested.

"What they always do when they know nothing. The situation is—how would the English say—fluid?" He snapped off the sound. "We'll check again in an hour."

Jean and I finished packing, working out what we would

argue when they told us not to go, which they certainly would. Not just going among Arabs now but Arabs on the warpath. We gathered again. I was torn. Weren't we here because we didn't want our existence defined by a man? Yet I had no more ambition than to stay at his side. Going away was unbearable. And with her as my companion? Maybe we could all stay in Athens until things settled down. One glance at Jean told me this was fantasy. There was nothing to keep her. If not Lebanon, not anywhere, not together. The news ended. Andreas' mother switched on the lamps.

"Well, what?" Jean was combative.

Andreas hesitated, weighing his answer. "The port is open, no information on how long it was closed. Nothing on the timing of any of it, when it began, when it was crushed, which they say it was. Rumors of casualties. The situation has become normal." Astonishingly, he chuckled. "Exact words? 'Returned to better than normal.' Whatever the hell that means!"

His mother looked at him reproachfully—either his swearing or laughing in the face of our approaching doom, hard to say. His father was talking so rapidly Andreas put up his hands to fend off the volley of words. "He asks me to tell you that if he lives to be ten times the age of his grandfather who lived to more than ninety he will never find words enough in Greek let alone English to describe how worried he is for your safety and he begs you to stay and they will care for you as their own daughters with the strength that is in them and the tenderness of their hearts until the end of their days."

When he finished Andreas put his arm around him. I followed, then Jean, and the four of us stood embracing in a circle, like the disciples at the empty tomb with the two Marys (one of them Magdalen), the father bathing us in his sorrow.

The row came after the family went to bed. Ismene kissed us

goodnight, convinced she would wake in the morning and find out that we weren't going away. Andreas was at the window, his back to us, smoking. "I trust you're not really thinking about getting on that ship tomorrow. At the very least wait to learn the true situation. Even if this coup was put down, who knows? Coup, countercoup—common as sand."

Stern but oh so reasonable, like my father when forbidding me to do something. For your own good. Taking over is how it felt. I disliked him for it. I disliked anyone telling me what to do like that.

"Of course we're going!" Jean said. "We didn't get this far to give it all up because of some coup. *Attempted* coup, one that's over with! So when that ship sails in the morning, you bet we'll be on it."

"If they have so many, like you say, they must be used to dealing with them. And the port's open. I don't think they'd let ships in if it wasn't safe." I hoped somebody tough was in charge. Isn't that what was needed at a time like this? What did it have to do with us, anyway? Besides, we had our introduction to *Time* magazine, almost as good as a diplomatic passport.

Andreas turned to me. "You're right, of course you are, how stupid of me. Not a thing to worry about. And if they can't do the job themselves, they can call in the U.S. Marines." Voice dripping with sarcasm. In that instant I thought it quite possible to hate him. "Which they did, not even four years ago. They landed on a beach near Beirut. Perhaps you didn't know."

To be honest we didn't know. How had we missed that?

"Have you really lived until now with so little to fear? No one will keep you here by force, I certainly won't, since you're determined to have heads like sheep."

"Pigs, Andreas. The expression is pigheaded."

"Thank you, Sirrine. How very kind to correct my

inadequate attempts to speak your language. Wrong-headed, that's what it is. You think this is some quaint ritual put on for the amusement of travelers, a bit of theatre you can watch from the back row. I hope you never have to find out how wrong you are. How arrogant. We have a word, *hubris*." He came towards me. "Sirry, please think about this, think about us …"

Jean jumped in between. "Haven't you done enough? You have no part in this now. Leave her alone, she's coming with me!"

"Does she belong to you, then?"

"Yes! For as long as this lasts. A solemn promise we'd stay together, no matter what."

I started to say something, but he didn't give me a chance, he was too angry. "Can't you see how reckless this is? Danger isn't a spectator sport. People who are willing to die, whatever the cause, they're ruthless. They don't care who gets in the way."

"All your pretty speeches." Jean was almost shouting. "Freedom this and honor that. You despise them. Admit it! From the beginning, ever since we told you about Alexandria. You think they're nothing but a bunch of infidels, leaping over the walls, swords drawn ready to cut our throats. Well, I don't subscribe to the stereotype."

His voice was colder than all Siberia. "I despise labels, I have fought them all my life. But I admit there are some that stick in my mind. You think you are so privileged, you Americans, going around with your naïve textbook ideas, thinking you can do exactly what you want and with luck it will turn out right in the end. Let me tell you it doesn't turn out right. For most of us it doesn't even begin that way."

I watched his jaw tighten. Had there been no other indication of how angry he was, the beating of that muscle against his cheek told it all. He let me know I was included in this. "I thought you were different. Go from here, go wherever you please.

And when you're through with your little experiment, go back to your soda fountains and your Elm Streets, your loyalty oaths and Senator Joes."

Loyalty oaths. Senator Joes. What had he been reading?

Jean laughed. "And I thought you were different, I thought you stood for something."

"You can't say such insulting things, not to him," I protested. My earlier thoughts filled me with remorse.

"Stay out of it, Sirry. This is between Jean and me." The expression on his face made me wonder if he would strike her, a look so terrible that for the first time I saw how it was possible for him to fight, even kill, if he had to. I hoped he would never turn on me the fury that was in him.

"Take her and go." He didn't even glance in my direction when he walked out.

"Hypocrite!" she yelled after him.

I slapped her, good and hard and very very satisfying, the ones outside the restaurant in Alexandria love taps by comparison. "How dare you! After all the time we've spent here with him and his family, all he's done for us, their hospitality. What the hell has gotten into you?"

She glared at me and walked out too. Well, let her. I lit a cigarette with shaking hands and just as quickly stabbed it out. I'd deal with her tomorrow, but if Andreas and I parted like this, shame would have the upper hand for sure. I made up my mind to go to him. In case I changed it, I crept down the stairs so he wouldn't hear me. Door ajar, I saw him at his desk. Seeing him preoccupied, too timid to knock, I was retreating when he said, "Come back."

He was at the door. I ran and threw my arms around him. "I can't imagine being in the world without you now!"

He started to move away from me. "This is what I was

trying to tell you."

Was. The past tense has a dreadful sound in the same room with love. I hung on to him. "I'm sorry, you know she didn't mean it. I don't know what it is, I've never seen her like this." But I did know. I'd warned us both, that night on the ship.

"There are words we can't take back, whatever our reasons for saying them. Choices have consequences, some very real."

What was he telling me? It sounded so impersonal. His words hadn't exactly been sugarcoated. *Oh God, forgive those things I thought about him.* Was that blasphemy beside the rest I was thinking? His hands on me, those hands that gave so much pleasure. I held my eyes tight shut to regain enough composure to leave without disgracing myself.

"Sirry, what are you doing? Your face all scrunched up, you look like … like Charlie Chaplin."

"Trying to pretend I'm not here."

"Trying to pass through it untouched?"

"Do you think so little of me?"

He shook his head. "I honestly don't know what to think. All that happened just now, all that was said—so much bitterness." He pulled me with him to the door, kicking it shut, then half dragging, half carrying me to the bed, where he threw me down, him on top of me, kissing me, not all that gently. A strangled sound. "I'm afraid for you, I'm afraid for you with her, wherever it is you're going I can't follow!" He tore at my clothes and his and turned off the light. "Yes," I said, figuring *I can join in this too, rough as it gets. I have fear of my own to get rid of.*

We were furious together until he exploded inside me. Afterward, we lay side by side, my face on fire. I looked down at him, spent. Dark lily on its pad. What was it to have the power of that weapon, only to lose it so vulnerably? Is this what made some of them cruel? He reached for me. "Can you forgive me? I don't …

this is not my way of behaving." The laugh was sardonic. "Great protector I am. What Jean said is true, I am a fraud." He turned away to hide his tears.

"I could have said no. I liked it." It wasn't a lie. Innocence isn't lost all at once, it seems, it takes more than one bite of the apple. Deep down I knew I could trust him with myself. His back to me, I pulled him close, to reassure him. That's when I saw.

"Andreas! Oh, my God, what is this?" *Welts.* Down his spine. Why hadn't I felt them? I thought my hands had been everywhere. Was I so oblivious?

"You were beaten! You said they knocked you around, that's all you said. Why didn't you tell me? Why? You were so young, what did you know? You didn't know."

"I did know. I knew the risk, we all did." He gathered me to him. "Forget about that. I love you, the rest doesn't matter."

I thought my heart would break. No one had ever said this to me, not my parents, not my grandmother, not anyone.

"I didn't mean to love you and now we must leave each other and I think that will hurt me more than anything."

We stayed together until dawn. The whole family came to see us off at Limassol with fear in their eyes, bravely waving their handkerchiefs as they watched us head out to sea.

Andreas kissed me goodbye. "I will remember us in this weeping night." No promise, no covenant but that.

What I remember is bending over him like the sky goddess Nut over the sleeping pharaoh and wrapping him in my hair.

PART FIVE

Beirut

15

This then is the story of what happened in Beirut, the chaotic chain of events, frightening and unaccountable, that led to our hasty exit and being held at the checkpoint on the way to the airport. The bit of theatre for the amusement of travelers, as Andreas had put it. No back row seats, either, we were right up front and center.

It would not be our last encounter with the forces unleashed in the region at that time. The extent of the intrigue we got caught up in did not become clear until later, after we had to flee for our lives into the desert, something Andreas never imagined when we first heard of the coup attempt and he sought to argue us out of sailing into it.

In Beirut. Holed up in a drafty, high-ceilinged corner room of the YWCA in a shabby villa off the Corniche. Madame Shoukri, a sour woman watching us from under hooded eyes, counted our Lebanese pounds, her face yellowing under a thick veil of powder. "Big trouble for you if you are caught on the street without passports," she warned. This would give her pleasure, I knew.

We didn't want to go out anyway. We wanted to tend our psychic gardens, our precious journals, and try to mend ourselves and the tatters of our friendship. We had only each other now, fragile company. What was going on in the world outside was trouble enough. We avoided speaking about what happened on Cyprus, Jean having made another tearful apology to Andreas at the dock and later on the ship to me. I would like to say that I recognized my own responsibility in this but I couldn't, not then.

Isolated with Jean in the besieged city, I tried to think about her in terms I could understand—her feelings for Andreas. Whatever they were, their angry confrontation seemed to have released something, seemed to free her in some way. With our separation from him, maybe we could arrive at willful amnesia. Looking back on it, I think we were both in a sort of emotional shock. Meanwhile, the book we had carried since Athens, our introduction to the *Time* correspondent and in our minds the entire Middle East, lay on a table under the window, reminding us of our mission. For the moment, it didn't seem important.

The days were rainy and windy, utterly dreary the way a Mediterranean city more accustomed to being blue and sunny can be in winter. Venturing forth one morning, we saw tanks in the streets and around public buildings, signs of the attempted coup. Farther away from the waterfront, groups of soldiers were milling around, handling machine guns as casually as little boys about to start up a game of cops and robbers. In the post office I was frisked, then searched by matrons in a dingy little cell of a room behind *par avion.* All this to send a letter to Andreas.

From the post office we walked to the National Museum—it would end up in no-man's-land in the civil wars to come. Dimly lit, dingy as the weather, it still did not obscure the wonders of the Phoenicians and their wooden ships. Those far-going seafarers imagined three impossibilities: a tiger kissing a gazelle, a gorilla walking behind a man, a fish marching behind a dog. The marching fish was my favorite. What impossibility did I imagine? Two friends in love with the same man.

Near the entrance, three monkeys elaborately heard no evil, saw no evil, spoke no evil, arms of stone covering the offending senses. This was a Buddhist idea, I thought but these sculptures from Byblos in the south Lebanon dated from some fifteen hundred years before Buddha.

On the first sunny day we left the coup behind in the capital and headed to Baalbek to see the temple ruins. We boarded a run-down bus along with a couple of live chickens, a goat, sacks of onions and pistachios, and stacks of flat bread. Along the way we passed roadside tents where shepherds sat drinking tea and puffing on water pipes. We crossed the Dog River where ghostly barking was said to warn of an approaching enemy—Ramses, Alexander the Great, Napoleon, take your pick. They were all here.

Climbing the mountains that formed the spine of Lebanon, we lost the sun in coils of mist and fog. The engine wheezed. At a roadblock we lurched to a stop, the surprised screech of a chicken joining the squeal of brakes. Soldiers surrounded the bus, pounding on doors and windows and shouting to the men to line up in the rain. They inspected our papers and those of the other women where we sat.

And sat.

The day wore on, increasingly cold and grey. We didn't dare speak, just elbowed each other from time to time. I don't know what was worse, the soldiers and their guns or our precarious position hanging off the side of the mountain. Finally the men were allowed back on. All but two. Their women protested, but the bus went on, the rest of the journey marked by the sound of their weeping.

At Baalbek, several of our fellow passengers invited us home, communicating in hand gestures and bits of French. We followed the women down a dirt lane in the shadow of the ruins and the last light of dusk filtering through the smoke of wood fires. It was a one-room dwelling, rugs and cushions scattered over the dirt floor. The bed would be ours, the honored guests. We all slept in the clothes we had on.

As night fell, other women wandered in to see the two Americans. They could not refrain from touching Jean's hair, holding the blonde strands up to the light and cooing. They squatted around the stove, told about husbands who had gone to Brazil to work. Good riddance, it seemed, they were pleased with their freedom. They nursed babies and children old enough to walk—obviously, husbands came back occasionally. They danced and sang. When it was our turn to entertain, they looked at us expectantly.

"There's nothing in our repertoire that would work with this crowd," said Jean. We managed a few weak choruses of "Don't Fence Me In." They looked at us blankly and giggled. It was a long night. In the morning we drank mint tea and watched as one of the women unwrapped her baby, bound so tightly we wondered how he could breathe—at that moment we understood the meaning of swaddling clothes—and bathed him in a tin basin. When we left to explore the ruins, they begged us to return. Back in Beirut I noticed the bedbug bites that covered me. Jean was untouched.

Apprehensive about another bus ride, we splurged on a taxi to the famous cedars. On the road north into the mountains we encountered no roadblocks. We wandered among the ancient trees towering dizzily overhead, holding hands and throwing ourselves on the snow to make silhouettes. The driver, laughing, joined in. At dinner that evening, there was a peace between us we hadn't known for quite a while.

Confident again in our teamwork, we decided it was time to deliver the book. On a morning again brilliant with sunshine we pulled together what was left of our glamour and stormed the St. Georges. The hotel faced the sea, its reflection washing over the windowpanes and flashing a thousand sapphires in its mirrors. The desk clerk told us that the man who belonged to the book, Graham Griggs, had left that morning for Damascus. "Some trouble, I believe. Student riots."

Reluctantly, I handed it over. "Perhaps you will leave a note? But wait, here comes Asif, they work together, why don't you speak to him?" An Arab. Could be even more interesting.

He approached, striding across the floor like a large but graceful animal. Something fierce in him too, I thought. He should have been wrapped in robes, leading camel charges in the desert, not bottled up in a grey suit and tie. Forty perhaps, skin the color of cloves, dark sloping eyes that were especially beguiling in the face of a man, a face that otherwise was not what you would call handsome, not conventionally so. His smile was welcoming but wary, making the harshness of his features more pronounced.

"*Ahlan wasahlan.*" It was a standard greeting.

"We have a book that belongs to Mr. Griggs. Perhaps you would give it to him, if it isn't a bother."

"No bother, atall," he said, ignoring the book I held out. "Call me Asif, everybody does. How about a drink? C'mon, outside on the terrace."

We followed him. It had gotten warm and he complained that he didn't like sitting in the sun, but we stayed anyway. Women in colorful bikinis lounged by the pool, chic in that self-contained way of foreign women, an ease of belonging unsettling to a bedraggle traveler. This Beirut was as much European as Arab. We would soon see why it was called Paris of the East, its smart shops and night life, its French Quarter with pale yellow buildings and iron balconies. The language widely used too, left over from French rule.

I felt drab. Better to have almost nothing on, like them. Even our chatter seemed to drop on the table like bricks. We told him we had been in Egypt. What did he think of Nasser? He said that other Arab leaders might not know what to make of him, but he was a hero in the street, especially after seizing the Suez Canal five years ago. We knew that the United States supported Egypt when Britain, France and Israel invaded to take it back, happy to be on the right side, but in the Middle East nothing is predictable. While we talked there was no mistaking the tension in him, as if poised for something to happen. The waiter too, standing behind him, flicking his napkin, watchful.

"Nasser's words have no caution. Then we get a big surprise, when he goes too far." Asif shifted his chair. "If only the Arabs could forget their differences. But we can be very foolish. Do you know the story of the scorpion and the turtle who meet at the riverbank? Scorpion asks if he can ride on Turtle's back to get across. Turtle does not trust him. 'Why would I sting you, for I too would surely die!' Turtle, persuaded, gives in, Scorpion climbs on, and in the middle of the river he stings. 'Oh, foolish Scorpion, why did you sting me?' Turtle cries as they are sinking. 'Because I'm an Arab!'"

Was this supposed to describe the coup attempt? Was this what he was really talking about? I looked over at Jean transfixed by his every word. And by him. His voice had a low resonant whine, like an exotic instrument, like the monotonous music wailing from every radio. He had a way of cocking his head to one side, as if he were in the desert listening for a distant sound. "Someday, we may have reason to wish that Nasser had succeeded in uniting us, for I see nothing good coming in the future."

A woman wearing a dress her appetite had outgrown, tottered past on high heels. "Nothing for you today, dahling!" he called after her. "Try again, you might have better luck." The taunt seemed gratuitous. Even the waiter was frowning.

"If my mother's a virgin, that one is," Asif muttered. He struck the table abruptly. "Time for lunch! La Gondola, good

Lebanese food. You look like you need some," he added slyly. Jean smiled as he took her arm. A handsome pair.

La Gondola. We drove past trash-littered dunes, a bleak landscape despite occasional glimpses of the sea along a deserted coast road. As we were going into the restaurant, a small boy, running with a loaf of bread, tripped and fell. The bread sailed into a pile of refuse. Asif was across the road in a flash. Lifting the tearful boy, he carried him inside, laughing and shouting, Jean behind him, clapping with delight.

"Bread! Can't you see this boy needs bread?" The waiters heaped his arms full, and he scampered off.

Jean watched him go. "You are kind."

"No, my dear, I believe it is you who are kind."

The restaurant was empty. We sat at a long table, the three of us at the end by a window. The waiter brought arak, the licorice-flavored drink that turns chalky when water is added, not enough to drown the fire that rises in your belly at the first sip. Then mezzes, small dishes of hummus and baba ghanouj and tabouli, and kefta and kebabs and mint-flavored yogurt, to scoop up with pita bread. We ate as if at our last meal, heads buzzing from the drinks. Never have arak in the afternoon.

He continued telling stories but said nothing about the coup. His attention was on Jean. And who could fail to notice her? The golden hair like a tropical bird in snow. Her presence seemed to sap the fierceness right out of him, made him boyish and appealing. The tension remained. Every so often he flashed his eyes around the room, as if checking to see that we were alone. As if the slightest footstep wouldn't have echoed like a drumbeat in that empty space.

He was busy making plans for the evening. "We will meet for dinner. I will bring a friend." Since he couldn't take his eyes off Jean, I understood the friend would be for me. When we left, it was nearly five, light already fading from the sky.

We met for cocktails at the Hotel Phoenicia, a gleaming high-rise at the other end of the Corniche from the St. Georges, a century away in style, more Las Vegas than Paris. Tired of our clothes, we had swapped. I wore her grey wool dress with a cowl neckline, perfect for pawing, I would learn. She wore my pencil-slim black skirt, the one I had made tighter so I would pass for eighteen when I went with my cousin to the Avalon Ballroom.

The "friend" was from Jordan. Hani Bishara, small, bald, one of the richest men in the Middle East, we were told. He kissed my hand and sat next to me. Asif, tall in a beautifully tailored dark suit, beside Jean, on my right. Immediately they were engrossed in conversation, deeply so. *Good, she'll find out what the mystery is all about.*

I admit a tinge of jealousy that he so obviously preferred her. Greedy, I suppose I wanted it all, in whatever colors and flavors. Still, he was making her happy. It would ease the tension over Andreas.

Hotel bars are usually tucked off to one side of the lobby. Perhaps the Phoenicia had such a bar but we were in the open near the main doors. All arrivals and departures held the attention of our companions. Soon we were all engaged in observing the traffic, the ultimate pastime in the Middle East. We had just ordered another round of drinks when two men came in from the street and looked in our direction. The shorter one, heavy-lidded, small staring eyes, sauntered over and put his hand on Asif's shoulder.

"So, this is how you pass your evenings." I thought I saw Asif recoil.

"*HamdulilLah.*" Thank God. Asif stood and gestured to include us all in the introduction. "This is General Osir." A general in a suit. The bulging eyes betrayed no expression, like a toad on a river bank, unblinking.

"From the Sureté Generale," Asif added. General Security, a cross between CIA and FBI, wasn't it? Vaguely familiar, from reading Camus.

General Osir removed a silver case from his inside jacket pocket, flicked it open, lifted the spring that held the cigarettes lined up, removed one, lit it and exhaled slowly, regarding us through the cloud of smoke. He studied his nails for a few moments, blew on them, then turned and left, his companion trailing after. Without a word the four of us got up to go too, our drinks left on the table untouched.

We went to a cabaret down a few steps off the street, Les Caves du Roy. Small, softly lit, just right for a seduction. A few nights ago we were on a dirt floor on the other side of the mountains. Apparently it showed.

"Stay with me, give me two days." Hani Bishara's tongue was lapping at my neck. "I will put you in the St. Georges, I will buy you beautiful clothes." *If he thinks all it takes is a decent wardrobe, I must look pretty shabby.* I thought of the women by the pool.

Was I going to create a fuss? Of course not, I didn't want to look like a ninny in front of Asif, or Jean either for that matter. "Tempting as that sounds, I really can't." What a silly response, one day I'd master the blasé patter. I glanced at her, focused on something Asif was saying. His eyes left her briefly to survey the room. I felt cheated, she got an interesting conversation while I got a boring come-on. Hani persisted. The thought of him touching me after Andreas was repulsive.

"Cut it out, I'm not that kind of girl, okay?" I could have slapped him, I was getting good at it. Before I could stop him, his hand had taken advantage of the loose cowl neckline and was sliding over my breast. I reached in after and flung it out. *There goes the fabulous wardrobe.* By now we were a little drunk.

"You little fool. I buy what I please." The hand that had been gentle squeezed my arm until it hurt. Charming as a teamster. "You're not a real woman."

I laughed in his face. "You'll never be rich enough to buy me!" This was getting serious. I gave Jean a frantic signal. She ignored it. The only way out was to pretend to be sick. This annoyed her, she didn't want the evening to end. In her shoes, I wouldn't either. In her dress, it was something else again.

After what seemed like a sharp exchange between the men—in Arabic, one is never quite sure—they paid the check and we crawled out of the Caves into the Beirut night. Fast Hands Hani walked off in a huff, a shocked Asif left to see us home. He helped me up the front steps of the Y as if I'd somehow become crippled by his friend's discourtesy. He kissed my hand. A million apologies were in that kiss. "I am sorry this man does not know how to behave."

I left them alone. When I turned at the door to call goodnight, I saw his hand on her cheek, heard him, it being late and the night so still, murmuring to her. "My dear Jean, trust me, I believe I know too well what is in your heart." I shut the door quietly, resisting the urge to eavesdrop further.

Pay attention, I told myself as I undressed, thinking over the day's events. *Something's going on here and not just between the two of them.*

When she came in, eyes bright, cheeks flushed, she didn't say a word. But her guard had fallen, this much was obvious even to a less practiced voyeur. We turned out the light and watched him walk down the hill, crossing under the arc cast by the streetlamp until he was lost in the shadows.

"What's pressing on him with so much weight?" I

whispered.

"I know, I sense it too."

"That nasty Peter Lorre character, I get the feeling he's tailing him."

"Osir? Foxy little character, isn't he?"

"Toad is what came to my mind. He's from the Sureté—that's like the FBI and CIA rolled into one, right? Maybe here it's more like the Gestapo and KGB."

"I don't know about him. But Asif has his finger on the pulse of the whole Middle East."

And on you. "All the same, I don't think he likes that Osir much, which makes two of us. He gives me the creeps. Worse than lover-boy at dinner."

We sounded so ominous, so much like Arabs, that we both had to laugh. "The intrigue around here is rubbing off. Could be a problem. By the way, what were you two talking about all night?"

"Oh, nothing really."

I lay awake wondering what the hell she was hiding.

16

We settled our account with Madame Shoukri, but we weren't getting out of town so easily. Not yet nine when Asif phoned asking us to lunch. If we would delay our little side trip to Damascus by several hours, he was more than willing to keep our luggage until we got back. Student riots didn't concern us. What Madame was going to charge each day for storing our suitcases did. It was a holdup, we were only paying seventy-five cents for the room. When we told her we'd made other arrangements, she eyed us with even more suspicion, spiked with unbearable curiosity when she saw the car outside. We caught her peering through the curtains. When we pulled away with Youssef, the driver, for the short trip to the office she was still at her post.

The Beirut bureau of *Time* was in a building near the St. Georges. It would be difficult to overstate the glamor surrounding the magazine then, the aura of the foreign correspondent (from those brave ones who covered the Spanish Civil War, including Hemingway?), intel reputed to be superior even to the CIA. The Beirut office had a balcony looking to the sea and the curving sweep of the Corniche and back to the roofs of the town rising to vineyards and the mountains, snowcapped, standing watch over it all. The secretary left for lunch, and Asif steered us down the tiny hall. "Here we can talk and nobody listens. My little secret, only Youssef knows." Little secret? As in a mistress? So much for Jean, then.

The apartment was the right size for a secret. A black

lacquered bar dominated one wall. It was laden with platters of food. A red leather couch flanked by matching chairs faced it. A bottle of scotch and dishes of pistachios were on the coffee table. We might not make the bus and we had checked out of the Y, but it was cozy, a place to talk, all right. And he did talk.

He was a Palestinian from the West Bank of the Jordan River. With the eastern half of Jerusalem, it had come under Jordanian rule following the establishment of Israel and the war of 1948. Most Palestinians who left the rest of the land that became Israel or were pushed out by force or fear lived as refugees in squalid camps on the West Bank and elsewhere in the Arab world. In a few years the region would be turned upside down again in the war of 1967, causing another Palestinian exodus and propelling Yasser Arafat onto the world stage.

Asif talked about the British Mandate, which had governed from the 1920s to 1948, about the fighting he and his brothers had done, the savagery of Arab against Jew, Jew against Arab, both against the British, gun battles near Jerusalem's King David Hotel, an informer garroted just inside Jaffa Gate, an ambush at night in the Kidron Valley, describing it with the intensity of Sheherazade staying alive by the urgency of her stories. He scooped up a handful of pistachios from time to time, opening them and offering them to Jean before starting on some for me.

"We know how to feed our hatred, though we ourselves may starve. Believe me, no side is without blame—have you heard of such a case? My wife was killed, blown up, they could not find enough even to bury. Two brothers killed, the others scattered, to Kuwait, to Panama. Palestine no more. Loss, so much loss. But one day, *inshallah*, we will go home in peace."

He picked up a box inlaid with sandalwood and mother of pearl. We'd seen cheap imitations in the Cairo souks. "This was given to me by King Hussein, in honor of his marriage. My beloved little king, my courageous little king. Only a boy of 18 when his grandfather lay dying at his side, shot by an insane Palestinian." His eyes filled with tears.

Hussein in his desert kingdom seemed far from us here in this apartment. With its glossy bar and modern furniture it could have been anywhere in Manhattan. No windows that I could see, perhaps there were in another room, no noises from the street. Sealed up here, away from everything.

We heard sounds then, many sounds, like people scuffling in the hall. The door flew open, must have been kicked open, and half a dozen men were pushing into the room. Even casual conversation can sound harsh in Arabic, as I've said. They left no doubt.

"Stand up!" one of them ordered, in English. "Up! Up! Get up!"

We stood. They separated Jean and me from Asif. They started to shake him down, roughly. His face flushed as red as the couch but he stayed calm, subservient almost, as he yielded to their groping hands. He mumbled a few words in Arabic. They ignored whatever he said and looked around. Glances fell on our suitcases, stowed in a corner by Youssef, the driver. They kicked them into the middle of the room and started rummaging, faces expressionless as they tumbled everything out onto the carpet—clothes, shoes, underwear, tampons, even Jean's pharmacy. Leafing through our journals, they pretended to read. At least I hoped they were pretending. I was mortified that they might, in fact, understand the words.

Jean was protesting. I thought the man near her might slug her but he took no notice, until she moved. It was only the slightest move. He shoved her. She stumbled against a chair, caught herself and did not fall.

"No!" Asif rushed from the other end of the room, arms

outstretched to shield her. "Stop! No! This can't be. She has nothing to do with this, nothing at all."

I saw the blood spurt from near his right eye before I heard the sound of the blow. He staggered and almost went down. What did that goon have in his fist that could make a hole like that? I was concentrating on that question. Despite the confusion going on around me, I kept staring at that fist, mesmerized.

Jean went to the pile of clothes and grabbed a blouse. She started towards Asif. An arm shot out, barring her way.

"Let me go to him," she pleaded. The man held her back.

Again Asif rushed to her. "You will not touch her! Before God, I swear to you …" He reeled from the blow. The next sent him sprawling. They kicked him as he fell, and again where he lay.

"You want trouble, we give it." They jerked him to his feet. He gasped from the pain.

More men came into the room, wearing uniforms, carrying machine guns, one pointed directly at me. I switched my attention from the fist. They were swarming and shouting. One raked his gun along the bar. Platters of lamb and rice splattered onto the carpet. Another swept glasses and bottles off the shelves. The sickening smell of liquor filled the room.

They herded us out into the hall. Some ran down the stairs. Others crowded onto the elevator, Asif in their midst. *Fish marching behind a dog.* A handkerchief, pressed against his forehead, was coloring bright red in his hand. He looked up at us, indescribable sorrow in his eyes. "Take care of yourselves." That was all he said.

The elevator gates clanged shut and he was gone. All of them were gone, leaving us in the empty hallway, staring after them. Youssef appeared, bringing us to our senses. Where had he been? Had he let them in? The phone started ringing, startling in the sudden silence. We ran to answer it.

"Don't!" he yelled. He was right. What would we say? I noticed the blood on the glass of the coffee table, a cocktail of blood among the half-empty tumblers of scotch. "Go into the office and lock the door," Youssef said. "I will get help. But do not answer the phone." He helped us gather our belongings and move down the hall.

"Let's get out of here," I said, as soon as he was gone.

"Abandon Asif? Not a chance. Besides, where would we go?"

"I don't know, but hanging around here seems … well, I don't know, maybe you're right, maybe it's the safest choice."

The mess they made in the office was methodical, some file drawers emptied, contents spilled out onto desks and the floor, the rest untouched. Throughout the long afternoon and into the evening we waited, trying to ignore the repeated ringing of the phone. Torture, that phone, as if someone out there were taunting us. The telex, at least, was quiet.

To pass the time we dug into the files, the raw material of so much that we had read. The squabbling tribes of the Hejaz in what is now Saudi Arabia, how they united to fight the Turks with Major T. E. Lawrence—Lawrence of Arabia—made famous by American journalist Lowell Thomas, a victory that allowed France and Britain to carve up the Ottoman Empire between them. The Balfour Declaration, another betrayal. Somehow they forgot to tell the Palestinians they had promised a home for the Jews in Palestine. Hitler had eventually made it all so easy. Intrigue among the Arabs didn't help. Scorpions and turtles everywhere. Independence when it came also brought coup and countercoup, common as sand, as Andreas said.

Nasser could have been the hero of the story, a nationalist who tried to unite all of them and keep the Western powers at bay. He had a hand in toppling King Farouk in 1952, going from major to general overnight—a rise through ranks that is automatic, it seems, when order is overturned. In Egypt, at least, the aftermath was civilized, Farouk allowed to sail into exile from Alexandria. Unlike young King Faisal of Iraq, who was murdered along with his family a few years later. His hated advisor Nuri Said made a desperate attempt to escape disguised as a peasant woman and was betrayed, his body mutilated by a mob. When Hussein, Faisal's cousin, took the throne of Jordan after his grandfather was killed, he immediately faced a revolt of his own army officers, possibly backed by the Syrians and Egyptians. This was 1958, the year our Marines went into Lebanon, as Andreas had reminded us. And Lebanon? A balancing act among Christians, Moslems and other sects, poised to unravel if they ever took a census. Beirut? A petri dish of spies and plots.

One file described white slave traffic into Saudi Arabia. If our imaginations were racing ahead of reason, what more did we need?

Long after dark Youssef returned, exhausted. "I have been all over the city and found nothing about where he was taken. I did find big friend of his, prince from Saudi. He comes soon."

"Swell," said Jean. "Straight from the land of white slavery. And what's this paragon of manhood going to do?"

"Protect us!" I said. "Money talks. We can fend him off for a night, then Griggs will be back and tell us what's going on."

We made a plan. Jean would sit behind the desk and do the talking. We'd let this guy know we weren't to be taken lightly. When he walked in, we were stupefied. Young, dashing, he could have been any college kid, even with the jaunty mustache. We expected fat, bald and shiny suit.

Jean started off prim, arms folded, the stern headmistress. The office was as bright as an operating theatre, fluorescent bulbs stripped color from her face. "You must understand how we came to be here. From America, traveling and studying." Each word enunciated, as if she were lecturing a class of lip readers. "Our fathers are lawyers. We are from one of the best schools."

"Run by nuns!" I hastened to add. *Nothing here for white slavers.*

"Nuns?" He looked at Youssef and shrugged.

"We met your friend Asif by coincidence." She raised her voice thinking he would better understand.

The prince got to his feet. "We go now."

Go? Had he understood a single word? "Go where?"

"Hotel."

"Hotel! What hotel?" Visions of being driven into the night, never to return.

"Excelsior."

Youssef nodded approval. "It's close, it will be okay for you."

The prince in his very long Lincoln limousine ferried us the few blocks to the Excelsior.

He came no farther than the lobby, a good sign. We were shown to a room grander by far than anything we'd been in since we left home. When he stopped by later, saying he had news, we let him come up. He sat on one of the beds and lit a cigarette. We scrambled for the pack, having smoked every last one of our own during the hours of waiting in the office.

"What news?"

"He is alive." *Alive*. The alternative had never entered my head.

"Where?"

"Prison. Here in Beirut."

"Prison," Jean said in a whisper. "But why?"

He shrugged. "Never mind, I have managed it. Blankets,

cigarettes. Lebanese prisons too bad."

"How have you managed it if you don't know where he is?"

"Some things okay … if money enough." If he knew more, he wasn't telling.

I changed the subject, asked him why he wasn't living in Saudi Arabia.

"My mother is here." No longer a favorite wife, we guessed.

"What do you do here?"

"I visit my mother at her villa in the mountains, I go to the movies, I love them too much, I go to hotel."

"You live in a hotel?" Jean asked.

"Yes, the Phoenicia. I go to nightclubs, I like nightclubs too much." He grinned. "You see how Beirut is too good for me."

17

When Graham Griggs called, I was on the balcony writing a breezy letter to Andreas about all the sights we weren't seeing. Back from Syria he heard what happened from Youssef. Jean stayed by the phone while I hurried to the St. Georges, excited by the prospect of getting some straight answers. He was waiting in the lobby, also younger than I imagined, visibly nervous.

"What got you involved in all this?" I reminded him about meeting our classmate in Paris and the book he had loaned her.

"I'm sorry it got you into trouble."

"Are we in trouble? If so, who with?

"Don't know, both counts.

"Is Asif a spy?"

"How would I know?"

"You work with him, you see him every day, how could you not know?"

"He has his sources. It doesn't really concern me."

Devastating, the man who was supposed to make sense of things, make us safe. Instead we were back to square one. Alarming enough, but I had also wanted to confide in him about what was going on between Jean and Asif, how that had as much to do with our staying as anything. What would he think about that?

"Look, we couldn't go merrily on our way until we were sure he was all right. I mean, we were with him when he was arrested, it seemed like common decency to stay. But if it's dangerous even to know him, if that puts us too far out on a limb, you've got to tell us. Tell *me*, right now."

"I don't know anything about it. They've arrested others for no reason, journalists too, just last night a guy from France-Presse. Another one for questioning this morning. Beirut's a crazy place right now. Everyone's got the jitters."

"Who's they?"

"Sureté? Army? It gets all mixed together. Not a lot of boundaries when something like this happens. This whole place is ripe to explode."

"But the coup is over and done with."

"Memories here are the longest and shortest in the world."

I recalled Osir's eyes, unblinking, the way he blew on his nails as if blowing us away like so much dust. I looked at Griggs sitting across from me. Maybe he was the spy, he knew the woman who'd gotten herself into Siberia. Nobody was allowed into Siberia, most of the people running the Soviet Union weren't allowed in. I made a last stab. "What do you think of all this? Of him? I mean if you had to give an opinion."

"I have no idea what he's been up to."

"This is *Time* magazine we're talking about!" I cried with frustration. "I find it really hard to believe you don't know if he's on the level, whether he can be trusted or not."

"Sorry, I'm afraid I can't help you."

Back at the Excelsior I ran into the prince. To get rid of him I agreed we'd go to a cabaret that evening. I went up to our room to tell Jean about Griggs. "It's a pretty strange reaction, don't you think?"

"Don't get me involved, that's all he cares about. So nothing's changed."

"No, we're stuck. It doesn't feel safe to go, or stay. But I guess we're all right as long as we have the prince. He was downstairs, he wants to go to a cabaret."

"With Asif behind bars? I don't think so."

"We're not doing much for him sitting around here fidgeting."

"But it feels disloyal, out having a good time …"

"Look, we can have a nice dinner. Doing nothing is bound to send us both over that balcony."

"Out with Saudis, don't forget! Out cold more likely, riding through the desert to Riyadh and into the arms of white slavery."

"Jean!"

"Well?"

"Okay, you made your point. You know if they catch a man thieving, they cut off his hand. So if they catch a man … oh, never mind."

She was actually grinning. "Okay, okay, we'll go."

We decked ourselves out in the really good outfits we'd brought along, hers a sleek black sheath with soft angora at the neckline, a knockout. Tough to beat a blonde in a little black dress. I was no slouch either in my tapestry skirt with V-neck black jersey top tied tight at the waist. Hourglass, one could call it.

Our prince almost lost possession of his jaw when he saw us, shocked at the transformation. Until we put on the dirty old trench coats.

"I have news," he announced when he could stop gaping.

"What?" We almost jumped him.

"They let him go. He's somewhere in Beirut."

"Are you sure?"

"Yes."

"And you'll find him." She smiled. "Now we can celebrate."

We drove in the rain through the streets and over the trolley tracks we were more used to riding to Le Casbah, Cinderellas and their prince. The driver, who looked like a thug, stuck to us like flypaper. Doubled as a bodyguard, we figured. At the table were two other Saudis, one taciturn, one talkative, a government minister he told us. Jean asked the quiet one what he did. "I'm a merchant." We didn't believe it for a second. From then on, if anyone was evasive about anything, we'd cry, *I'm a merchant!*

The place was full. Half the people in this city were in nightclubs, the other half in jail. Le Casbah was decorated like one, arches and colored glass and carved stone railings separating the upper level from tables surrounding the dance floor where an "alcoholic playboy" was making a "spectacle," according to the minister. Waiters in Moorish costume fussed over us, bringing scotch and champagne, flaming meats, flaming sauces, flaming desserts. We were sketched and photographed and reproduced on matchbooks. It was after three when we got back to our room. We talked until dawn, close, almost like before Cyprus.

"You've vamped the prince," she said as we fell asleep. "He called you 'ho-nee.'"

It was late when we woke up. "Wow, I could get used to this—wine, dine, sleep till noon!" I opened the curtains, stepping over clothes tossed in a heap with the souvenirs from the club. Our faces looked up from the matchbooks scattered on the carpet.

Jean yawned. "I think princey is sufficiently smitten with 'ho-nee' to buy breakfast in bed, what do you say? Crème Chantilly? Meringue glacé?"

A peculiar whim, but it suited our spirits as we cavorted in and out of bubble baths, singing all the kept-girl songs we knew. The ringing of the phone put an end to it. Asif. I could tell by her face. "He wants me to come to him right away. The St. Georges."

What about me? Hadn't I stayed too, to make sure he was okay? I tagged along. Jean didn't care, didn't notice. She'd forgotten about everything, even meringue glacé.

* * *

We would be directed to the bar, no doubt. Instead we were sent to a room. Strange. His own apartment, clearly no longer under wraps, was almost next door.

The corridor of his floor was filled with goons, some in civilian clothes, some in uniform, all of them in dark glasses. I cringed. Jean ignored them, marched down the hall and knocked on the door.

"*Ahlan*," we heard from within. He didn't come to greet us. One look and we knew why and that it was bad. He was propped up in bed, pale against huge white pillows. Yellow draperies were closed, bathing the room in perpetual sunset. He lifted his hand and beckoned. Jean went to him.

"You have come."

She bent to kiss his forehead. The side that had taken the blow was bandaged. He grimaced when she sat on the bed. "What have they done to you?"

"Have a look. Have a good look. See how we do things in the Middle East." Pushing the covers aside, he rolled over and lifted his pajama top, all that covered him. I averted my eyes. Not modesty, I assure you. I looked instead at the oversized pajama top, so big it was almost comical and he was a big man. I braced myself and I did look. His back and his buttocks were red and pulpy like raw meat. Dark purplish stains spread where he was bruising. His legs ended in bandages. Hobbled—like Chinese royalty or courtesans.

Jean slowly reached to touch him, drew back and bit her fist. "Oh," she cried. She lurched to the bathroom. I went after her. She was staring into the mirror, eyes wide, hands gripping the sides of the sink so hard I thought her knuckles would pop right through her skin. "I want to scream. I'm holding it in so tight I can't breathe."

"Jean, don't do this. I'm sorry, I don't know what to say. I do know we should get the hell out of here, get out of Beirut, right now, before it's too late!"

"I will not let it show," she said. "I was going to be sick in there. Now I'm just mad. At him for making me see this … this mess. At whoever did this … who could do such a thing? At whatever he's done to make this happen. What has he done? He didn't do anything, he couldn't possibly …"

"Please don't get involved in this. Promise you won't. It's dangerous. He's out of prison, he'll be okay. We stayed to be sure, now we are sure so let's say goodbye and go. We'll just walk out through that door and keep going."

"I should have done something, I should have helped him."

"What could you have done? We hardly know him."

"Oh, but I do know him." Her face blurred with tears. She went back to sit by his side, stroking his hands, his face, his shoulders, any place she could find that was not sore to her touch.

He opened his eyes. "My dear Jean, don't waste your tears. We only make these people bigger. In fact they are no bigger than this." He flicked his finger, then was quiet. He stirred and reached for her hand. "Water, please, if you don't mind." She gave it to him. "We lift to our lips whatever He pours into the bowl, the wine of paradise or the cup of hell." He smiled weakly. "Better in Arabic."

He dozed, fell into a deep sleep. Painkillers probably. Nothing more from him, only an occasional groan rising from the nightmare he had endured or one still buried in memory. Jean had made up her mind to stay. No matter what I said, how much I begged, the consequences I threatened, I could not get her to budge from his side.

I left her there, holding his hand against her cheek, still

stroking him, still murmuring to him. "Whatever you have done, I know you can't deserve this pain."

"But who is he? We know nothing about him, nothing, zilch!" While I was sitting around waiting for her, my suspicions had run rampant. Now she was back, and I thought she ought to think about entertaining a few of her own.

"Yes, what happened is horrible. But this subterfuge, not knowing what's what, it's spooky. All the blah blah about courageous little king and harmony in the region and who knows what other bullshit and the whole time he could be a spy! Involved in the coup, even, did you think of that? You don't want to hear this, but we might really have gotten ourselves into something. You saw the way those goons looked us over, how we were treated when they arrested him."

"What do you suggest? That we return to the loving arms of Madame Shoukri? If we walk out of this hotel, there's no one to protect us, you said so yourself."

"We could go to Damascus like we planned. Before any of this got in the way."

The phone interrupted our argument. The front desk. The prince had sent his car to take us to the Phoenicia. Our other life, revolving in a galaxy of nightclubs and hotels, Casbah, Caves du Roy, St. Georges, Excelsior, Phoenicia. "We'd better humor him, I suppose. Can you pull yourself together?"

"Yes. Besides, I need a drink."

"Okay, we'll go, but don't leave me alone with him. I don't feel like being his 'ho-nee,' not tonight or any other night."

The penthouse the Prince occupied with his retinue was spacious and full of light. From the balcony we watched the sky turn color in the setting sun over the sea. He was receiving a long line of visitors in a room behind us. They were deferential as they waited their turn. What a charade, who could possibly take this guy seriously?

"What's going on, what are they doing?" I asked the minister.

"They are needing help, money or child sick, something like this."

Resplendent in white robe and headdress, the prince was listening to each person make his case. We'd been treating him like an overgrown kid but he apparently wielded some power. When the last supplicant was gone, he came looking for me. I tried to get Jean to take notice. Short of shouting like a circus barker, I couldn't get her attention. He took my hand and before I knew it we were in a room on an enormous bed, rolling around and almost suffocating in his robes. With an enormous shove I got him off me.

He was glaring, his fine robes a shambles. I didn't laugh, afraid to make him angrier. "This, my sweet prince, is not in the cards. I'm sorry you got the wrong idea."

"You will go now."

Fine by me. I hustled Jean, sputtering in protest, into the hall. "What's the rush? I thought we were having a nice time."

"I'll explain." The elevator was slow but no one came after us. Out in the street, we looked for the driver. Nowhere to be found.

"C'mon, let's find a taxi," I said.

"Taxis aren't in our budget."

"You want to stay and grapple with him, be my guest. Me, I'd rather pay and scram. Besides, he might send someone after us."

"No longer his 'ho-nee'?"

"No." I described the bedroom farce. "Our prince could use some work on his technique. Like a little familiarity with the concept of foreplay."

"Guess you would know."

"And that's supposed to mean?"

"Whatever you want it to."

"Jean, I'm very much hoping it means nothing. How about you taking on the role of sacrificial lamb? Our room has to be paid for somehow."

We stopped sniping and hailed a taxi. She directed it to the St. Georges. "I'm going up to check on him."

"You're nuts! It's dark, we've had no dinner and you're probably tight as a tick." I didn't pursue it. If she had too much to drink, that was her problem. I went on with the taxi. Of course I paid.

During the night I woke in terror, hearing what sounded like shots far out across the bay, our balcony door slamming shut in a gust of wind. Huddling in a blanket, I waited for her and the storm. Which first? She didn't come until dawn, long after the storm was spent. I was fuming until I saw her face, exhausted and sad. I'd have to be made of stone to hold a grudge.

"You'd better get some sleep," I said.

"We both should. He wants to see us later, says it's important."

"How nice to include me."

The tables had turned. I was the one left out and I felt it keenly.

18

Close to noon before we started over to the St. Georges, clouds coming in off the sea. I went over and over in my mind what to say to him, determined to get answers. His room still basked in the yellow drapery sunset, his visitors evaporating as soon as we appeared. One stayed, an official from our embassy. A woman in her mid-thirties, though she could have been older, short, solid, glasses perched at the end of her nose so she could peer over them, the better to intimidate when questioning us.

Which she did.

"What on earth do you two girls think you're doing here?"

Not once had we considered going to the embassy for help. I don't know why. We told her about the book, how we had met Asif.

"That's all very well. Now tell me what you're *really* doing here."

"We just did," I said. "We told you exactly what we're doing. And we didn't swim here either, we came on a ship from Cyprus, like anybody else might."

"If you *girls* are this ignorant, this willful, you're a risk to yourselves. And others. Coups are deadly serious in a place like this, especially the ones that fail, nobody to pin it on, everybody fair game. Gives folks lots of cover for settling old scores."

She glanced at Asif. His eyes were closed, his breathing shallow. "This is not a good place for you to be." She frowned, was going to say more but thought better of it and left without so much as a nod to him.

He was up like a shot, had been pretending to be asleep. “You see how dangerous it is? You must leave from here right away. Not to Damascus, not now. You will go to our friends in Jordan. Our prince will help, *inshallah*, he can get the tickets.”

Was this a plan hatched before or after the skirmish on the bed?

“But what about you?” We both asked it.

“*Maalesh*! Don’t worry, *halas*, they’ve finished with me. You see who goes in and out of here, the Sureté, people from the government. Even the prime minister, right after him the opposition.” The names beat an exotic cadence—Chamoun, Jumblatt, Boustani, Husseini, Rashid, Rashad. “But I will rest easier when I see you gone from here. You must get to Amman before they shut down the airport. Believe me, you must do this.”

Time to go, he was tired. But if all those prominent people had been here, making apologies, I had one question, one I was sure she would never ask because the bond between them might break if confronted with too much cold reality. “Tell me, why did they do this to you?”

“They don’t know who their friends are. Over and over they ask, who is it I met on such and such a day, such and such a time? Front of the St. Georges, Paon Rouge, Romano’s. I tell the truth, I don’t remember. They beat me. They ask again, I cannot answer, how can I? It is months ago. I meet too many people. They smash my feet with rifles, they want to make me a cripple. Other things they did. This is how I am broken.”

He fell back against the pillows. “Stupid people. Like a family with too many brothers, each too much concerned what the other one is doing.” He drank some water.

“They have taken my dignity.”

I thought of Uncle George. “A man we met on Cyprus told

us dignity is only a word. Said it's nothing but a whore."

He managed a rueful smile.

As I walked back to the Excelsior—Jean of course lingered—the woman from the embassy weighed on my mind. If she didn't believe us, then what about anybody else? And Asif? Was he a victim of events or was it worse than that? An American official had come to see him, did that count? Was she hedging bets too, like the rest of them? We were putting ourselves in his hands, flying to Amman just because he told us to.

Around and around I went, but it always came back to the same thing. What choice? Wherever we turned—Griggs, the embassy woman, the goons—we were met with suspicion. At least we'd be out of Beirut.

An army jeep was parked in front where a limo for hire usually stood. Jeeps were all over the city but never one at our doorstep. I hurried inside and straight to the bar to buy cigarettes. Maybe Sami the bartender knew if something was up. There were few guests, and we were pretty well known around the place.

"*Bonjour, mademoiselle.*" Sami flashed me a smile full of white teeth. Bored, standing around with no business.

"Hi, Sami. Pretty quiet, huh?" I looked around the dark room.

"Too quiet. What can I get for you?"

"Just a pack of Player's." Someone came up beside me, standing so close I had to notice him. Grey suit, bland face, nothing alarming, just that closeness.

"Aren't you Pamela Johnson? Stewardess with Pan Am?" No accent, could even be an American.

"No, I'm not."

"You were on your way to Damascus. Change of plans?"

"Excuse me, sir, but this lady is a guest of the prince."

Sami had a nasty scowl on his usually pleasant face.

"Soon to be a guest of King Hussein?" He regarded me calmly and was gone.

"Who was that, Sami? Do you know him?"

"Never saw him in here before."

No one knew about Damascus except Asif, maybe the prince. We hadn't told Madame Shoukri. And Jordan? We just found that out.

"Put these on the bill, Sami!" I grabbed the cigarettes and ran from the bar. In the elevator, I started shaking, my heart pounding, floor buttons a blur. If only I could reach Andreas, at least someone in the world would know where we were. He could help us. Our parents? They wouldn't have a clue what to do in a fix like this. They would never get into one in the first place.

Selfish bitch! Putting herself in danger, again, couldn't wait to get back to him and the rest be damned. In his room murmuring at each other, the two of them, those awful yellow drapes, he telling her to go away, the whole thing already too complicated.

I went out on the balcony. The evening was fresh, the way it is after a quick, hard rain, a breeze sailing off the Mediterranean, wisps of cloud running back and forth over the moon. Strange how the night sky was never totally dark here. It wasn't the lights, there weren't that many looking towards the sea.

It had seemed like an eternity before Jean followed me to the hotel and I could tell her about the jeep and the man in the bar. Within minutes she had showered and announced she was going back to have dinner with him. What did they say to each other all this time? That was the real mystery. Her hand shook lighting a cigarette.

"After what I just told you. And his warning earlier? Don't do it!"

"I have to. I'm not sure what's happening between us but I can't stop it." Tears started. "Don't you see, he knows what I am and …"

"And what?"

"He cares for me anyway."

"Why shouldn't he? You don't have leprosy."

"I'm not any good at this. It's so intense it scares me. Wasn't it that way with you?" I thought of that last night with Andreas, his passion, my response. I thought the question meant she had forgiven us.

"Yes. But you're not being cautious. What about that guy in the bar? He knew everything, Jean. About our plans. How could he? Our plans keep changing. We don't know ourselves what they are. And don't tell me Lebanese security is that good. Those creeps crawling up and down the hall outside his door? Come on! They couldn't find Damascus, they couldn't find their butts with both hands and all the lights on."

"It's not the way it was before, everything's turned on its head."

"You need yours examined if you go out there again." I wasn't going to beg her to stay, but I didn't like being left alone. "Are you two …?"

"No! How could he, in the condition he's in? Anyway, we could spend all night and he wouldn't touch me. Don't forget the dead wife."

"What's that got to do with it? He can't mourn her forever."

"The whole business terrifies me, you know that."

"I see the way he looks at you and that terrifies me."

"It's not like that."

"Then what is it like?"

"I'm sorry," she whispered, and closed the door behind her.

* * *

Selfish bitch!

The ringing phone brought me off the balcony. The prince. Not a peep since we took a powder, so to speak, at the Phoenicia. "Come to the bar," he commanded. He had our tickets, I supposed.

There they were, squeezed around the small table, a tiny candle in the middle—the prince, the retainers. At least I wouldn't be alone with him. It was clear they were all on tenterhooks. The minister joked in the usual way but as soon as he stopped, his face collapsed in gloom. I tried a few pleasantries. The prince had taken care of us, for that I would always be grateful. I could have handled him better before, but the harder I tried now, the worse it got. Nice seemed to encourage mean.

"When nothing better, you will see me, ugly girl." He finished his drink, snapped his fingers for another. "Beirutis no good, I spit on these people, they are no-theeng."

He was drunk. Our unhappy prince, living on an allowance, nothing to do but visit his discarded mother, go to the cinema, hang out in clubs, unable to change any of it because uneducated or spoiled or scared. Holding court the other night was a charade except for the favors he could hand out.

The minister tried to distract him. "His Highness is very good at reading palms. Perhaps he will read yours, *mademoiselle*."

I turned over my hand. He traced a line with his fingernail. "I see many lovers." I wanted only one, the one I'd found, but in that dark bar, under his spell, I had the feeling that he was right, that Andreas and I were doomed.

He grinned and traced another line. "You will come back to Beirut. First a desert, very hot." He bent my fingers one by one into my palm, then covered my hand with his, pressing hard, forcing my own fingers to hurt me. Eyes dull. Not even cruelty excited him. I tried not to wince but I couldn't stop the tears.

"You like it too much," he said.

"No, I don't like it one bit." He let go.

"My girlfriend, she is Danish, she likes it too much."

He lit a cigarette and put the burning end on his palm and held it there. He locked eyes with me and didn't flinch. I could smell the burning flesh. "I do this to her here and here and here," he said, waving the cigarette like a wand over my body. What was this? Some kind of demented ascetic, castigating his flesh and hers to rid it of passion? He started laughing. The others too, forcing it. I got up to go and there was Jean.

"Hello, everybody!" she said brightly. Why not? She'd spent the evening with someone she could actually talk to.

"We're a little out of control here. If I were you I wouldn't stick around." Tickets or no tickets I wasn't going to.

When she came to bed, I must have been sound asleep, but she was ordering coffee when I woke up. I described the incident with the cigarette.

"Swell. A kinky prince, just perfect."

"Along with the other sadists and spies and godknowswhat."

"What about the tickets?"

"Nothing. I went down to meet him because I thought he had them."

"Asif wants to see us before we go. Maybe he does."

"What'd he say about the guy who came up to me in the bar?"

"I didn't tell him."

"You can't be serious! Too much gritty detail getting in the way of romance?" I thought of a painting I'd seen, a masked man holds out his hand to a woman while a monstrous winged creature tugs on a thread of his cloak.

"You're involved in something! Something's going on here—besides falling in love, I mean."

"You don't know what you're talking about. It's this place, it's Beirut, making all of us jittery. Look, if we can't trust each other ..."

"Then what is it between you?"

"I told you, he sees what I am and he understands."

"What are you then, that he sees?"

"He needs me, that's all I can say. I admire him, he stands for something. C'mon, let's go and see if he's got the damn tickets."

This time we had to check in with the Sureté before being allowed upstairs. In the hall the usual assortment of men talking, smoking, clearing out as soon as we appeared.

Asif did have the tickets and a thick wad of Lebanese pounds. "Listen to me, Sami is arranging a car to the airport." He knew Sami too? "In Amman you will go directly to Hotel Philadelphia. Speak to no one. Ask for General Jamal, Sharif Jamal."

Walk into a hotel in Amman and just ask for someone? They must use hotels like the English use their clubs.

"A man followed me yesterday. Came up to me in the bar, as if he knew me."

"Our man, as a matter of fact, the prince's own man."

"Wait. Asking about Damascus? Jordan? As if he knew our plans."

He frowned. "That would not be our man, as a matter of fact."

"Jesus! How about just one little matter of fact, for a change? Prince's man, your man, what the hell are you talking about?"

"Leave! Go to Excelsior at once. Jean will be right behind you."

"By myself? Why should I, I'm not …"

Good God, was Jean staying with him in Beirut? No, of course she wasn't.

"Go and go quickly! An army officer, high up, arrested. They say he's connected to the coup so rumors begin again. Beirut is more dangerous. Do as I say."

Running most of the way, I made it in seconds flat, lobby empty as usual, Jean not far behind. Another jeep outside, she told me, a soldier at the wheel. I hadn't seen it. She double-locked the door, took a stack of letters from her bag, lightweight, airmail type.

"He asked me to take these. Said to give them to no one but General Sharif."

"And you took them? Are you one hundred percent fucking nuts? Like your mother, you've got a death wish!"

"What was I supposed to do? The way he asked, it's important."

"Know what? I just thought of this, they questioned him about us."

"So? He wouldn't have told them anything … nothing to tell."

"Think it makes a difference, think it clears us? Thank you, gentlemen, for letting this fine upstanding citizen vouch for us, the one you just finished beating the crap out of because you think he's up to no good."

"Sirry, he begged me to do this."

"And waited until I left because he knows I've got more sense. What is it with you? Out saving the whole damned world?"

"I couldn't refuse him."

"*I* can! Watch me. We're way past due on smarts here,

Jean."

"It's not what you think. He's writing friends in Amman, telling them what's happened …"

"Horseshit! He's using you, using us. Nothing personal, just business. We can get out of here to do his dirty work. If it's even true that we can get out. Give me those letters, I'm going back over there."

"No!"

"Like hell!" She darted away. I lunged, got my hands on one, ripping it.

"All right, don't destroy them. We'll go, we'll find out what the story is."

"Don't you dare pull a fast one because I'm up to *here* with this crap."

We raced back to the St. Georges. No one in the hall, no one to leer at Jean, not a soul. We barged into his room, everything the same, draperies pulled shut, perpetual sunset still. But the bed was empty, the room was empty.

"What the …" Jean looked stunned.

"Holy shit! C'mon, we've gotta go!"

As the elevator doors closed, we saw General Osir coming down the hall.

We ran back to the Excelsior as fast as we could. To Sami with the beat up taxi. First thought: the prince, angry again, wouldn't spring for anything better. Second thought: anything better meant attracting attention. We were learning how to read the signs. We grabbed our bags and made for the airport.

PART SIX

Into the Desert

19

I heard you, from the car—that scream. What were they doing to you?"

Her eyes, frightened. "Nothing."

"I always scream over nothing. Do you think I'm that stupid? They were questioning you."

"They asked what everybody does. 'What were you doing in Beirut?'"

"And?"

"Didn't believe the answer."

"Same as I don't believe you now."

"They asked if I heard of Asif, aka Riad Teffari. He never told me he had another name. I figured I'd better not lie about the Asif part so I said, yes, if it's the same man, I know him a little. They jabbered away, looked at our passports some more. I made a fuss, I'm sure that's what you heard, they left to get you and then that officer came. He was upset, I mean, he really let them have it, in Arabic. And hustled me out of there. *Et fini*."

"*Fini*, my fanny. All that time with them and that's it?"

"That's it. If he hadn't come along when he did … well, like the driver said, we're lucky peoples."

"They didn't seem too disciplined, those guys."

This cozy conversation was taking place on the last plane out before the airport shut down. We had been brought up short when minutes after takeoff the plane shuddered, the seat belt sign came back on, and the passengers, very few, grew still. Mechanical trouble? Or had we been fired at? Already near hysteria at being free of the checkpoint and in the air, when the pilot pulled out of it. Jean and I found ourselves holding hands so tightly that letting go we saw imprints our fingernails had made.

Before long we were over the hills of Amman, *jebels*, seven as in Rome, pastel villas nestled among them like outsized Easter eggs, a striking contrast with the sprawl of dun colored souks and baked mud buildings in the ravines below. It looked little more than a village, spare after the excesses of Beirut. Not much importance since the Romans who called it Philadelphia. A little brotherly love would be nice for a change.

We passed through airport controls and took a taxi to the Hotel Philadelphia. It stood across from the ruins of an amphitheater, fragments of columns scattered about like cut logs. Following Asif's directions we asked for General Sharif Jamal. Whether Asif was in prison or hell, we decided to stick with the general who might at least have a few guns in his possession to protect us. Lobby deserted, only one man at the desk. We were given a large room on the ground floor at the back. Our passports were not held for the routine security check.

It wasn't until we shut the door of the room that we really fell apart. Jean, lighting a cigarette with trembling hands, paced. How thin she was! Colorless as a plate of scallops. Like The Countess, I realized, those hollows at the temple, transparent, so you had to shut your eyes against the pitiless throbbing beneath.

Never mind all that, I was seething. We had made it out, sure, but at what cost? The chance she had taken. But, damn it, once again I had to hand it to her, the way she walked into that checkpoint, head held high. I would have been begging for mercy. Best not to think about it. I turned my attention to the room. One wall dominated by a wardrobe, warped doors, mirrors opaque, seeing nothing. I sat on a bed, the one nearest the windows, and looked out at the dusty paths. More ruins beyond. In another part of the world, this might have been a garden.

A muezzin called prayers, a sound like the wind whining in the desert. *La ilaha illa-l-Lah.* There is no god but Allah. Her pacing was driving me nuts. "If you don't stop, I'm going to go bats!" She stopped. Started again.

Muhamadun rasulu-l-Lah. Muhammad is the messenger of Allah. The chant had gotten louder. Or another muezzin had joined in.

"For heaven's sake, Jean, sit down!"

"If I do, I'll start thinking." She cupped her elbow, cigarette aloft in a V of fingers. What victory? "How long will it take before I stop seeing that mush of flesh, that other injury his eyes speak of?"

How long before I shove your teeth down your throat so you'll shut up? That's what I wanted to say. What I did more politely say was, "How long will it take for you to stop being a total idiot?" She didn't see it was all an act? Romancing her so we would accept the letters? She had to suspect this was true or she'd be a lot more concerned about that empty room.

"He tricked us, Jean. Tricked us and disappeared. Start thinking about that. Here's something else to think about. What the hell we're doing carrying these letters in their cockeyed script with the dots and curlicues nobody can read but them! Why did you go along with it?"

"Don't be a fool!" She jabbed the cigarette into the ashtray.

"Who's the fool?" I looked at the ceiling webbed with cracks. The prince would have a field day reading fortunes in those patterns.

"Like mountain climbing, isn't it, Jean? Roped to one another, no chance to pull out and go it alone, not when you're halfway up. So the first choice is the crucial one. After that you're stuck. All you can do then is pray nobody takes a wrong step."

"Let's stop this. I went along out of fear, that's all. Fear of being afraid, for one thing. Most of all fear of showing it."

"Wanting to be so sophisticated. I'm afraid we've gone too far this time."

"What else did we have to do that was important? Until he showed up."

Andreas wasn't important? No, of course not. I let it go. "Well, we have our own personal general, presuming he shows up to claim us. Nothing to be afraid of now. Who knows, maybe he'll have some answers."

"He's an Arab, don't forget. Since when do Arabs deal in answers?"

I couldn't believe my ears. Cynicism making a comeback? A good sign. We'd pull ourselves together, do what we had to and get out of here. I yearned to be in Paris, Philadelphia even. "Let's hope he's not like that other general, Osir." The minute I said it I was sorry.

"Don't bring him up." She lit another cigarette and started to cough, wound up in a fit of coughing, couldn't stop until she was almost throwing up. "Nerves."

"The last time you almost threw up, it was Ahmed's mother making buffalo butter."

"They had the right idea, Ahmed and his brothers, not letting us out of their sight."

"Why are we sitting here staring at dust?" The afternoon was folding, a feeble sun on the way to setting. Jean was smoking her way through an entire pack.

"I don't give a good goddamn about any of it!"

"Fine! Tell me again how you don't give a good goddamn. Let's hear it."

"Go to hell!"

"We're in hell."

I saw that there was a door behind the curtains. We didn't have to go through the lobby to get outside. Into the half light of dusk we went, depressing unless you happen to be in front of a fire listening to Cavafy, knowing your lover is near, feeling close to him because you're with his friend. Would I ever see either of them again?

"Don't!" I heard myself shout. She jumped a mile. "Honestly, for a second I thought that fence was … I was actually thinking you might get electrocuted."

"You're in worse shape than I am."

What did she expect? We turned back to the hotel. The upper floor windows were dark, only a few dim lights here and there. A figure, silhouetted in one, disappeared.

"On second thought, maybe there's not enough electricity in all of Amman. To give you a shock, I mean."

"It is spooky out here," she said. "Like crawling around inside an old photograph."

We met in the bar at seven. General Jamal wasn't a tall man, but he had the bearing of one, trim in a dark blue suit, body tense, on total alert, thin nose pointing to a neat—well, military—mustache darker than his sandy hair. His eyes? Couldn't tell. They were hidden behind tinted glasses that gave him a sinister look, a look that was subverted by round cheeks as benevolent as pancakes.

"This is Khalil Rafeir." He indicated the man beside him. They traveled in pairs, where women were concerned anyway.

"Welcome," said Khalil. Just this side of plump, cheeks you want to pinch, the picture of a good-natured chaperone.

We ordered drinks and exchanged pleasantries as if we were meeting on a holiday tour, their English fluent and easy, Khalil's punctuated with what he assumed to be British expressions. Balderdash was a favorite, which he dropped into conversation with abandon and no apparent link to meaning.

Jean grew impatient. "We've come from Asif and—" General Jamal stopped her with a jerk of his head and a sharp click of his tongue against his teeth. "*La!*" he said. Two distinct syllables—*lah ah!* No. "Not now."

We tugged at our drinks, the only sound the amber worry beads sliding over his knuckles. He left briefly. When he returned the dark glasses were gone, unveiling the most amazing eyes the color of bluebells. Amazing on anyone, but especially an Arab.

He motioned us up. "You will come to dinner!" Great idea. We hadn't eaten all day. "You will call me Sharif." He let us see a hint of mischief.

We went to a nightclub of sorts, in the hotel, a huge space like a gym with about as much atmosphere. At one end was a balcony where we sat above the crowd, a bottle of Johnnie Walker Black on the table when we arrived. A waiter filling our water glasses looked away, distracted, spilling as he poured. Sharif snapped his fingers and an army of waiters surrounded us.

"Tell me what happened," he commanded when they finished mopping up. "Why did he send you?"

This time Jean hesitated. He nodded towards Khalil. "He can be trusted." She told him everything then, about Asif's arrest, how we met, how we happened to be there when they came for him. When she described how badly he was beaten, Sharif sucked in his breath, swearing in Arabic. We didn't need to understand the words. When she finished, both men were silent, stunned.

"You have told everything?"

"Yes."

After a long pause, he shook his head. "Those bastards! We didn't know any of this stupid business. Stupid people! Thinking we had anything to do with it!" He slammed his fist into the table.

Glasses jumped. “God have mercy on them. I will not.”

We. Meaning Jordan? The Lebanese suspected Jordan had something to do with the coup attempt? Everybody’s fair game, the embassy woman had said. Then why were we allowed to fly here? Did the prince bribe our way out, through that checkpoint? Once again, we had to see him in a different light.

“I will inform His Majesty of all you have told us and all you have done. You have shown great courage. We seldom see this, *yanni*, in two so young.” Courage required a degree of choice I’d always thought, but I didn’t argue the point.

“He sent these.” Jean handed over the letters.

On our way into the bar, I had suggested we tell how we tried to take them back and what we’d seen—hadn’t seen—when we got to his room. “And say we chickened out?” she’d snapped. For a moment I thought it possible Asif wasn’t the villain after all, that he might be in trouble again, and we should report it.

“Let’s wait, make sure what we’re dealing with,” she had said.

Sharif rifled quickly through the pile, selecting several to read. When he finished he lit a cigarette, lost down some wadi of the mind.

“You will be safe with us,” he said finally.

Others dropped by. Some lingered. To a few, Sharif seemed to tell our story, or parts of it. Listening they made that same click of the tongue. The table drifted into a low buzz of Arabic. Jean and I turned our attention to what was going on below.

Most of the crowd were men, most of them in robes, strolling among the tables like customers in the souk, sipping orange drinks or something stronger, cadging cigarettes here, stopping for a light there. A band, perched on a platform at the opposite end, played Western music, a singer in a skin-tight gown twinkling with sequins under the lights. It was a welcome respite from Oum Kalthoum, the neighborhood's Billie Holiday. A steady dose of Arab music demands occasional respite.

A sedate foxtrot was ending when the singer jumped up, grabbed the microphone and belted, "Come on let's twist again!"

Onto the floor they came in their robes and headdresses, twisting like windmills in a storm. We didn't dare look at each other.

Our companions didn't notice, weren't paying attention, kept muttering, clicking tongues and fingering worry beads. At midnight we ate huge steaks and went to bed in the arms of Johnnie Walker to sleep a dreamless sleep. Out of the nightmare of Beirut, no more thought of trouble or torture, unless it was the throbbing heads that would greet us in the morning.

20

The smell of garlic and roasting chicken brought us back to reality. General Sharif's driver had appeared before dawn to take us to Jerusalem, less than two hours' drive. Sharif would meet us for a late lunch but first we would go to the Garden of Olives, to the dark church of the Agony of the Garden in the hills covered in cedar and eucalyptus and pine, and to Bethany, where we came upon a roof-raising, men shooting pistols in the air, women ululating, an ancient sound. Then into Jerusalem, down the narrow streets and steps, under arches and through tiny doors into rooms where Jesus was scourged and spat upon and crowned with thorns, Calvary above, tomb below. It's where they told us these things had happened, and what difference? If it wasn't there, it was somewhere nearby.

From the moment we drove through St. Stephen's Gate, the rising sun burning away mist and turning golden everything in its path, we were caught up in the atmosphere of the place. We could imagine how people got carried away, believing themselves to be prophets, the Virgin Mary, even Jesus Himself. The place was alive with mysticism and miracle.

The restaurant was a cocoon of couches and cushions. The proprietor fussed over us, bringing water flavored with orange blossom and tiny dishes of nuts. Sharif bounded in, holding out his hands, a small box in each. "Take them!" Inside were crosses encrusted with rubies or garnets, who could tell? "My driver has told me how much you are affected by this place."

"But you're a Moslem!"

He laughed. "My dear girls, I am not so foolish. God is God, isn't He? Same for all of us. If this is not so, then He is not God. Simple. Let's eat."

It was after five when we finished, the street coming alive with the fall of evening and the raising of shutters as shops reopened after the midday break. Our host was talking heatedly to Sharif, his worry beads falling on the little brass table, tears in his eyes. Sharif translated. "This man is a Palestinian. It is about his father he speaks. He cannot die, he tells his son, until he again eats an orange from Jaffa. It is time, he wishes to die, but he cannot. The old man's orchards are over there, on the other side. He will never see his home, but it is of oranges he dreams." Sharif shrugged. "This is how we live now, dreaming of oranges."

Brightening a little, the man asked if we would allow him to tell our future in the dregs of thick black coffee. "Me too good. I see everytheeng!" I thought of the last time my fortune was told. We'd just as soon not see everytheeng, thanks anyway. He was cast down again.

"Where does his father live now?" Jean asked.

"Here, with the son, as a matter of fact. We do not send our old people away, *yanni*, to live among strangers like you Americans. Never! You think you are civilized but for us this is uncivilized above all."

We left the restaurant, walking past the barbers and cobblers and moneychangers, peering into dim recesses of cafés where men gathered to smoke and play backgammon. Sharif stopped in the middle of the street and threw up his hands. "What does this man think, that we can send our army to steal an orange?"

He stood with his palms up, a gesture made in prayer. "We know how to mourn the past, how do we learn to bury the future? We have all become prisoners, prisoners of broken dreams."

* * *

"Get up you lazy girls! *Wallahi!* What do you think, *yanni,* you can come here and wear out our beds? They will make us pay extra!" Gone the somber Sharif of the evening before. "Get up," he shouted into the phone. "You have an appointment to see His Majesty. *Yella!*"

His Majesty! King Hussein! We would actually meet the dashing figure we'd read about in the Sunday supplements—maybe not tall but he was handsome, he flew planes, he was a daredevil. He was, as Asif said, courageous. Nothing bad could happen to us now. We danced around the room, singing, *We're off to see the Wizard* ... A date at the palace and one pair of nylons between us. Jean won the coin toss.

Up and down the hills we drove in a Rolls-Royce so polished we could have used it to put on our makeup. We didn't see the tanks until we were through the palace gates. Not only tanks, but jeeps, two and three deep along the sides of the road and across the ridge of the hill we were climbing and massed around the buildings.

"Quite a welcoming party."

"Are these usually here? These tanks?" I leaned forward to hear the driver's response. There wasn't one.

Jean took up the challenge, raising her voice in case the problem wasn't language or obstinacy but simple deafness. "All these military vehicles, is this *ordinary*?" No answer.

This was Oz, couldn't be too serious. But sands shift under you, even when you don't feel the wind. We had seen this in the desert.

Soldiers were everywhere. Those files we read had described the Arab Legion, most of them Bedouin and fiercely loyal, officers trained at Sandhurst, the famous military school in

England. They had a reputation for professionalism, which was reassuring as we passed by all the guns. An Englishman, John Bagot Glubb, known as Glubb Pasha, helped build the legion but had been relieved of duty, a link to colonialism and too dangerous for King Hussein to keep around, an excuse to do to him what was done to his cousin Faisal. He had already survived assassination attempts. This too happened in Oz.

The man who came out to greet us introduced himself as chief of protocol. Protocol? With all that metal lined up to worry about? He asked us to wait, indicating a row of chairs against the wall. Men sitting there melted away at our approach. Others, black-robed, heads wrapped in keffiyehs, stood sipping glasses of tea. Bedouin from the desert, we were told, tribal elders from the look of them, faces deeply rutted like country roads in a spring thaw. They circled like crows, nodding and murmuring. "Where from?"

"America."

"*Eioua.*" The Arabic word for yes sounded like Iowa.

"You are the newspapers!" Newspapers? If they thought we were journalists, what was the scoop?

"No, we're students." Blank stares. I enunciated more clearly. "*Students.*"

"*Helou!* Top page!" *Helou* we'd heard often enough to know it meant pretty, pretty enough to make the front page. The definition of journalism. They were grinning at us through blackened teeth, uneven like a stand of trees after a forest fire.

"*Eioua! Helou!* Top page!" they chanted.

It was chilly inside the stone palace. We were shivering when the protocol chief returned. His Majesty would be a while, would we like to tour the royal garden and zoo? We followed him into the warm sun. Not a large garden, not a large zoo either, though we only skirted the edges, glimpses of racing camels, royal lions from Ethiopia, gazelles, all gifts from heads of state. "His Majesty has pressing matters," Protocol was saying.

Heading off a revolution, for starts?

"Most kind showin' us around, smack in the middle of yore busy schedule." The word *schedule* dragged a city block before she let go of it.

Now what was she up to? I hadn't heard the drawl since we left home. He blushed. Enough to keep her going. She was flirting outrageously by the time the monkey leaped onto the path in front of her, swinging his long arms in the direction of her long legs. A dance, she backing away, the monkey advancing, coming closer, clawing at her, connecting. Enchanted, he studied the nylon unraveling in his paw.

"Fuck!" shouted our southern belle. The word flew from her mouth in a perfect arc, along the path, through the windows where the elders stood sipping their tea, on to the soldiers lined up beside the tanks and jeeps on the crest of the hill. Who would be on their way to arrest us for defiling the precincts of the king.

"Jean, not that word! They obey commands around here, remember?"

"Filthy little bastard!" The little bastard squealed with delight as she hopped around him. What a great game!

Groundskeepers came running. They managed to get between her and her tormentor. She stopped shouting, realized what she'd said. "Oh, dear, I'm so sorry …"

"How did this creature come to be here?" said Protocol, as he and the workmen, barely containing their laughter, shooed the monkey away. "I do apologize."

Jean inspected her leg, naked beneath flaps of torn nylon. "Did he break the skin?" I was worried about rabies. Nothing in her pharmacy for that.

"I don't think so. But I'd like to kill the …"

"Don't say it!" I took her arm and we followed Protocol back inside.

"What was all that southern shit about?" I said, when he excused himself.

"Just thought I'd flirt a little, get him on our side."

"As in, can't we complicate it? Don't we have our hands full?"

Protocol came back with a grim expression. His Majesty was unable to receive us. General Jamal would contact us. Hiding our disappointment, we thanked him, he and the Bedouin bowing us out. The sun was casting wide shadows over the neighboring hills.

"You cursed like a heathen, that's why we didn't get to see the king."

"Wait a damned minute, I'm not going to get blamed for this one! While we're at it, I'd like to tell His Majesty what he can do with that evolutionary dropout. It's a threat to the kingdom. What if Nasser comes to call?"

"Nasser doesn't go in for kings, remember? He's already toppled one."

"You can't mention them in the same breath, that fat Farouk and King Hussein?"

"Think General Nasser makes distinctions? Maybe you'll have a chance to discuss it with the king. Then again, maybe not. A thoroughbred jumped the fence today, as my grandfather was fond of saying. And it wasn't the monkey." We laughed nervously as we rode through the gauntlet of tanks.

"Jean, I have a feeling the king's got bigger problems on his hands than that renegade monkey. Just when I thought we were home free."

"Who organized this contest anyway?"

"Huh?"

"Trouble is, we're the only ones who entered."

"Trouble, my friend, is exactly what we're in. Again."

21

Message at the front desk, "Bar promptly, quarter of seven." Almost that now. Sharif was waiting with his sidekick, same table.

"*Aahlan wasaalan.*" Not nearly as cheery as the morning. Difficult keeping up with the mood swings. No mention of the monkey or our disgrace at the palace, nothing about tanks either.

"*Aahlan,*" Khalil added. "Have something to drink, my sisters."

Sharif was fiddling with a radio. "His Majesty soon makes a statement. Everyone in the country will be listening."

"So that's why tanks were lined up at the palace," said Jean.

Sharif didn't answer. I looked around and realized that again the bar was empty. Did he have the power to shut out everybody else? He checked his watch, played with the ice in his glass, checked his watch, minutes marked by the drone of the radio and the clatter of worry beads. He slipped a finger under his watchband, rolled it back and forth, stopped to check the time once more. The radio voice turned solemn, like the one in Cyprus announcing the coup attempt. Sharif raised his hand to hush us, although no one had said a word. "Now. *Inshallah.*"

King Hussein spoke, another broadcast we couldn't understand. After ten minutes, maybe longer, patriotic music came on. Sharif switched it off. "So, my friends, a new prime minister. *HamduliLah!*"

Because of what happened in Lebanon? The whole region ripe to explode, Griggs had said.

"Cheers to the new PM!" said Khalil.

"This is why all those men were at the palace," I said.

"Yes. His Majesty consulting with the people. It was necessary to wait for the Bedouin to travel."

Bringing in the loyal Bedouin to shore up the throne. Meaning the choice was controversial? Now I was reading the coffee dregs.

"They come from far away, then, if the journey is long," Jean said.

"Yes, they walk far." Khalil looked happy that fate had not chosen him to be a Bedouin.

"They do not like to rush. They say it brings sorrow and sickness in its path. We try to follow their example, *yanni.*" Sharif's face had a wistful expression. "The secrets of the desert, its rocks and dunes and resting places, are as familiar as the tattoos on their hands. It belongs to them, we only visit. The desert is absolute, its demands are absolute. And its loyalties."

We finished our drinks. Outside the air was crisp, any star bright enough to follow to Bethlehem, not so distant from where we stood. Sharif took the wheel. We sped through empty streets to the Amman Club, jammed with people crowding the bar, women too, for a change. Sharif led us to a dining room, comfortable with its big leather armchairs. Khalil settled in happily and winked. "More like it, eh? More your cup of tea, wouldn't you English say? Balderdash and so on."

"These girls are *mejnouni*, yes. English, no!" Mejnouni, meaning crazy. Sharif in a teasing mood, upbeat again. We all laughed. Anxiety eased. No longer in Amman but transported on a magic carpet to a supper club back home, the Elks, for example, ordering the roast beef special with my father and his friends, organ music drifting in from the cocktail lounge was all that was missing. Sharif with his worldliness and humor, his power—more Sandhurst than Wormwood Scrubs—fit more easily into this setting, into most settings, than Andreas ever would. I must have flinched, because Khalil touched my arm and said, "Don't worry, Sis, you are safe with us."

Sharif clapped his hands. "Coffee!"

"Turkish coffee!" I said. Strong enough to launch a counterattack on the scotch we'd been drinking.

"Turkish? Are we in the souk?"

When would we be near a souk again? I yearned for the days of simple travel. Sharif left the table, reporting in to someone, no doubt. Khalil noticed that we had lost Jean to her thoughts. "The weather of your friend, very changeable, isn't it?" I decided not to point out the mood changes of his friend Sharif.

He shook her gently. "I do not believe it is only concern for our friend in Beirut that brings you sadness." Tears were instant. Give in to your feelings, I'd told her once. Wasn't this going too far?

He pulled out a handkerchief. "My dear Sis, I assure you God is taking care of you, even if He does not feel close to you now."

How did God get into this so fast? "Do you truly believe that?"

Khalil looked at me. "Of course! Do you not believe it?"

"I always have, with all my heart." I didn't think this was the place to confess that any idea of a benevolent divinity had faltered badly in the face of so much contrary evidence. He turned back to Jean.

"You are young, your whole life in front of you, but you cannot blow on your hand and say, poof! it will be a good life. Think how many saints were fallen. But goodness comes out of recovery from moral failure. Isn't this the point of redemption?"

His redemption had none of the fire and brimstone we were used to. He patted her hand. "Be thankful we do not have to place ourselves in a universe with no intelligence behind it, no resources of eternal goodness to back us up."

"But this is exactly the universe we're in!" Jean said.

Khalil, taken aback, was considering his response when Sharif reappeared. "Come, meet the new prime minister! *Yella!*"

We jumped up and followed him to an elevator just big enough for the four of us. "They've got him stashed away upstairs?" I whispered to Jean.

"With the Wizard?" A second chance to meet the king turned her spirits around.

The prime minister was in the middle of a long narrow room, seated at a small table, alone except for men making shadows on the wall at the opposite end. Security people, I surmised. The air was close, smell of stale cigarettes and morning-after scotch. Draperies were pulled shut, chairs pushed up against the folds. So he wouldn't be seen from the street outside? Surely not because they were here smoking hashish like the last time we were behind closed curtains. So he was in hiding. Or was I again thinking like an Arab?

"Good evening, Mr. Prime Minister." Sharif beckoned us forward. "Come, meet Wasfi Tel." No explanation of who we were or what we might be doing there.

Sharif said, "You are tired."

Yes." Expressive eyes, more like Dr. Thanos the poet than politician. "Many visitors. Just now His Majesty." Not again! We'd just missed him.

"Everything is quiet and in order," Sharif reported.

"Yes, our friends have managed things quite well." They

switched to Arabic.

Sharif stood and signaled time to go. We left the new Prime Minister behind in the small, airless room. He survived whatever lurked outside the window that night. A decade later he was gunned down on a street in Cairo in broad daylight.

What a relief to be out in the fresh night air. We rode with the windows down.

"What did you think of our new PM?" Sharif shouted.

"Office not much to look at," Jean said.

"What danger is he in?" I asked.

"None. If we do our job." He was driving fast, heedless of the Bedouin creed about rushing. Villas and trees and pinpricks of light in the hills no brighter than fireflies disappeared as we sped out of town on the open highway.

"Hey, slow down, y'all think we're in Texas?" Not the time for that stupid drawl. Was she tipsy?

"Maybe you want to see the Dead Sea by moonlight." There was no moon. Even the stars had dimmed.

"How far is that?"

"Minutes, the way our friend drives!" This from Khalil.

A doubt flickered as to their intentions. Olive groves and fields whizzed past, nothing else on the road, not a car, not a sound in the huge night except the whine of our tires on the macadam. We dropped to the valley floor. Without warning, Sharif pulled over. He pointed to Jean in the back seat with me. "You drive."

"I don't know this car," she started to protest. I started to say she might be drunk.

"No different from your crazy American cars." The words were bantering, his tone was not.

Khalil slid in beside me. Jean got behind the wheel and drove until we reached a bridge and the inevitable checkpoint. A soldier came up to the car.

"Tell him Dead Sea Hotel," Sharif said to Jean. Khalil reached for something, flash of metal. A gun?

Jean did as she was told. The men turned their faces away. *Won't be fooled for a second,* I thought, as the soldier checked me out in the back seat. Then again he might assume this was a tryst, our companions prominent, not wanting to be recognized. Maybe that's what it really was! He hesitated, then waved us on. We crossed the Allenby Bridge to the West Bank. Any effect of the drinks vanished. We drove in silence. Dead silence down to the Dead Sea. We could demand to get out of the car, but then what? Hitchhike back on a road with no traffic?

The hotel was small, boarded up like any out-of-season resort, parking lot deserted. Sharif banged on the door until a heavyset man in pajamas and slippers opened it, not bothering to stifle a yawn. I fidgeted with a stray cigarette, crumbling it in the pocket of my trench coat. The man nodded us inside. It was cold, a smell of damp cement from being closed up. Avoiding my eyes or Jean's, he led us to a room. Beds covered in thin blankets, a dispirited pink, a single light bulb behind plastic in the middle of the ceiling. No carpets. Gathered up to mold elsewhere. The men continued down the hall. We locked ourselves in. Before long, a knock and Khalil's voice.

"At least it's only one of them." I got up to open the door.

"Sharif is asleep! He needs it after what he's been through."

"And what might that be, exactly?" Jean was off the bed in an instant. "What was all that business back there?"

I never saw a face go so blank. "What do you mean?"

"You know what she means! The bridge, remember, checkpoint, guns, that's what she damn well means!" A sweet man, but he was really irritating me now.

"I'm not used to driving around with a gun poked in my ribs," said Jean. So Sharif had one too. Of course he would.

"I don't know how to answer this," he said wearily. "Remember who he is. Trust that, if nothing else."

"And who is he? Little Bo Peep?" I had to laugh in spite of myself.

"You don't know?"

"How enlightening. He's a general, so what? This part of the world is crawling with generals." I felt like clapping. This was a lot better than tears.

"Security. His Majesty's own chap, you see."

"Security? You've gotta be kidding! He just ran himself out of town!"

I groaned. "Not another Osir!"

"I don't know who is this Osir but Sharif is like no other in our part of the world. He is the best, I can assure you. Our intelligence is the best in the region. This is why I know you will come to no bad end."

Bad end! What on earth was he talking about? His Majesty's own chap, that much had to be true. We had met the prime minister, almost met the king. We heard the slap of plastic slippers coming down the hall and a tap on the door. Fatso with tea, already lukewarm.

When he was gone, Khalil sat on the bed and patted a place beside him. "Sis, let us finish our talk. I know I can help fortify your faith."

"'I know I can help fortify your faith!'" she mocked. "Leave me out of it, I didn't ask to join this circus!"

"Jean!"

"Get off it, Sirrine. I have no use for this business, you of all people know this. Where does it get anybody? Where did it get my mother, on her knees every day of her life? Eyes empty, staring at nothing. You want me to believe in a God, love a God who does that?"

Khalil turned his face away. Submission to Allah was the very essence of Islam. I raised my eyes, waiting for the thunderbolt. I wasn't ready to take this on either. I'd leave that to her and Andreas. But what were we doing, sitting around in this godforsaken dump discussing God with His self- appointed propaganda minister?

"Listening to you and Sirrine, oh, how wonderful it all is. But it's not, just another cliché out of a cereal box."

"I say, oh, dear, this won't do! No, old chaps, this won't do at all! We must try to remain calm, yes, all will blow over in a jiffy. Much the better thing, eh? Jolly good, let bygones be bygones." Poor Khalil, wringing his hands and spouting his clichés, one expected him to start hopping about, still unable to let go of the notion we were British.

Jean ignored him. "I can remember the exact moment when I decided I could fix this. My father raving drunk, yelling all over the house, usually just sat there and drank, but something snapped. My mother cowering. I hated the power he had over her. Why didn't she stand up to him, prove she didn't need him? I know how to end this, I thought. I will never marry, never have children, and that will put a stop to it. This madness will end with me. This idea got me through.

"Only my mother and I loved each other. But she wasn't strong enough even for that." Jean was on the verge of tears again. "I haven't much talent for it—this business of living. Something got left out."

Here we go again. Weren't we in enough of a mess without this? What had happened to my glamorous Jean? I wanted her back. Why had I ever tried to change her? Or was it what I'd feared, something breaking in her too? Or was she grandstanding?

Another drama to get attention.

"I'm like that sea out there, dead."

"My dear Jean, be careful not to fall in love with your despair, carrying it around with you like a pet bird feeding on the worms of your doubt. You think you have plenty of time for this. Too soon you will stand before God and you will have to answer to Him."

We heard slippers shuffling back and forth in the hall. More tea? For whom? The place was empty. Must be close to dawn. Then Sharif was pounding on our door, suddenly in a hurry to get back to Amman. "*Yella!*" he shouted.

He was startled to find Khalil with us. "My dear boy, what are you doing here?" He looked at the beds, still made. "No one slept? Well, no time for that now. *Yella!*"

First light, just light enough to see grey salt flats leading to the sea, the sea grey too, motionless under a flat, milky sky, not a ripple disturbing the calm, there being no wind and nothing living in its depths. The sea you could not sink in. Just light enough to make out a few black Bedouin tents scattered here and there, goats and camels tethered nearby, fast asleep on the winter ground. Light enough too to see the distant hills, hills of Judea, wilderness of biblical temptation, lure of madmen, home of hermits. No sound anywhere, not a horn honking, not a dog barking. Not a single bird noticing the dawn.

We were climbing out of the valley, Sharif driving much too fast, we too tired to care, when a car, the first since clearing the city's outskirts the night before, came up behind us. Close. Any closer and it would ram us. I caught a glimpse of Sharif's face in the rearview mirror. Something was wrong.

He drove faster still, zigzagging wildly, yelling at Khalil in Arabic. Jean grabbed my hand. More yelling, some kind of horror happening in Arabic, us caught in the middle, no translation. I began to pray that we'd get out of this and not die. I talked to God, to myself, to nobody in particular. Grow up in the Midwest and you trust people, protected like Andreas said, Griggs right not to get involved, not a coward as we suspected, just not foolish like we are, Andreas warned us, we wouldn't listen. Whatever it takes, if it takes everything in my power and all the money I've got left, I promise myself to get out of here and never again get into a fix like this, risk my life like this, she can do what she likes, if she wants to die let her …

She was thrown against me. We were in the hills, swinging side to side across the road, narrowly missing the ditches. Sharif slammed on the brakes, whipped the car around, rocking and skidding before he could control it and speed in the opposite direction. We drew even with the other car. It swerved to hit us. Sharif swung wide, braked and turned around, spinning and coming out of it quickly this time, heading once more in the direction of Amman, into the rising sun after the other car, gaining on it, a noise like popping corn, Jean reacting fast, yanking me roughly to the floor, Sharif shouting, "Down! Dammit! Get down!" The other car screeching and skidding, more popping noises. Then quiet, the utter quiet that falls after something bad has happened.

I struggled to sit up. I looked behind us. No car, vanished. We were hurtling along, terrifying speed. I was thrown against the front seat, banged my forehead. A sound came from there. Khalil, slumped against the door, its window shattered. Sharif's hand was on his chest, inside his jacket. Was he hurt? No blood, not that I could see. I reached for Jean's hand. "Is he … is he …?" Jean was looking at him too, her face ashen.

"Fainted. He's all right," Sharif said.

"What about those other people?"

"What other people?"

In the outskirts of Amman he slowed down and turned off the highway through residential streets until we came to a road carved out along the top of a hill, just yesterday from the look of it. He stopped in front of the skeleton of a villa going up, pulled something from the glove compartment and passed it under Khalil's nose. A sharp smell filled the car, like ammonia, or mildew, turning my stomach. Khalil moaned, his eyes fluttering open. Sharif forced something into his mouth, got out, helped him out, half walking, half carrying him, and settled him against a tree. He hunched over him, holding his face in his hands, talking to him. He kissed him on each cheek, came back to the car and drove off, yelling out the window in Arabic. Something ending in *bahd bucarra*. After tomorrow.

"You're dumping him there?" Jean said.

"My dear girl, I know what it is I do and it would be much better for you to be quiet now and listen to me. For the moment you are not secure. Those foolish people may be the only ones who wish to make trouble. In that case, there will be no further trouble for anyone. But we cannot be absolutely sure."

"Who … were they?" I could hardly get it out.

"Enemies of His Majesty. And Jordan. We have more than enough of them. I will turn you over to my people. They will see that you get out of the area. Today. I am sorry you did not see more of our sights. Jerash, Petra. Next time, maybe. *Inshallah*."

Next time? Not on your life, *inshallah*. I seemed to be very cold, my jaws chattering, unable to stop. Jean looked like somebody had belted her and she was trying to decide what to do about it.

"Listen to me. Khalil will soon be on his way to hospital. You know I love him like a brother."

We were in the *jebels* still, circling aimlessly it seemed before changing direction and heading south, or what I thought might be south. Free of the city on that side, we drove until we came to a fork in the road, dominated by a Bedouin camp. Sharif stopped and got out, men gathering around him. Glasses of tea were brought. There must have been something sedating in it, because soon I was more calm.

"This is where I leave you, in the hands of my man, Abu Moussa, as I would gladly leave my own wife. He will take you from here. Believe me, it is for your security."

I was having a hard time concentrating, it was a quiz I was supposed to know the answer to but couldn't think fast enough. I grasped a piece of it. "Where will we go?" Forgetting the second question, How long?

"To the desert. Until it is safe to return."

Abu Moussa, bearded, powerfully built, was giving orders. Jean was asking how much time it would take to get there. I thought of asking about our things at the hotel.

Sharif was ahead of me. "All that belongs to you will be secured." Then, "I am dishonored for allowing danger to come close to you. Do not be troubled about Khalil, he is not used to such things but it is only a flesh wound. I know, I have seen plenty."

He managed a smile. "You will come back to us, *inshallah.* Someday you will come again and we will kill a sheep in your honor. Two sheep, one for each, right? *Mazboot?* Until then I hope you will think well of us." He was struggling to hold back tears but they came anyway. More tears. These people shed enough to reclaim the desert!

"Go now, you crazy girls! Really you must go, Allah be with you. We will tell our children the story of how you came to be here, and the Bedu will sing of your kindness for us, who are after all only Arabs."

22

The road south to Aqaba and the Red Sea unwound before us, a black line painted on sand. We couldn't see how it dipped and fell into the wadis until we crossed them. The sun was high and hot. Abu Moussa, stern at the wheel, shifted his weight and grunted from time to time. A car appeared, coming towards us, silver like the one that morning. "It's coming right at us!" But there was nothing. Only a spiral, rising and disappearing like a genie released from a bottle. A mirage. As was the lake shimmering on the horizon. Deeper into the desert, tiny birds, seduced by the sun's reflection, smashed against the windshield. No mirage, their carcasses littered the roadside. "Slow down, please!" we begged. But he had a job to do. Misguided birds from whatever oasis they came seeking death were not going to stop him.

We sat sideways, legs crossed in front of us the way you do as children, facing each other, talking to keep from hearing that thump.

"I could have been hit like Khalil, could have been killed even. You pulled me down in the nick of time." My tears came as a shock.

"I don't think our friend Sharif's got this security thing buttoned down, do you?"

After several hours we were approaching Aqaba. A smell of the sea, but before any sign of the town we veered off and drove over the sand, the track not even noticeable. When we could no longer see the highway left behind, Abu Moussa stopped. "He will meet us here." What could possibly distinguish here from any other place?

We got out, stretched and drank from a bottle of water buried under blankets in the trunk. It was surprisingly cool. We were leaning against a fender, smoking, when Abu Moussa said, "He comes." The speck on the horizon became a form. Then he was in front of us, in a long black cloak, a cloth wrapped around his head and face. He reached for the water held out to him and drank slowly but steadily until the bottle was empty. Only then did he look at us through sand-hooded eyes. "*Salaam aleicham.*"

"*Aleicham ma salaam.*"

He gestured in the direction from which he had come. "Men and camels," Abu Moussa reported.

"Does he have a name?" Another "merchant" no doubt.

"Never mind." More of their beloved secrecy. How could a barren landscape like this produce such mental jungles? Was it the solitude, so unrelieved that the minute they banded together they were compelled to concoct plots and intrigues? Was this why they walked arm in arm in the streets, clinging to each other, always in a crowd, talking, gossiping, afraid of finding themselves alone in the silence of the desert?

"His men guide you to the soldiers and the camp. These are the orders of General Jamal."

"How far?" Jean asked.

"Several hours' ride, not more."

"Are there women in this camp?" Do you recruit monkeys, she might well have asked?

"I have yet to see a woman in our army." *And never expect to,* said his expression.

Dark shadows had settled in the dunes by the time the camels arrived, led by "the men"—two boys not yet into their teens. They looked away as we climbed up onto carpet-covered saddles, hangings and tassels in lurid colors not found in nature, the two of us still dressed in what we'd worn to dinner the night before and our trench coats. Abu Moussa handed up rough blankets against the night chill and red and white keffiyehs to wrap around our heads. He did not hide his pleasure at getting rid of us. The lone Bedouin was again a speck in the distance when the boys jumped up behind us. They made that clicking sound, tongues against teeth. The camels uncoiled themselves, snorting and belching. They lurched off, noses disdainfully in the air.

"*Schwayeh, schwayeh*!" Slowly, slowly, Abu Moussa called, with the hint of a smile.

The ride was not a comfortable one, but I was lulled by the swaying gait of the camel and the soft air of dusk whispering about my ears. I gave myself up to the stillness, broken only by an occasional shout from the boys. The one with Jean turned from time to time, to make sure we were close. She never did. I signaled my boy to draw even. "How long do you think we'll have to stay out here?" I was surprised by my voice in the vast emptiness. *What's going to happen to us?* That's what I really wanted to talk about.

"How should I know?"

"Pardon me, I just thought you might have something to say about it."

"When you'll get back to Andreas?"

"Yes. I admit that thought had occurred to me. Whether we'll be swallowed up here, lost without a trace like yesterday's footprint. Whether a lot of things." I started to cry, tears blinked back fiercely, then let go.

"Maybe that's all we are, a few footprints in the sand, then gone, just like that."

"Ever the optimist," I said bitterly.

* * *

We rode, lingering sun low at our backs, east, the direction of Saudi Arabia. Scattered clumps of growth threaded their way through the sand, a few scrub trees in the depressions where there was underground water, deep hollows high in the hills rising on either side, like huge eyes staring blindly from under the brows of overhanging cliffs. The passage narrowed, and we rode between arched peaks, as if down the aisle of a ruined cathedral with no roof. The sun threw a last red flare and disappeared, leaving behind a landscape as bleached as old bones. I gathered my trench coat and blanket more tightly around me.

Alone under a vast, implacable sky, insects under a bell jar, robbed of context, no one from our world having the least idea where we were. Retribution for the lies we had told? Our *hubris*, as Andeas accused? Closing my eyes, I could picture him, studying, sitting in a café with friends, could almost feel him wrapping his arms around me, sorting himself against me like spoons in a drawer the first time I stayed with him through the night. Could picture my parents too at any given hour, moving through their lives, the streets they drove, the rooms that held them. I thought of my grandmother, my beloved river. I drew them close to comfort me.

But this? Who could picture this? See me framed in it? Did God know we were here? Or had He turned away, irritated by the dabbling in disbelief, the flouting of rules supposed to govern unruly flesh? Did Jean feel as isolated? As scared? Or was this how she felt all the time? We rode in darkness. A deeper stillness fell, not even a breath of wind. I turned around wondering if there was anything in this endless expanse to see, to mark where we had been. The first stars appeared, one by one, then the rest all at once as if turned on by a master switch. Nothing in them to reassure.

Mute sand, mute stars.

I fixed my thoughts again on Andreas, willing him to think of me, folding myself up in him. Hours must have gone by. We were nearing camp, the boys chattering away. I could make out a building, whitewashed and incongruous out here on the sand, and enormous black tents like those of the Bedouin. Nothing else. Where was the oasis with hanging gardens, date palms fanning the air? The love-sick sheiks alone on the sand under a full moon, like movie posters or the covers of my mother's sheet music?

The boys spoke to the camels. They dropped to their knees, throwing their heads forward in a low moan of homecoming. A man in uniform emerged. We staggered, stiff and hurting, as he led us, fugitive squaws in our blankets, into a tent. My eyes grew accustomed to the light. Soldiers surrounded us, wrapped in red and black woolen cloaks. Whether because of the cloaks or reflections cast by the fire, they looked like a race of giants, white teeth gleaming in faces darkened by desert sun. Like Alice, we had fallen down a rabbit hole. Shouts greeted us. Invitations to join them were cut off abruptly by their commanding officer. He allowed us to stay long enough to warm ourselves and drink coffee spiced with cardamom before leading us back outside and up steps to the roof of the building. "You will sleep here. Under the heat of the stars."

Heat of the stars. Some joke. Carpets were laid and more blankets brought and we were left alone to sleep. Which we did as if drugged, despite the cold. Burrowing in, I didn't even feel it.

Sitting on their haunches the boys were watching me. Jean was already up, the sun hot, the camp deserted. I shook myself awake and climbed down to find her, smoking a cigarette. She had on a long white garment. On her it looked glamorous.

"When did you wake up?" I asked.

"A while ago. Amazing how much goes on in the desert if you start paying attention."

"Yes, how nice this little dilly-dally in the desert. Frankly, I'd rather enjoy it from a distance, with a way out when I feel like it."

"You'll get the hang of it."

"Oh no I won't!" If I did, I'd never give her the satisfaction of knowing. "I'm sure they've got a fancy bathroom just for us." She pointed to a low ridge a couple of hundred yards off, thick growth trailing through rocks and sand, enough to shield us. "What happens if we get the runs?" I was the one panicking without the pharmacy.

"End of civilization as we know it. A good thing too."

"Somehow, I don't picture you spending the day squatting in sand."

She handed me a garment similar to hers. "Here, put this on. You can get rid of your clothes in that tent over there."

The boys brought a tin basin of water for washing and glasses of sweetened tea and bread. They gave us clean keffiyehs to cover ourselves against the sand and sun. That day we walked in the desert, not straying far from the tents. They looked like giant fossils left by the receding of the flood. We took a short ride on the camels, still so sore we could hardly sit, our legs aching too. Mostly we sheltered in what shade was offered, watchful of scorpions until we learned they stayed under the rocks unless disturbed. The smell of goat hair used for the tents repelled them, so the officer assured us. The boys tried to talk, mystified that we didn't understand, seeming to grasp, finally, the concept of different languages, eyes widening with the idea. Soon we were teaching them words in exchange for Arabic and inventing games to play for cigarettes.

Jean and I talked less and less. At first I thought it had to do with the boys hovering. Personally I didn't care, and besides, what would they understand? Anything to keep from being swallowed up in the silence. A welcome friend once, but this, marked only by the rush of wind, was a fearsome stranger. The desert had no dimension, no subtlety, only a high merciless sun. I longed for dusk, the outline of shapes it brought, for darkness that would bring with it a moon. But with night came the cold. We wrapped ourselves in cloaks and went early to bed under coarse blankets. Sometimes, when smoking a cigarette, I managed to take myself away, and then it was painful to return. In any romantic fantasy of the desert, I never imagined such desolation.

The commanding officer was dismissive, as if we'd gotten ourselves into this jam because of some foolishness of our own. Not that far off the mark, I suppose. His men were disciplined and polite, and for this I was thankful. We had been moved to a small field tent at some distance from them where we had toilet facilities, sort of. We bathed once out of buckets the boys hauled in. As soon as we were settled for the night, they threw themselves down at the entrance to sleep instantly and soundly. Meals, alone except for the boys, were in one of the large tents, bread and strong-tasting lamb smothered in yogurt. I picked at it. Jean was oblivious. What was put before her she ate, with neither relish nor revulsion. Mostly she smoked. We heard the men return, but usually after we'd crawled under our blankets to sleep. At dawn they vanished again like ghosts. I might have fallen into the rhythm of it, appreciated the adventure even, had I an inkling of how long this exile was to last or someone to talk to or a book to pass the time. Always the undercurrent of fear, wondering what other nasty surprises were in store, if she had told me everything.

The relentless sun was hateful. I wondered if the Plains Indians ever prayed for it *not* to come up. At its strongest we were forced to stay in the tent. When we tried to brush dust from our faces, the boys gestured for us to leave it. I understood it offered some protection. Sand swirled and blew into our eyes and noses, stinging our skin, grit in every crease of our bodies. Again, Jean seemed not to mind. Admirable? Or so removed from reality it was dangerous? I did not know. Hour after hour she sat gazing into the desert. The more solitary she became, the more the boys clung to her. Fiercely. They were devoted to us both but especially to her. I resented her for withholding any shred of companionship, able to remove herself while I was being defeated by the almost total isolation. I resented her for getting us into this. If she hadn't become involved with Asif, if she'd refused to have anything to do with those letters, we'd never have heard of General Jamal. This wasn't what I bargained for. The rose red city of Petra, yes, but we'd managed to fix it so we'd never get near the place. So much for our journey of discovery. If she was discovering anything, I certainly didn't know what it was. The way things were now, I might as well have started out alone. I began to regret more than anything else in my sorry list that I had left Andreas and followed her.

One morning I woke to find her leaning over me, hair tangled and wild, her hot breath on my face. I sat up in alarm. "Jean! What's wrong, do you have fever?" She shrugged, but when I felt her forehead, it seemed all right. I woke again to find her gone, one of the boys with her. The other one avoided looking at me, frightened, unable to say where they'd ridden off to. As the afternoon wore on and still no sign of them, I was beside myself. I supposed she wasn't in any real danger, the army had patrols, but anybody could get lost out there. When they rode in at dusk, the boy left behind with me let out a joyful whoop. Jean, wrapped in her keffiyeh, looked like one of them. She gave no explanation, which made me furious.

"What the hell do you think you're doing?"

"Nothing." The inscrutable gaze, everything receding before that gaze.

"What is nothing? Jean, talk to me. I'm going to go out of my mind with this silence!" I was yelling. The boy who'd gone with her tugged at my sleeve, but I pushed him aside. "You can't do this, you can't just wander off deserting me."

"I can do as I please. I belong with these people."

"What kind of nonsense …?"

"Their life has simplicity." Said with grim conviction, the conviction of martyrs hellbent on sacrificing themselves. Fanatic. It made me shudder.

"It's cleansing."

"Cleansing! What a concept. We can't even take a hot shower."

"It matters? You're so concerned with your creature comforts."

It was more conversation than we'd had. "Where have you been? Who's got this simplicity you're talking about?"

"Bedouin. Not far. They invited me to stay with them. I know there's something important for me here."

"Come off it! You're from New York City, USA, not remotely related to any of this!"

"But I want to be one of them."

"What on earth for?"

"Why would I want to be me?"

"Well don't mutate until I can get the hell out of here."

Later, before going to sleep, she said into the darkness of the tent, "You can put an image of all you ever wanted to be on this place, all you've missed."

"The desert can have great beauty, Jean, I agree. But not like that. To visit, like Sharif said. Only the Bedouin belong. You'd end up mad as a hermit and a hatter if you stayed here.

Nobody to talk to, nothing to do, nothing to read. Not to mention the food!"

"I really don't care."

Sure, babble your nonsense, go out on a limb, be reckless as you please, you know I'm here, good old reliable Sirry, making sure you don't go too far. What if I want to be the one to slip over the edge for a change?

She rode off again at dawn. Leaving me alone in this vast sand trap.

Midafternoon. Loosely wound tornado of sand rushing towards us.

I watched, transfixed, until I realized we'd better seek shelter, then realized it was two riders on swift camels. Bad as desert storms were rumored to be, this was more ominous still.

The officer was instantly at our side. Where had he come from so fast? Nothing alarming in his face. Maybe they were bringing our stuff. At last I could brush my teeth, pour my loneliness into my journal. What they brought was liberation. General Jamal had proclaimed it safe to leave. We would ride out with them to a waiting car to take us to Amman. We changed into our clothes and were about to mount when Jean said, "I'm not going."

"Get on that camel, goddammit! Grow up!"

"I do not wish to go."

"Stop the drama, Jean, I'm sick to death of it!"

"What is this?" the officer asked.

"I wish to stay," she told him. I looked away, mortified.

"Out of the question, of course."

"I am not one of your men to be ordered around!"

His response was a curt nod. No appeal in this court and she knew it. The boys who had watched over us, who never left our sides except when we were in the dunes, refused to look us in the eye, refused to say goodbye, refused even the last horde of cigarettes we offered. They stood by the animals, tears cascading down their cheeks. When we started off they could hold out no longer and came running after us, shouting and waving their keffiyehs in the air.

We rode hard this time. When we reached the highway it was dusk. We were spared the suicide of the birds.

Back in our old room at the Philadelphia. The most luxurious place in the world as far as I was concerned, and God willing, *inshallah,* no one would call about an audience with a king or a meeting with a new prime minister or a midnight drive to the Dead Sea. Coming out of the desert was like plunging into a pool, washing away weariness if not the ache of the sun and the ride. That would take longer. Miracle of water. Water flowing from a tap, a flushing toilet, a shower. Reunited with our belongings, untouched. Miracle of clean pajamas, soap, sheets, a real bed. Face cream slathered on so thick we looked like geishas.

We weren't exactly Chanel Number 5 when we'd landed at the camp. By the time we rode out it was eau de camel, we could have cleared Yankee Stadium in five seconds flat. Taking pity on the driver, we smoked all the way in an attempt to fumigate. By the time we got to Amman we smelled like ashtrays. Jean, denied her whim, had sulked. Now she too seemed pleased to be back in civilization, embracing the comforts she had scorned. I only observed the contradiction, too exhausted to even try figuring it out. As soon as we cleaned up, we were ravenous. A room service call brought a tray with cold roast chicken, bread and fruit. That meal was the gold standard for a long time to come.

When we opened our journals, I realized my desert eternity had lasted only five days. I called the front desk to make sure I had this right. The man on duty told me an American had gone around the earth in a spaceship in our absence—he thought the name was John Glenn—had we heard? My laughter was a little too close to hysteria. Around eleven a packet came with tickets for a flight the next afternoon. *To Beirut*.

No! A thousand times no, I wasn't going back there, I had vowed to get out and I meant it. Soon after, General Jamal phoned, friendly but formal. How had we gotten on, apologies for the conditions, any complaints about the hospitality of the army and so on. This opened a floodgate of gratitude to those tall men in their enormous cloaks who had sheltered and kept watch over us and we hadn't even said goodbye. He reported that Khalil was "mended" and wanted to know how was Sis and Other Sis, "Tell them I love the one and adore the other." Nothing about balderdash. I was rather nostalgic for it.

Only then did I hear a slight chuckle in his voice. He himself could not come round but was pleased to report the situation calm, no problem whatsoever, anywhere. "Our friend is expecting you in Beirut with some eagerness."

"You've talked to him? To Asif?"

"Yes. And believe me, this is the best thing for you to do now."

"Let me get this straight. You've actually talked to Asif and he wants to see us?"

"I told you, situation normal."

Normal? Normal could mean a three-headed camel singing "Jingle Bells" outside our window.

"But … why should we *ever* go back there?"

"My orders are not usually questioned. You cannot go anywhere you will like better. Unless you wish to visit Riyadh."

"I'll give that a pass, thanks."

"Believe me, Beirut is absolutely safe. This crazy business is finished."

"Whatever it was to begin with." Again angling for an explanation.

"Do not ask, Sirrine, for I cannot tell you."

"But how was Jordan involved—can't we know this at least?"

"The milk turns sour, all the children become sick." Another proverb. Trotted out like checkpoints on the roads. I gave up.

"Must we really go back?"

"Yes. This is the right way. From there you fly to Istanbul." He paused, letting that sink in. "Why, after all that has happened, should I let harm come to you now? You are dear to us." His voice broke when I asked if we would ever see him again. "Who knows, maybe in New York! *Inshallah.*" Then he laughed. "*Mejnouni!*"

"Beirut?" Jean was bewildered too and seemed just as frightened at the idea.

"Yeah, Houdini's back. Eager to see us. Translate, eager to see *you.*"

"But why?" I gave her the look, the look we exchanged when one of us asked the unanswerable.

"Apologize maybe? You know him better than I do. Unless we want to fly to Saudi Arabia, Sharif says it's the only way out, as good as an order, he made that clear. Says everything's okay." There might be satisfaction in confronting the bastard and letting him know he had never fooled me.

"Then it's Istanbul."

"That wasn't on the itinerary, ever."

"The middle of the desert was? It's in Europe at least!"

Finally, she could not hide her pleasure at the prospect of seeing Asif again. I knew how she felt. I would have given anything at that moment to touch Andreas, to see his face. And I was ready to do anything to make sure I got that chance. A good thing he wasn't there to touch me. Odd bumps were coming out on my skin, the effect of what we'd been eating—or not eating—maybe the water. It took a week to be rid of them.

23

Evening, the velvet hour before the lights come on and streets fill with people hurrying to dinner, hurrying home. In this, Beirut was like any other city in the world.

We did not fly, as it turned out. Instead we were driven, through Syria, starting early in the morning. No reason forthcoming. Now we were outside the St. Georges, waiting for Youssef to take us to the apartment that was no longer a secret to anyone. He managed to seem glad to see us and at the same time disapproving. Scared stiff, no doubt, at what might trail in our wake. Who could blame him?

"What the hell …?" I couldn't believe my eyes, didn't even try to control my mouth, when it wasn't Asif who answered the door, though we heard the familiar voice from within calling, "*Shu, shu hada?*"—What, what is it? No, it was the dreaded General Osir of the Sureté Generale who stood before us, the smile that made no connection with the eyes, like halves of two different faces sewn together by grotesque accident. Osir still holding him prisoner? House arrest? What ambush had we walked into now? I didn't want to look at Jean. She would be devastated.

"It's not what we thought," I said to her quietly. "Third time lucky." Her face betrayed nothing.

"So you have come back, finally." Asif rose to greet us, looking only at Jean. "My dear, how very thin you are. Why? Were you ill?"

She managed to smile at him. "No, not ill. And you, you

seem—remarkably well."

Yes, he did, remarkably. He took her hand and looked so long into her eyes I had to turn away. "Tell me, how are our friends in Amman?" Asking this in front of Osir?

Jean said, "Maybe we should come later, you seem busy."

No, apparently the plan was dinner at the St. Georges. We walked back, Osir with us. Not only him, we were joined by two Lebanese couples, Hind and Amina, Nadia and her husband, whose name I didn't catch. And a heavyset man, Perkins, one of those types who could be from anywhere. On the way over, Osir and Youssef stationed themselves on either side of Asif, carrying him along, his broken feet dangling above the pavement like a puppet's. From Osir the gesture was hypocritical. Or proof of his control.

A private room had been booked for our little party. Covered in Chinese wallpaper, pagodas and birds with long tails, the green and silver colors giving the impression we were under water. Osir kept pestering with questions we didn't know how to answer. By the end of dinner, Perkins was beyond knowing much of anything. He was drunk. I found myself actually feeling sorry for Asif—his first outing, I assumed, and this buffoon making a mockery of it. The more he drank, the louder he got, until there was no ignoring him. Haranguing about Nasser, banging his fat fist on the table, "I could buy the Lebanon, buy this whole goddamned country from the cedars to the sea, all of it, kit and kaboodle—every minister, every towelhead, every arak-swilling whore!"

You could hear the ice melting in our glasses. Someone stirred. Osir. He shoved his chair back and was on his feet, moving quickly down the length of the table to where Perkins sat, Jean beside him in a flash. Now what was she up to? I reached to stop her, tell her for Christ's sake sit down, don't make a spectacle of yourself, hasn't that jerk's outburst been enough? She was too fast for me. In a tableau unfolding in the light of a dozen candles, the two of them stepped forward and yanked the chair out from under him. He pitched forward onto the carpet with a thud. A napkin fluttered after, settling on his back like a snowflake. Osir kicked the chair and it toppled over on him too. "That, *monsieur*, is for the arak-swilling whores!"

The hand at her side, shaking, gave the lie to the calm triumph on Jean's face. The others began to cheer, one by one, then a crescendo of cheering. I didn't join in. I was busy watching the look they exchanged, two old comrades, Jean and that disgusting toad. Osir was watching me, as if … what? I turned to Asif. He was smiling at her, at them both.

I got it. The way it happens sometimes, an inkling, then full-blown conviction. They were in this together, all three of them. Stunned, I sat back down. Bit by bit things fell into place. Why she wasn't nearly as shocked as I was when we took the letters back and found the room empty. As alarmed when we saw Osir coming down the hall. Or when we saw him earlier tonight at Asif's. We *had* been used, as I suspected. Taking the dammed letters. But she'd been in on it, making me the one used, the real patsy. That business about how we had to get out of Beirut, another lie. Sending us to Amman, into worse danger. Had the prince known? I didn't think so. How much had Jean really known?

Somebody, Osir, I suppose, signaled a waiter to get Perkins off the floor and out of the room. The Lebanese couples, murmuring apologies as if the whole thing had been their doing, shook hands and left. We sat in the subterranean glow, candles still flickering. I was so angry, so hurt I was trembling. On the verge of tears.

"You lied to me, Jean, you and your buddies here. You fucking well lied."

"And you lied."

"Surely you're not comparing Andreas—if that's what you're talking about. Not putting that in the same league! What the hell did you think you were doing?"

"You don't understand."

"A few things I do understand. You knew damn well he'd be gone when we took the letters back. You put me in danger without bothering to ask how I might feel about it, not once."

"True."

"All the time knowing what we were walking into."

"Not true."

"Bullshit! You betrayed me. How can I trust you ever again?"

"He needed our help."

"C'mon, now who's playing Lady Bountiful?"

"You agreed we'd never done anything."

"What you've done is almost get us killed!"

"What is the meaning of this?" Asif was looking from one to the other of us.

Jean stood over me. "I wanted one thing that was mine, one legitimate feeling of my own. Without your controlling it. Let me escape with that, at least."

I was on my feet. "You want to destroy yourself? Good, be my guest. I don't care this much!" I snapped my fingers in her face. "Don't drag me down with you."

"Are you that selfish? I needed to come away with something, for any of it to have meaning. Don't take this from me."

"Take what? Your great romance? How naïve."

"It was. Just not your kind."

"What is my kind? They've been using us. You don't see it yet?"

"You don't know that, Sirrine."

"I don't know anything. You don't either. Remember the women on the ship? 'You don't know what it is you do.' They were right. Nothing makes sense. Why should it? No one'll explain anything. This man's beaten, people arrested every day, people shot, we don't know what for, and we pass through amusing ourselves, like Andreas said. Looking for experience. Meddling like missionaries. It was a mistake, Jean, coming here. That part's my stupidity, I admit it."

Asif rapped on the table. "You're hissing like snakes. What's going on?"

"A good question. Why not ask your pal Sharif?"

"Sharif? We discuss nothing, the lines are not secure."

"Is anything, ever, in this damned place?"

"What is it I should ask?"

"Ask him what a nice time we had in Amman, he was in charge of the entertainment. Tanks at the palace, chased, shot at, riding for our lives into the desert. Imagine what that was like, what we thought? We'd never get out, that's what I thought."

He looked genuinely shocked. "Believe me, I never realized it would go so far. My dear friends, what have I done?"

Another good question. I was sick to death of questions. Terrified of not getting out, terrified also of being left out, alone on the sidelines when the teams were chosen. I always made sure this never happened growing up, learning to run and field and bat like a boy, but I was out of my league now, benched in the high-stakes game of Middle East intrigue. Did I still care so much? The truth is, I did. He had chosen her, placed his confidence in her. I wanted to be considered trustworthy too, not pushed aside, oh, God, not now. The decision hadn't been mine, but I'd gone through it, same as Jean. Defying the desert and the desolation, with her to worry about on top of it. Yes, I had a right to know, everything.

"What has this been about?"

"A mistake."

"People died, you were tortured. For a *mistake*?"

He shrugged. "Somebody reported me, that's all, who knows the reason?"

"But General Osir …?"

"We have always been together. We pretend otherwise. He came under suspicion too. You were in danger, because of me. I had to warn my friends in Jordan. People are alive because of those letters. Jean knew the importance."

Oh, Christ! Pour it on. Alive because of her! Jean, the hero. I, the coward who tried to stop her. Maybe I didn't want to know, after all. Would she give me away?

"More I cannot tell you. The situation has many faces." The oppressive secrecy again. She could have it! He cocked his head in that peculiar way of his, as if listening for a distant sound. "Now you have seen what a friend to me is Sharif! But two jinns cannot play on the same rope. We know each other too well, no one of us can fool the other.

"One day you will find it easier to accept that reasons are veils covering what we do not understand, may never understand. One thing only, I would never put you in the way of harm. Harm Jean? I would sleep with the Devil first." He sighed. "Injustice gives wings to hatred. We have only begun to do our violence here. Wait and see and pity us."

We fell silent. Then he said, "What does it mean to give up this life with all its sweetness? Spring in the groves of Tyre, snow in the Cedars, the love that transports us to paradise. We call them heroes. Are they not insane? Or are they saints? If we begin to think this way, where does it lead?"

We helped him to his apartment. I left Jean there and walked back to the St. Georges alone. No moon, no stars, the sky filled with that ghostly light, the way I remembered. Whatever nasty surprises the Middle East might hold, a woman can safely walk the streets in the dead of night, all other things being equal.

We met for lunch the next day, our last, on the terrace where first we had drinks together, Asif hobbling along on Jean's arm. The day had begun dark with storm clouds, waves lashing over the St. Georges jetty. By midmorning sun was lighting up the red tile roofs and the high stone wall of Faron's villa with its Corinthian crowns surrounding a courtyard of palm trees, lighting the tumbledown shacks tucked in among the balconied apartment buildings. Sun high in the clouds now, chasing them out to a calming sea, a quiet Sunday morning. Even the hawkers and beggars were stilled.

"There are two things left in the Lebanon. The ruins of Baalbek and me!" A voice, not stilled, from a group around the pool.

"Chi-Chi, the town gigolo, sniffing after everybody like a goat," muttered Asif.

"Chi-Chi, darling!" The woman's accent was French. "You were a ruin before ever you leave the womb of your mother. She wanted to be finished with you, pushing you out before you were ready!" They howled with laughter.

"We don't care about him," said Asif. "What is this I hear about your Greek?" She had told him, then. "Forgive me, I put my tongue on the other side of my mouth."

"I don't know that he's *my* Greek."

"Jean seems to believe in this love of yours." She had never told this to me. He touched her cheek gently as he said it. She was looking out to sea, the look of someone contemplating thoughts more intriguing than the rest of us could conjure. He looked at me shrewdly. "You are three sevens, bright and well educated, you must decide for yourself about him. All we can do is wish you the best in the world."

Why is it, when you desire something for a future time, when you are so sure, does anxiety come? And in the midst of anticipation, the thought of loss. "There are complications, not least that he might have forgotten all about me."

"Love is always complicated—wait until it has been going on for some years. See around you people who feel nothing, who only chew on the rinds of love."

Like the woman he'd taunted that first day? He'd insinuated she was a whore. Was this what he meant? He laughed and laughed. "Oh, that one! That was one of Osir's best men. Bloody good disguise, no?"

Good God! Could we believe a single thing we saw in front of our own eyes? Jean said not a word. She was beautiful, the skin she'd been careless of in the desert flowering into freckles, tiny and golden and so at variance with her fragile looks that they were like something wild blooming in a garden. What had drawn me to her, the loneliness, the sadness, formed the deeper bond between them. He understood it. She had found her guide to interpret the silence around her, to interpret her own silence. Displayed beside this gravity what were my feelings made of? Even then I wondered.

I left them and walked in the direction of the museum, around the Place des Canons and Riyadh Solh Square before turning back along the waterfront, past All Saints jutting into the water, its bells mingling with calls from the minarets, past the men in their jaunty blue caps fishing off the jetty. Urging the hours on. With the passing of each, we were that much closer to getting out.

"Of thee, I sing, baby," Gershwin in Beirut, at the top of my lungs I sang into the wind off the sea. Nearly five months since we'd left home.

PART SEVEN

Another Stranger

24

Out of Beirut for good. Farewell to the desert. Farewell to intrigue and our strange company of men. On our own again. Not even a checkpoint on the way to the airport, as if everyone in uniform had grown tired of the game, gathered up their toys and gone home. I thought Jean might stay—for love of Asif, the desert, who could say? By now her behavior was beyond anything I could predict. Up to the last minute I wasn't sure how it would go.

In Istanbul we found a cheap pension in the old section across Galata Bridge with its throngs of men and donkeys, beasts of burden alike. One man, bent double, had a refrigerator strapped to his back—where was Ahmed and his taxi? A ship at anchor flew the hammer and sickle of the Soviet Union, that fear-inspiring symbol of the Cold War enemy. Not a hint of spring, clouds low to the ground, winds off the Bosporus straight from Siberia. Back to the spartan mode of travel, the cold-water walk-up we had been used to before we acquired friends in high places.

Reports of unrest, even a coup, swirled around us. Not again! After what occurred on our first night we needed to move on, no matter what. We were in bed, so cold we were wearing sweaters, so cold hot baths hadn't warmed us for long. This dump we were in had hot water for half an hour, at dinnertime, when everybody was out. Everybody? Who was I kidding? The only other person in the place was an old man who shuffled up and down the stairs clutching a small bundle. Jean mumbled something about him looking like a revolutionary. They were usually young, I reminded her, unless she knew different.

I began to badger her. Out of the clutches of Asif, she might tell what she knew. But how much had he revealed to her?

"A lot of the time he didn't say anything," she said. "He never asks for an explanation, never asks for anything."

No idea what she meant. "So? If he did ask?"

"If she let him, he could love her. She's frightened, she refuses."

She! As if talking about somebody else.

"He tells her he understands. She is not sure of herself. He could be her lover. He won't want her when he's healed."

Jean, in the bed next to mine, referring to herself in the third person. Isn't this what crazy people do? Alone in Istanbul while she sails around the Golden Horn of her mind.

She got out of bed in her nightgown and socks and sweaters. "It isn't any good, it never will be any good, she'll crawl out of the cave and she'll always crawl back. So let's just say this didn't mean anything. Next time and there will be a next time and another one after that and they will all be the same and this is how this little farce ends."

I turned away, wanting to remember what had been so appealing about leaving order behind. We needed to get back to what was familiar, to letters from home and no more subterfuge, no coups, no rumors of coups, a place where we might see spring again. Everything would be all right then.

"I'm going to sleep now," I said. Late in the night I saw her in the dim light from the street, standing in the middle of the room, still as a stork.

"Go to bed, Jean, please."

Her voice sounded like it was from that cave she mentioned. "That time we were talking about death, how it got fearful when they moved away from the Egyptian idea of a journey—guided, safeguarded. This is the journey she wishes to take now."

Not with me. And wasn't all that death rigmarole of the Egyptians precisely because they did fear it? "For God's sake, Jean, get some sleep." She did not sleep, I heard her tossing, but in the morning there was no more talk about death, no more talking about herself as *she*.

We hit on the novel idea of being tourists again. We'd go to Topkapi and Hagia Sophia and the Blue Mosque. As unreal as stage sets, they seemed to us. Then we boarded the Orient Express to Munich, run-down, no heat, as much resemblance to the glamour train of the movies as we had to Ava Gardner. Maybe it had something to do with riding third class.

Our plan had always been, once we left the Middle East behind, to go to Germany, buy a used Volkswagen, and head south over the Brenner Pass to Italy and on from there to France. The direct rail route from Istanbul was through Bulgaria. Isolated behind the Iron Curtain, Bulgaria did not issue transit visas, even if you never set foot off the train. I made up my mind to try. I could promise we wouldn't even look out the window. I found the consulate, set back behind a high iron fence near the Hilton. I walked past several times, not a soul on the street, before screwing up the courage to go in. I begged for visas, said my friend was sick. They scowled behind their desks in their shoulder-padded, shiny brown suits, unmoved, unmovable, Communists out of central casting.

So across to Greece we went, then up through Yugoslavia. In Thessalonika I had the temptation to bolt for Athens, but I couldn't abandon her, not now. I was anxious about Andreas too, all this time without contact, wondering if he cared whether I existed or not. The train skirted the snow-shrouded villages of Yugoslavia's bleak winter, wisps of smoke rising from wooden dwellings, the conductor coming back to us again and again, tearfully pointing to the crosses around our necks, the ones Sharif had given us. "Communism nix." This didn't do a lot to lift our spirits.

Munich. Even colder than Istanbul. We pulled into the station in evening fog, our breath mingling with clouds of steam as we stepped out onto the platform. Hissing engines and the sharp whistles of departing trains reminded us of Nazis and spies and lives hanging by a thread—one wrong move, a delay, a suspicious travel document. "We're back with the cement people," Jean said, clutching my hand.

We found a small pension, run by a widow according to the gospel of clean, neat and orderly. We found piles of mail waiting for us at American Express, and what a joyful sight. Our bribe had worked, the night man at the Athens hotel had paced our letters as instructed, but of course the supply ran out before we got out. More recent letters from home spoke of concern. Otherwise, Jean's mother described a swirl of activity, gossip about the social scene, the latest plays, notes from life on another planet and totally at odds with my view of her. One day I would understand this as a manic phase. My parents described the winter they were having, how they too looked forward to spring, who died, who got married, while my grandmother, working the same territory, added who was left out of the will and who left a trail of broken hearts on the way to the altar.

Jean's spirits lifted for awhile, in spite of the cement people. Mine went flying when I saw letters from Andreas. I could forgive anything now, even her treachery. I would have him and our summer in Cyprus. He hadn't forgotten.

Thayer, atheist godmother and journalist, the one person to whom Jean had told the truth about where we were going, turned up on assignment in Salzburg, virtually next door. The widow called for Jean to come to the phone. She refused, adamant.

"Afraid of *her*? You've got to be kidding after what we've been through."

"She won't like me, she'll laugh at me. A Dorothy Parker type. One thing I can say about myself is that I'm no longer burdened by irony. I'd like to find another way to be in the world."

"I'd say a few things have happened since people were able to laugh at us."

"Won't matter. She has a cruel side, both of them."

"Both of them? You mean The Countess? Wait a minute, I thought—"

"Let's drop it, okay?"

"Okay, let it ring, but sooner or later you'll have to talk to her. And let's stop talking in riddles. In other words, stop talking like an Arab."

I didn't think more about it, in a rush to get to the post office to call Andreas. His last letter had told me how to reach him. Downstairs, the widow asked if we were running away from home. "Not anymore," I assured her.

After waiting in line and finally getting through, I didn't say a word about Jean or the Middle East. There was a definite chill at first, but he warmed up. Relief did it.

"I wondered would I hear this voice again."

"I wondered too. So many times wishing you'd come find me."

"How? By searching the stars? Are you all right? Nothing from you for weeks."

"There's a reason. And a lot to tell you."

"Then come, tell me. Do they have ships in Munich? My kingdom for a ship!"

"Andreas, stop. Don't make me laugh when I'm crying. I'm all mixed up!"

"You are so mixed up in me I don't know who I am apart from you. What can I say to bring you back to me? Love you more? Yes, let's try that, beginning this moment, do you feel it? Not yet? Then summer had better hurry."

"I will hurry."

"I will use the time deciding."

"Deciding?"

"How to make love to you."

"Oh, God, Andreas … don't say it."

"I want to say it, I want you to think about it, wherever you go. Are you the same, has anything changed?"

"No, nothing." Tears splashed the receiver. People in line studied their boots. "Sirrine. Come to me, soon."

I made my way out of the post office. I could not have talked to anyone.

Turning the corner into our street I saw that the room was dark. Jean must have gone out to avoid the phone. Thayer seemed the kind of person who'd be persistent that way. A ringing phone would forever be nerve-wracking, the sound that had punctured those hours we waited, by ourselves and frightened, after Asif's arrest. The hall light was on a timer, set by some sadist to last exactly five seconds. Before I could reach the landing it clicked off and darkness. I ran a race with it and lost, nearly killing myself tripping over the last stair, shorter than the rest.

Fumbling with the lock, I got the door open. I knew she was in there, in the dark, even before I turned on the light. When I saw her I screamed. She was sitting in the middle of the room, looking straight ahead, her face smeared with mascara and lipstick and eye shadow, lurid blues and greens and reds and purples, rings circling her eyes. The face of a clown. She didn't stir, didn't seem to breathe. She was so still I imagined for a terrible moment that she was dead. Finally she moved. A cigarette burning in the ashtray. A bottle of wine on its side at her feet dribbling onto the carpet. I picked it up. Empty. I felt like throwing it at her. Behold our hero!

"Jean, what the hell? Can't I leave you alone, even a few hours? You could've burned the place down. Look at you! What if someone found you like this? Oh, you can complicate it, all right." She started to cry, mascara dripping in the wake of tears streaming down, making the whole mess that much worse. The glittering eyes pleading. I couldn't stand the sight of her.

"And what are you doing with that stupid scarf on? Intending to go out with a mug like this? Drunk like this?" She started babbling about spoiling things and sickness infecting everybody, bad dreams and finding a way out, all the time asking, "She here, she here?" Leaning forward, moving her hands at her sides, then over her head, chanting like some ancient priestess. "The sand … the journey …"

"*Shut up!* I don't want to hear any more of this! I've stood by you all this time. Now I'm stuck with you and you've gone away again and I'm alone." I started to cry. "I never left you. Did I? Answer me, did I? I wanted to, how many times, oh, yes, I wanted to, but I never did. I don't have to stay, I don't have to be your goddamn babysitter. And stop talking about dying. I don't want to hear it. Die! Get it over with!"

I got rid of the cigarette. Got rid of the lipsticks and eye shadows strewn all over the bathroom. Tried to clean the carpet but the wine stains were unrelenting. I knelt in front of her and took her hands in mine. "Please don't leave me, don't talk like this, you scare me. Do we have to go through this over and over? Can't you … I don't know … find a way, somehow? Okay, we didn't do so well as Clea and Justine, so let's drop them. Let's just go back to being our ordinary selves and try to forget what happened."

She just sat there, a blank. "We're going to Italy, remember? We're going to Florence and Rome, we've got the underwear for the germs! Remember how we laughed when Lucy's mother gave it to us? And Paris. We dreamed about Paris, you and I, you couldn't wait to dazzle them with your French. All Europe waiting for us. Like we planned."

I don't know how much time went by before I asked if she would drink some coffee. Still no answer. I stood to rouse her, to get her to clean herself up and go to bed and that's when I saw what she had done. The scarf slipped and I saw her hair, what was left of it. She had chopped it off. That beautiful hair, golden again under the sun of Greece and Egypt and the desert, the golden hair everyone wanted to touch, that transformed her into a goddess, turning the heads of men and women too, wherever she went. No more. Nothing left but that tear-streaked, circus clown face.

Our golden dreams gone too. I wanted to hold her. I couldn't do it. I sank to the floor at her feet. *You did this to her. You had to have your adventure and look what's come of it.* A universe without goodness, she told Khalil. It was true. It had turned against us.

I had no idea what time it was when I put through the call. "You better come right away and get Jean." That's all I said. I sobbed until I thought I would break.

Thayer did come, sometime after dawn, pulling up in a car with a driver. From the window I watched her get out in her wide Katharine Hepburn trousers, complete with a cape slung over her shoulders, ensemble in grey.

She sized us up with one glance. "I guess no one told you girls about the desert and quicksand." I guess that's what's meant by irony.

She took charge at once. We packed Jean's belongings, all

but her journal, which I had enough presence of mind to hide, sure Thayer would ridicule what was written there even if it sounded like Hemingway. Especially if it did. She refused Jean's share of the extra cash General Jamal had given us. I wanted to wash Jean's face, but no, the doctors should see her just as she was, no matter what she looked like. She snapped at me when I teared up. "Get hold of yourself, there's no time for that now!"

All the while, Jean said not a word, not even when Thayer came through the door. Flinched a little, a quizzical expression on that mask-like face, that's all. Didn't put up a struggle either when Thayer led her out to the car, didn't ask where she was taking her. I followed them down the stairs, grief suffused with relief at getting rid of her, the fearful responsibility. Another betrayal. But I had no choice, did I?

At the curb she fought free of Thayer and came back to where I stood by the gate. She looked at me, her face smudged under the ragged, chopped-off hair. "I wanted to love someone too, I wanted to be part of it. You have everything now, I have nothing."

She fell to her knees and clawed at the frozen ground. "I'm more than this. Tell them. I'M MORE THAN THIS."

The driver helped get her into the car.

25

I don't know how many days I stayed curled up in the fetal position, in the bed I had shared with Jean, sleeping, or when not sleeping going over every detail of what had happened, in Beirut, Amman, the desert, wondering what I should have done differently. The same words churning in my head, over and over: *I loved her, I betrayed her*. The widow finally came pounding on the door, threatening to call the police. There had been no way around her finding out what had occurred. How else explain Jean's sudden departure, the stains on the carpet? She too took responsibility, this had happened under her watch and not a shred of order about any of it. Let alone clean and neat.

I got hold of myself, settled the bill and squandered the money on a plane ticket to Andreas. But first I had to phone my parents. When I heard their voices, alarmed at getting a transatlantic call, though *not* the middle of the night, I almost lost my nerve and begged for a ticket home instead. I hoped they wouldn't be angry, and they weren't, not until I talked about Greece and summer in Cyprus. Not thinking straight, I blurted it out.

"But you've spent weeks in Greece. Or have you been lying to us?"

"No!" I lied.

"Who is this character? And what in the Sam Hill is there to do in Cyprus?"

"It's beautiful. I hear."

"We'll hear no more about it, you're not going."

"Please, Dad."

"You're always sticking up for the underdog. I cannot figure out for the life of me why you want to spend the summer with one."

"He's not an underdog. He's a hero!"

"That will do, Sirrine."

He might be a hero in Cyprus. He was not going to be a hero in Minnesota. "If you're through traveling with Jean, you'll come straight home, do you hear me? And that's final!" I was tempted to say just how salubrious it had been, traveling with her.

"We'll be with his parents, if that's what you're worried about."

"We'll talk about it when you get here. Remember, your grandfather …"

Thoroughbreds over the fence were coming next. I said goodbye. He had ordered me home. How could I do that without seeing Andreas? I made up my mind to go to him, convinced the plane would crash, catching me in yet another lie.

The first glimpse of islands rising from the sea told me I was right to come. Running down the steps of the plane, the rush of balmy air caressing my skin, Andreas coming towards me, white slacks and shirt as blue as the sky, opening his arms to me, filling me with the scent of lemons, the memory of each time he had ever touched me. "You have been gone for what seems like my whole life!"

"Never mind, I'm here now. People are staring."

"Let them. Who cares?"

"I do. No, I take it back. I don't. Of course I don't."

An earthquake wouldn't have distracted him. He looked at me, so serious an expression, I thought, *Oh-oh, what's coming now?* "I have been fighting and fighting you, trying to erase the taste of you, the feel of you but you are in me now and won't let go. Inside my head, every moment thinking of you."

"Good, I don't want you to fight me. I want to be with you, that's all I know." In that moment it seemed that I could shake the dread I'd carried for so long, I could stop thinking of Jean and steal a few days of pleasure. My turn to be reckless.

Athens to me then was a wonderful place. The orange trees of Kolonaki, its cafés where people argued politics long into the night, the tavernas and soft lights of Plaka, the fragrant pine woods of Lycabettus, the blue mornings before the heat came. Walking early along Sofias, the boulevard near the palace where flower vendors set up their stalls, I was offered a rose. "For you, the first beautiful woman I see this day, it is our custom."

Andreas took me to hidden beaches where we walked barefoot in the shallow lap of the sea, to restaurants lining the little harbor of Tourkolimano where we ate grilled fish and drank retsina before going back to his rooms in one of the smaller buildings above Omonoia, that ugly square where you catch the little train for Piraeus. The house was shuttered and silent, its owners away in the islands for Easter. We spent almost no time below, wanting instead to be up where we could climb out the window onto the roof and see the Parthenon, white and shining under the moon. To find each other in its light.

I told him a watered-down version of what happened in the Middle East. About Jean, I only said that her godmother had shown up, that they'd gone off together and I was waiting to hear. He didn't question me. The little I did say frightened him, and he held me more tightly. He told how his mother and father had watched us sail from Limassol, "so fearful they asked a hundred times inside of five minutes if I thought you would be safe, weeping, muttering their prayers, white handkerchiefs raised in surrender. Surrender! To the two of you who had stormed and captured their hearts. "What were you thinking of, taking up with those men?"

I assured him that there was no "taking up with those men," not the way he meant. "But you gave them your trust. Based on what?"

"I won't even try to explain, not if you're going to be this way." I gave him a playful punch. But there was no mistaking his jealousy along with his fear.

"I should never have let you go, I should have done something to prevent you."

I took his hand and kissed it. "You must always let me go."

Time ran wild, the way it does when happiness drives days to their ends like runaway locomotives, while sadness does the opposite, stretching them to unendurable lengths. I had to tell him about leaving. And the truth about Jean. We were downstairs, the two of us at one end of the table in the dining room, shuttered against the afternoon sun. He was going out for something for dinner. The last time he had come back with a fish head. I told him I hoped he didn't expect me to eat *that*!

"We consider it a delicacy." I told him I thought there was nothing more revolting, failing to appreciate the gourmet qualities of fish cheeks.

"Things you will get accustomed to."

Not on your life, I had said then. Now I said we'd better talk about the fact that I had to go home.

"What do you mean?"

"My parents will have Interpol after me. They don't even know where I am!"

"It's Beirut where you needed Interpol, not here with me. And why don't they know, how can you do that?" What if he knew how I'd deceived them all along?

"I told them about you. They ordered me home."

"What about Cyprus, our summer together …"

"I can't, Andreas. I can't defy them like that. Not now, not my father."

"But you can do *this*? To me?"

"I'm sorry. I'll come back." I had no idea how, but I couldn't bear the look on his face or the feeling in my own heart.

"And Jean? What about her?"

The story tumbled out, all of it from the very beginning. About Asif and the strange connection between them from the moment they met, how he seemed to understand her sadness, pulling her out of herself, and all the rest that followed. How she refused to leave his side after he was freed, the letters, the scare at the checkpoint, how that attempted coup had tentacles that reached into Jordan and the desert.

"She was so determined to prove something, to find something to believe in, and Asif was part of it. I realize this now. I have no idea what she knew or what was at stake, but she didn't care about the danger, the risk. The only time she ever faltered, even the slightest, was at that checkpoint when they made her get out of the taxi and go with them. In the desert she retreated into herself, worse than in Cyprus, much worse. Maybe it was the torture, his injuries, the sight was enough to unhinge anybody. Maybe it was finding King Hussein in his palace surrounded by tanks when we thought all that was over with and we were out of danger and under his protection. Did she know something different? She didn't trust me either, she said as much.

"She got it into her head she wanted to stay out there, in that godforsaken place. But as I tell you this now, it makes a certain kind of sense because whatever else it was, it was safe. I mean we had the whole damn army, well, a battalion or whatever it was. Or was cracking up the most reasonable response to the craziness around us? In Beirut, there had been a furious purpose about her. When I found out how she had deceived me, taking those letters … who knows what the hell else she was doing? Going to the St. Georges all hours of the day and night. They saved lives, those letters. That's what Asif told us."

This was far from easy. I was not the hero of this story. I didn't enjoy proving him right either, with his angry warning not to go anywhere near Beirut in the first place.

"I was sure she'd be fine, that we both would be, if we could just get out and leave all that sinister business behind. No more secrets. And when she fell apart …" I stopped to regain control. One thing left to be said.

"Andreas, I keep asking myself over and over and over, was what she felt for that man real? Or was she trying to bury her feelings for you?"

His answer was silence. Finally he asked, "Where did they take her?"

"Thayer talked about a clinic in Switzerland. She never called."

"Why didn't you tell me before?"

"Because I wanted you to myself." There, it was out. "I was afraid you would blame me, think us criminals like you said in Cyprus. That would have spoiled everything. I was blaming myself quite enough already."

"We're together. That's one way."

"And now you're going." He started for the door. "I will bring something."

The whole time he was gone I didn't move from the table. He had opened the shutters to let in the evening air and sounds came in from the street, the city shaking off afternoon lethargy. It got dark but still I sat. I waited so long without moving that when he did return, when I heard his footsteps on the tiles and saw the light go on in the hall, it was like coming out of a trance.

He came up behind me and kissed my hair. I turned and saw that look of his, that brooding intensity I loved but that frightened me too. He put his hand on my cheek. "We will marry. Then they can't take you from me."

"Andreas, be serious."

"I can't let you go, Sirrine. If that means we marry, then let us marry."

"Just like that?"

"Why not? We love each other. Most people do marry … who love each other."

"Most people don't have the situation we do. I mean, how would we live? We have no money. Even Thanos pointed this out." Why was I saying this? Wasn't this what I wanted, the certainty I'd craved?

"We'll live on the wind like butterflies. Must everything be reduced to columns of figures, statements from banks? You need faith—in me, in us." Odd word for him to choose.

"Faith isn't … something I have a lot of faith in anymore." Street sounds had faded. I could hear his breathing.

"Without you, my life is unthinkable to me now, it would seem unbearably long. Don't you want me? Your letters, everything you said …"

"But you have no idea what this means. My parents. There will be priests and promises of all kinds, are you willing to do that too?" To break with them was something I couldn't even contemplate.

"Yes. You found the courage to come to me, that first time we were together. I wanted so much for you to come, I willed it every night, but it had to be your choice and you did choose." I heard the teasing smile in his voice. "We talked about the summer and you said we should see how it goes first, remember? Before we knew how we would be together. Even then you couldn't hide it." I did remember.

He pulled me to him. "We know now, don't we? We know how it goes. I have nothing more to ask of it. Or of you."

During the night I woke to find him outside on the roof, leaning against the parapet, smoking. I joined him, cool fingers of breeze playing on us. "What are you thinking?"

"Nothing. Everything. How you looked the first time I saw you, coming up on the deck of that ship, your hair falling around your face, drowsy from sleep. How your eyes grow big each time I come into you. How your name sounds all around me like soft rain falling … Sirrine. I want to go to the farthest corners of myself and you and discover all there is in the world to know."

"And bring it back to me. And I to you. Can we do that?"

"Yes. You are making me believe in many things." He stroked my face in that thoughtful way of his, drawing it slowly, drawing me back inside to the warmth before starting on the rest of my body. "I want to remember you just as you are now for all of my life."

"Don't let me go," I said, pulling him down to me. "Andreas, don't let me go."

Afterward, I found myself hanging on to him, weeping. Weeping for everything, for Jean and The Countess, for Asif and his smashed body, for Dr. Thanos and his beloved island, for all the suffering and how we seem condemned to go on and on, the needle spinning wildly from country to country like a roulette wheel, with as little purpose, changing nothing. Weeping for all of us but mostly for Jean.

26

How quickly we fell apart.

Marry in Athens and then fly home, what a great plan! How did I get swept up in it? Andreas was the dreamer, but me? Forget running to extremes, I was crossing the finish line of whatever extremes there were. Like that ride at the fair, slowly up around the first curves, hurtling down at terrifying speed. That's the ride we were on, soaring one minute, everything possible, plummeting into despair the next. What I had thought about Jean and Asif, that confronted with too much reality their bond would break, now applied to us. We began to build walls of misunderstanding and in the cracks of those walls rancor, like weeds blown in on the wind—an ill wind to be sure—took root. One afternoon we had tea with one of his professors, a distinguished-looking woman who told me how talented he was, how eloquently he spoke not only modern Greek but also the classical form. I was filled with pride but as soon as we left I asked why he would go to her for help, an academic who lived modestly with her books. A waste of time.

"You think this person a waste of time?" he said sadly.

At the embassy, the official was dismissive when he heard it was a Greek I was planning on marrying, but this could have been my imagination. He said I would need a copy of my birth certificate. What excuse could I drum up to ask my parents for that?

Andreas wasn't bothered. "The captain can do it on the way

to Cyprus."

"Sure, just like in the movies."

"There's a reason they do it in the movies. You only need a passport."

"We still have to get home," I reminded him. The nagging question had taken hold, the one that gives rise to all the others and brings an end to the dream. I turned into a harpy. Day after day we chased money and came up empty-handed. One afternoon he returned with pockets full of drachmas. I danced around as he turned them out, not realizing the gesture was one of futility. It added up to no more than a hundred dollars. His face told me what the cost had been, the humiliation. Living on his stipend was becoming difficult, barely covering him, let alone me. The passage of time was worrisome for another reason. I'd now been out of touch with my parents for weeks. A last chance was a position teaching English in a secondary school in the suburb of Psikhiko. The headmaster was sympathetic but it would be at least a year before an opening might arise.

"So many Americans in Athens?" I asked.

"My dear, it takes but one or two, and we have the British, don't forget, whose accent, never mind what I might think, is generally preferred." *Ouch.*

Consoling ourselves we splurged on coffee at Zonar's, one of those grand cafés that exist in most European capitals, testaments to bourgeois prosperity and contentment. Secure. Unassailable. Not a worry in the world about money. Unlike on other occasions of bad news, Andreas left me without a word of encouragement. I watched him walk along the treeless avenue, shoulders slumped the way Asif's had been that night Jean and I watched him pass under the streetlamp and disappear into the shadows of Beirut. The burden he carried was me.

It was hot for April, the midday sun stripping all contour,

reminding me of the desert. The isolation too, so oppressive that, like Jean, I wanted to escape into oblivion. I turned towards the park hoping to hear a nightingale, a good omen. I walked in on the palace side, past the Evzone*s* in their white kilts and tights and shoes with the black pompoms, and sat on a bench. Nearby a group of mothers watching their children, one in particular catching my eye, not more than my age with three of them in tow. I vowed to be more careful.

Careful. The word went off in my head like a cannon. Startled, I opened my eyes. Had I said it out loud? Then came words I did say aloud, heedless who heard. *What am I doing here? I can't go through with this. Whatever possessed me to think I could? How long before we regret, before we come to hate each other?* I thought of Thanos and the Pied Pipers. We needed friends. Or was it only Jean we needed?

What had gone wrong? I had no ambition but to be with him, I once told myself. Athens was dull to me now, the way a city can be when the novelty's worn off, tourist sights exhausted—unless you have a more solid reason for being there. I was drifting through the hours, no real life to fit into, living with a man to whom words were everything in a language I didn't comprehend, a language it would take me a lifetime to learn, nodding and smiling at people as they went by on the street, nothing in return but more nodding and smiling. Unlike Cyprus, his companions here spoke only Greek. While they talked and argued and joked into the morning hours, I smoked and drank retsina, finally squeezing his arm to remind him I was there and it was time to go.

How were we to reach those far corners of ourselves without common experiences, the common references that make up everyday life, the stories and the jokes? I thought of living without snow. I began to long for autumn in New York, the song and the season, for the wide river of home, for home itself. I was with this man I loved. Why did I feel so alone, wanting only to get away from him and the web I was entangled in. This frightened me more than any machine gun I had faced. I was responsible, I had said things, I had made promises.

Choices have consequences, Andreas told me that last night on Cyprus. I had taken our lives and flung them into the void to shatter into a million pieces. I looked at my watch. Late, time to start back. I would make the climb to Dexameni for a last look at the Acropolis in the late sun. But first a stop at the Grande Bretagne for a drink, a *real* drink. Enough of retsina. You needed a barrel of it to numb the pain and by that time you'd be retching in an alley.

As I sipped a scotch in the dark bar, chiding myself about the cost, a man came in, looked around, took the table beside me. An American, I knew it even before he ordered, attractive in a Wall Street looking way. After some sparring, fun when you don't have to explain every other word, he asked what I was doing there.

"Besides having a drink, you mean?"

"Yeah, a spy? Under cover?" What a suggestion.

"Getting married. It's what I do wherever I go. In the larger cities, anyway." What a smartass. And who was I laughing at, if not Andreas?

"Have a prospect?"

"Depends …"

"Lucky guy." Stirring his drink, deciding what to say next. "Why not come to a party this evening?"

"With the prospect?" This threw him.

"Sure, let's see how he goes up against the competition." He wrote an address on a napkin, said to show up around nine, wrote his name, Rob Smythe—Smythe as in smoothe. I bolted, half of my expensive drink still in the glass. He was staying in the hotel. I was capable of doing something really stupid.

Andreas had zero interest in a party, especially one at the invitation of a man I'd picked up in a bar. Not anything a respectable woman would dream of doing in Athens. We argued. I threatened to go by myself. Anxious to put off the inevitable, I told him we could use the distraction but as soon as we got there I knew it was a mistake, not his scene at all, social chitchat being a foreign language to him. I, on the other hand, was determined to have a good time. When Rob steered me to the bar where we started drinking champagne, I was more than willing. Andreas watched from across the room. I didn't care, I wanted to be lighthearted for a change. I also wanted him to see me this way. Easier to let go.

It got to be too much for him. He pushed his way through to me. "What are you doing?" he demanded.

"Getting drunk, what does it look like?"

"You're making a fool of yourself. And me." He grasped my arm to pull me away. The men near us were laughing, general merriment and champagne all it was, but I could feel his anger. I asked him how he could be so primitive, told him he could leave if he wanted to, I was having a good time, and returned to Rob.

"Your prospect?"

"Depends, like I said …"

"On?"

"The weather, the stars, how should I know?"

"He could tone down the tan." *Tan*? What tan? I looked at his face, a few freckles the only color it would ever see.

"Not your type, you're more worldly, something you may have lost sight of since going native." *Going native*! That was Jean's trick, not mine. I looked at him, smug self-confidence in his tweed jacket and loafers. "Unlike you. Who go away but never leave home!"

"Some of these guys are after a passport, you know."

"News flash, and it may come as a huge shock, but not

everyone's lined up to get into our country. In fact I've met quite a few people who are proud of their own. He happens to be one of them. He was willing to die for it."

"Whatever he's one of, Greece is piss poor, years before they're on their feet. You don't look the type for hardship."

"Big on types, aren't you?"

"Think about it, you and the bearded guerilla—he doesn't have one now but he will. Then it's widow's weeds."

"Go to hell!"

Andreas saw and turned away, assuming it was what it looked like, a kind of lovers' or would-be lovers' quarrel. I hadn't had so much champagne I didn't realize how hurtful this was. We walked home through the empty streets. Was any city quieter after midnight, only the politicians of Kolonaki awake? Had we fought, had he accused me, it would have been a relief. Instead we were merely polite. Even The Scold went mute. Sometime in the night he tried to rouse me but that intimacy between us, never failing to thrill, stirred only sadness. All I wanted was sleep. The human heart is a monster.

27

This is how we lost each other. Nothing left but to undo all that had been done. And what about Jean? I had forced my way between them. For what? This hollow victory. She had accused him, but again I was the fraud. If I wanted to salvage anything I had to let him go, to find her if she got well, or someone else with the courage to love him. Or was this another lie, justifying what I was about to do?

It was a Sunday. I remember how early it was, the house not yet open to the morning. I remember how the sunlight was coming through the narrow windows on each side of the door, the patterns it made falling on the stairs. I remember his face, how weary he looked bringing coffee from the kitchen, his feet bare on the stone. He had not touched me since Thursday, the night of the party.

"Andreas … I have to go."

"I haven't forgotten."

"No, not what you think. Alone."

"So this is what he was trying to tell me."

"Who?" He didn't want to tell.

"A conversation with my father. Ever since I failed to keep you from getting on that ship, my father was troubled, I had no influence over you, half a man in his eyes, but now, worry for your safety gone, he started on his other one." (Her father is a judge, you say?) "Did I say? If I did, I said something to do with the law." (My son, how is it their law will judge you? They place importance on money, the Americans, so I have heard but this could be unjust.)

"And later, as if conversation between us had never stopped, we were walking along the sea wall, that place you loved so well. (You know how I feel about her, my son, how we all feel, about the two of them, but she is young, it could be that she does not see clearly into her own heart. Perhaps only God can do that, for any of us.) We walked on, each wishing to find lighter thoughts. (Andreas, you of all people will understand what it is to give up your country. It is a large decision. I myself believe the story of Ruth to be little more than an old man's foolishness, a romantic dream, and when you wake from that dream, my son …)

"When you wake, what?" I interrupted. Something in the words of his father might give us wisdom.

"When you wake from that dream, he said, I will be afraid. What could I say then to ease his heart?"

"You'll never know how sorry I am. I don't have the courage Thanos hoped I would. I don't even have the courage to tell you this."

"Sirrine, I …"

"No, Andreas, your words won't save us now. The truth is, I'm not what I thought I was."

"You are still the woman I love."

"No. You're disappointed in me, admit it. And I'm disappointed in you. Look what's happened to us. If we could have loved each other for a time without tying ourselves up in knots, maybe then … But we had to domesticate it, make it fit into the neat package of marriage. You compromised who you are. Now we can't find a way back into each other." I was talking to a statue. "Andreas, for God's sake, say something. This is hard enough."

"The song I translated for you, that song you loved, do you remember? *I give you milk and honey …*"

"... *in return you give me poison.* Yes, I do remember." I had sung it in Greek first, without knowing what it meant. "You fought for Cyprus but you didn't fight for me." Unfair and I knew it.

"I'm weary of fighting, Sirrine. It's time for something else. I see only bitterness now. What do I do with my love for you? Take it back? It would be easier to gather the rain. I didn't ask for you to come to me, why then did you begin? To play with me? To add me to your adventure?"

"I wanted to be free, to go wherever the dream might lead. I thought there'd been this great transformation. But I'm not really different after all. Your father's right. I never once understood what it would be for me to do the leaving. And that place I always wanted to escape comes now to ambush me and pull me back."

I looked away. I felt I would die before I got through this. "I wanted to be like you but I was wrong about that too. How can you love me when I'm trying so hard to become someone else? You would despise me, the one thing I couldn't bear."

The room filled with silence, the silence of dead illusions. He knew I was telling the truth. All we could do was stare at each other, strangers again. "I want to go home, Andreas. Maybe then I can find something stronger in my character … to live my life."

No more tears. We were beyond the comfort of tears.

28

Idyllic homecoming, another illusion shattered. All hell broke loose, the town criers relaying the gossip that landed before I did.

Got herself mixed up with some Greek, Greeks bearing gifts.

Fought in some kind of uprising.

Communist, likely.

Too big for her britches, that one.

Dad's fit to be tied.

Tougher'n a rattlesnake, her dad. He'll run him out of town faster'n you can say Jack Robinson.

Darn tootin'.

My pal Sam was hearing this talk out at Elmer's and up at Frankie's Café and the bowling alley.

"So what did you say?"

"I said it's all Greek to me."

"Very funny! Why didn't you stand up for me, tell them to mind their own business?"

"Because I don't know what you're up to either!" We were sitting on the curb outside my house. A light flashed in an upstairs bedroom across the street. "I hope this guy's worth all the grief he's causing."

"Who appointed you conscience of the world? One year of law school and now a know-it-all. Who asked you?"

"If I'm not mistaken, you did."

"Sam, if you've got an itch to preach, build yourself a church. Anyhow, this gossip's way out of date so you can tell them the town is safe from the Trojan Horse."

My father wasn't running anybody out of town unless it was me. Fit to be tied? You bet, as Jean would say. He knew I'd defied him. He was no fool about what I'd been up to either—his rapid response to my cable asking for money to get home told me that—but he would never confront it. Left unspoken, maybe it hadn't really happened. In that, he was one with Andreas' parents. During the long trek home, all twenty-three hours, counting layovers, I had not slept, consumed by the pain I had caused Andreas, my own pain, the pain of leaving Jean behind. I had booked a flight through Vienna, hoping to take a train into Switzerland to say goodbye. Twice I telephoned her mother, twice she refused to speak to me. Thayer's report was none too kind, I guessed, the crybaby with a lot to learn about quicksand.

I carried a note from Andreas crumpled in my hand. *I had nothing to offer you but myself and like any man I thought this was worth something because I had not offered it to anyone before. I didn't believe in foolish concepts, love, but you brought your innocence to me promising everything and with it came back my own. When you came to live in me you cleansed the hatred and in its place, when I stopped fighting you, was something so sweet it still has the power to surprise. How could I know I was walking into another prison, willingly this time, and that it would be more secure than any I had been in? It never occurred to me that I might be the one needing courage.*

It is half past ten and I am still in love with you but the bird has flown.

I had shot the bird out of the sky. All that was left was the idea of home. One look at the faces at the airport, my parents grim, my grandmother smiling gamely, and I knew I had miscalculated yet again. In the back seat of the car, my grandmother squeezed my knee reassuringly. We could do no wrong where she was concerned, not me or any of my cousins. She even faked a heart attack when my cousin Kitty ran off and got married, days after graduating from high school. When my father got wind of it, he barged in the front door shouting, "What's this nonsense I hear all over town?" scaring the daylights out of the housekeeper who ran out the back door, knocking over the ironing board. My grandmother, roused from her nap, came out of her bedroom. "Zachary, what on earth's gotten into you, raising Cain like this? Why, I do believe I'm having a heart attack," hand fluttering to her chest. That's how she saved Kitty, never another word on the subject.

The inquisition was held at the kitchen table. Any thought of confessing all and putting an end to the secrets and lies was quickly dispelled. I would never be able to tell about Andreas, the whole blistering experience, how the thought of them had been my solace that night riding into the desert. Or about Asif and General Jamal and how brave we had been, yes, both of us. Above all, I wanted to tell them about Jean, how much I needed their solace now.

"You deliberately disobeyed me, running off with that character." My father, tougher than a rattlesnake.

"I was going to bring him home."

"*Him!* Who you knew, what, for a few weeks? No man alive respects a woman of easy virtue."

"Dead ones do?"

He slammed the table, demanding an apology. "What were his prospects?"

"Have I missed something?" my grandmother interjected

sweetly. "Why are we talking prospects, are we getting him ready for the Kentucky Derby?" It was her husband who began the saying about thoroughbreds and fences.

"I don't think it's unreasonable to ask what they were going to live on," said my mother. "If we knew she was going to be so irresponsible, we would have thought twice about permitting her to go on this trip."

"He has talent and ambition. Anyhow, what difference? It's over."

"Ambition that began with marriage to you, getting his hands on an American passport."

"Christ! You too?"

"Sirrine! Your language." Despite this, my mother wanted to relent, I could tell from the expression on her face, but she didn't know how. "None of us has much experience with guerilla fighters, dear. I suppose he's a Communist too."

"Because he fought the British for the freedom of his country, this makes him a Communist?"

"Dear me, I've never met one of those!" My grandmother actually seemed disappointed. "Senator Joe would turn up his toes, all right." Senator Joe. Exactly how Andreas had referred to him.

"Time to be going, isn't it, Mother?"

The dagger her eyes delivered let him know she'd sooner crawl home than get in a car with the rattlesnake.

"Sirrine knows it's for her own good."

"Fiddlesticks!" She leaned on me as we walked to the door. "Ride it out," she whispered. "And don't forget, there's another heart attack left in me before the jig's up!" I heard her chuckling above the sound of the crickets all the way to the car.

29

I rode it out all right, out of town and straight to New York. It was all that prevented giving in to the despair that threatened to engulf me, the fear that anything I attempted now was sure to end badly. All was confusion. I saw omens everywhere, I saw Andreas everywhere. My haste to run from him turned into a regret so profound I was reeling. Over and over I questioned what I'd done, what I'd lost. Through lack of nerve (and, I suspected, an even greater lack of character, my love being so full of self-congratulation) had I given up that chance at transcendence I yearned for? That aliveness I so passionately felt? Had I sentenced myself to a life of dull compromise?

Hour after hour tormenting myself, remembering the lovemaking until it was seared into me, until it spilled over into my dreams from which I woke feverish and empty. One of those nights, unable to sleep, I thought *there's only one place for me now,* her door never locked, the light on the stand by her bed burning day and night, the radio on too, stations coming in from all over the South, from Memphis and Nashville and sometimes as far away as New Orleans.

"Sirry, is that you creeping around out there?"

"Yes."

"I thought so." My grandmother, swallowed up in the old Victorian bed with the fat scrolls rolling over the top, the bed my grandfather died in. The whole room smelling of Vicks and talcum powder.

"What time is it?" She reached for the alarm clock. "After midnight. Anyone at home know you've flown the coop?"

"No, I didn't make an announcement."

"No, spose not. Never mind, they'll figure it out." She drew back the covers and I snuggled in next to her. "It's Andreas, isn't it?"

"Yes."

"Eyesight goes, hearing goes, hunch comes along to compensate." How delicate to put it this way when I was as obvious as daylight.

"He seemed like the luckiest thing that could ever happen to me. I was so sure there was a purpose in it, both of us existing at the exact same moment in time, both of us on that ship of all the ships sailing around the seas of the world, me from the opposite side of the world. So much between us it seemed like a miracle. Then nothing at all, I couldn't hold on to it. Now it feels like the unluckiest thing that ever happened to me."

"Bad as that?"

"I loved him and I hurt him. How do I forgive myself?"

"Time takes care of that. He'll get over it." My grandmother put her arm around me. "You can't see this now, Sirrine, but we look back with sorrow, every last one of us. Then we pick up and go on."

"It's the whole point, isn't it? To remind us never to be too happy because sorrow's always there, waiting."

"Anybody tells you they know the whole point, don't you believe it. The meaning of this journey won't come clear till the end of it. If then. So many compromises to make along the road, only eternity can sort out which ones are worth it."

"But you're always sure about things."

"No, and wouldn't want to be. I never trust those people who go around saying they're sure, jaws set, determined not to let in a single unexpected grace. They're the ones lacking faith." She drew me closer. "Faith means carrying on without being so everlasting sure all the time."

We must have dozed, because the next thing I heard was the clock in the living room. I wasn't sure what hour it was chiming. My grandmother stirred too.

"I'm awfully thirsty," I said.

"All those tears!"

I hadn't given a thought before to my grandmother and tears. For the first time she seemed frail, lying alone in that big bed. I hurried into the kitchen.

"Bring some ginger ale while you're at it."

"I thought you were supposed to cut down on sweets."

"Fiddlesticks! All those quacks know is what *not* to do."

When I came back, she said, "Tell me about Sam. You know there's worse to look for from a man than friendship, a little comfort. Like coming home, that's how I always thought of it."

We had spent the day together. I was in the backyard when Sam came by, leaning out the car window, calling, "C'mon, let's go to the river, it's a nice day for a change." It had been unusually chilly, Andreas would have called it winter. He crossed the lawn and pulled me to my feet, a newly forceful, grown-up Sam. "Get your bathing suit, you can't mope around here all day!"

With a giddy burst, like a kid playing hooky from school, I did as he said. It was twelve miles to the river on a gravel road that wound down through the hills, so it took longer than twelve miles might suggest. Still, Sam often drove it in less than half an hour. Not today. Today we were happy to poke along, sun streaming in, grass humming in the heat, fat clouds shuffling aimlessly along their own highway.

"I suppose you won't be sticking around." His eyes stayed fixed on the road.

I didn't answer.

"Any damn fool can see you're miserable."

Again, no answer.

"You told me once to butt out. Guess I don't need a second time." Johnny Cash on the radio was reminding us how up against it life can get when you're not even paying attention. Sam switched it off and lit a cigarette, offered me one, punched in the lighter a second time. I caught it as it popped, the ritual oddly comforting. I looked at his profile, the strong, clean lines. Why couldn't I fall in love with him? It would be so simple. Or was there too much familiarity, too much that lacked mystery?

"Have you told your parents all this weird shit you got yourself mixed up in?"

"You kidding? They'd lock me up. Didn't tell about Jean either. I wanted to. Get rid of one guilt, another rises up to take its place."

"Screw guilt! I'm sorry, I know how you believed in him." Sure I was going to cry, he pulled over to the side of the road and put his arm around me. "Sirry, if it was meant to be …"

"Bullshit. I don't believe in any 'meant to be.' Just lets you off the hook."

I looked out at fields thick with corn and hay stretching as far as the ridge, flatness broken only by silos (Midwestern minarets!) before yielding to the far-off hills toppling one by one all the way down to the river. Our river. By the time we reached the top of the ridge, up where we could see through the notch to the blue of water in the distance, we were delirious with expectation. A few months more and those hills would be on fire with color. Fall again, time to go away again.

"Sometimes I wish I'd never left."

"But you've gone farther from this town than anybody!"

"And what was the point? To get a glimpse of something

only to find I couldn't choose it. I wanted to change my life. I changed nothing."

"The point is you did it, that's all. And will always see things differently."

"While *they* stay the same, prejudices intact."

"Listen, you're always preaching tolerance, why not try some? Your parents were scared, that's all." He rode the steering wheel, fiddled with the lighter. "I know it's not a good time right now, but I can't help wondering if …"

I leaned over and kissed him lightly on the cheek. "I've done enough damage, Sam. I'd like to understand a few things before I give myself to someone again."

He turned away and the very air stopped breathing. But when he turned back he was smiling. "Let's get up to the ridge where we can see the blue."

"And dip my toes in. One last time." What I said every time and knew it would never be true. As my grandmother predicted, the river always brought me back again.

"We spent the day together," I told her now, climbing back into bed beside her. "Like coming home, you said. Is that how it was with you?"

"Yes. I don't know what you remember of your grandfather, such a long time ago." She took a sip of ginger ale and settled herself on the pillows.

"I remember how he looked sitting on his horse, the smell of his pipe, how he used to tinker with that old car, the one with the rumble seat Kitty and I loved to ride in. I can hear his voice, how gentle it was."

"His gifts were quiet ones. I'm thankful I found the silence in myself, finally, to hear. I was a lot like you. Headstrong, near thirty before I married—one foot in spinsterhood, the other in the grave, for those days." She laughed. "But I fooled 'em. No one seemed right until he came along, and then it seemed like peace was declared all over the world and I was safe at last."

Her breathing changed. Fast asleep. I nestled in closer, listening to the music struggling through static from one of those faraway places down the river, country and blues, lyrics heavy on heartbreak.

PART EIGHT

Jean

30

In New York and desperate to have a job and the financial independence it would mean, I took the first one offered, at a small publishing house, a cut above a typing pool at eighty dollars a week. We didn't get on well in the beginning, New York and I. My mother understood and tried to warn me. Despite the sympathy I thought she displayed at the conclusion of the dining table inquisition, she had said nothing. I was no longer the apple of anyone's eye, that was clear. On the contrary, all the dire prophecies uttered over the years were fulfilled—I had overdone it, I had most certainly jumped the fence—so it was a surprise when she came to me in my room as I was putting the last odds and ends into a suitcase.

"I'm glad you're going away to make something of yourself, Sirrine. Just be on guard against asking too much of life. You do tend to get carried away."

"Oh, Mom, isn't it *you* we're talking about?"

"It's a question of ... you've had so much choice, perhaps too much. Try to grasp how it was in the Depression, everything shutting down, a future imposed more than chosen. I was after a different kind of life. Then I met your father. It didn't seem like giving anything up, at first. Call it my failing, but yes, I wanted a bigger world, I never could get used to this one. God knows I tried."

For once I didn't protest, didn't cry out, *What about Dad? What about me?* All of it existed together, I realized. No one thing canceled out the other.

My mother had more to say. "It begins a niggling little thing, a shadow that comes to sit on your shoulder any old time of day, when you're walking down the street or reading, playing the piano, or doing something as innocent as putting wash on the line or clearing the table, it hounds you, and it builds and builds until before you know it this desolation swallows the rest." Dante's dark wood.

I poked around in my suitcase so she wouldn't know I saw her tearing up. I heard the defiance in her voice. "I'm glad you're going, with or without your father's blessing."

If only I could have thrown my arms around her, kept her there talking, but I knew that if I drew near, she would find an excuse to withdraw. She did anyway. Maybe one day we will have that conversation, I thought. (We never did.) *Thank you for not holding me here*, I whispered after her, thinking of Jean and The Countess.

Like my mother, I had trouble getting used to the world I was in. Manhattan seemed dreary, bereft of intensity, none of the blatant emotion, even an afternoon with that gang of rascals in Alex, so exasperating at the time, would have been cherished. Walking the streets, men and women scurrying past, talking of nothing at all, of stocks and bonds and summer rentals, nothing of interest to me anyway, poles apart, in every sense, from where I had been. Wanting to stop them and say, *Listen while I tell you about islands rising from the sea and about people dreaming of oranges.* Coming to terms with regret, the hemlock of Dr. Thanos, thinking about Eve and the wheel going round once more, wondering if she would have gone back into the garden given the choice and what might have been revealed to me had I chosen differently.

When the sky was so blue it ached, I was back in an instant, in Athens or on the island. I would turn expecting to see Andreas, to feel his touch. I would turn to speak to him but there was no one. Not a day went by when I did not remember him. This went on for a long and anguished time.

31

A letter from Jean. Shock at how much I missed her, the only one who could possibly understand the tyranny of memory, my sense of loss. What happiness to know where she was finally, where I could go to be with her. I would make up for my absence. I would send her journal to her and funny cards to make her laugh and lighthearted descriptions of what life was like in her city—even if I had to borrow them from someone else.

Her handwriting looked like that of a monk working over a manuscript or a child in an old copybook, letters large and meticulously formed. *She wants to make a garden for you. She has drawn a butterfly. Called it Margaret.* Third person. Again.

Right there, in the lobby of my building, by the bank of mailboxes, the doorman in a fit of coughing, pretending not to notice, I lost it. Wailing, wailing into the elevator, into the apartment. What a grand sense of adventure we had started out with, how much we had gone through, to end up like this? One mad, the other mad with regret. No, I would not be sending the journal after all. If the doctors got hold of it, they would judge it to be, what? Delusional? I could have sent an affidavit. My father knew all about them. Hers too. Patient not hallucinating, what you read herein is the truth and nothing but. *Habeas mentis*. Don't bother with the *corpus*, not implicated. Names not changed to protect the innocent because we have no fucking idea who they are. If any.

I answered the letter, doing my best to make her city, now

mine, sound appealing, a place she might like to return to some day.

That fall President Kennedy was assassinated. All over the world people entered into the country of my grief, all those who had revered him wherever we went, who had saluted and raised a glass and chanted his name, who had welcomed us because of him and whose hopes died with him too. That November day in Dallas—the brutality of it, the rumors, the conspiracy theories, the murder of the murderer in police custody, all of it as shocking as anything Jean and I had read about in those files in Beirut or anything we had been through or witnessed. Such things happened *over there*. Not anymore.

At the turn of the year I had a letter from Andreas' mother, telling of conflict on the island at Christmas. He had come home. Beside herself with worry—"whispers of ships coming from Turkey"—she pleaded with me to write to him and tell him to go back to Athens. I didn't do it. I had meddled enough in his life.

A decade later the ships did come. Turkey invaded Cyprus. Once more, prophecies fulfilled. The island was divided, the town of Famagusta sealed off in the Turkish sector, as it remains to this day, Andreas' family refugees in their own country. I did not think his father could have survived this but by then I had lost touch. I had not lost my ability to grieve for them.

Within months, Jean was writing fast and furiously and what a difference. Talking about herself in the first person, droll comments sounding like the Jean of old. If ever I knew who that was. She said how much she missed me. *It seems forever since I saw you and yet again it seems as though you have just gone out to buy some cigarettes and that you will be opening that door any minute. Which is it? It is hard for me to have you so far.*

Exactly what I was feeling. Almost two years since I had

asked Thayer to come for her on that grey winter morning in Munich. My life was changing too. I recovered laughter. I started dating, although this did not begin well. On the first attempt, I excused myself to go to the restroom and kept on walking, right out the door and home. What a farce. This is how alienated I felt. It did not endear me to the friend who had arranged it.

General Jamal did come to New York, not once but several times, emotional reunions made more so by drinking into the wee hours, listening to lugubrious Russian folk songs that musicians in the bar of the Volney Hotel near my apartment favored after midnight. When I told him what had happened with Jean, he was irate, so upset—stupid godmothers, stupid doctors, stupid friend meaning me—I was afraid he'd go back to Jordan and plan a commando raid to free her. I seem to remember the two of us plotting one. On several of these trips he was with King Hussein. Alas, we were not destined to meet then either.

The Countess wrote to me too. She lived not far away, on a block I assiduously avoided. She'd forgiven me, it seemed, if indeed she had ever blamed me. "Jean talks about going to Thailand to meditate with nuns," she said in one letter. "I never knew Buddhists went in for nuns, did you, Sirrine? Seems they live in a temple in a place called Ayudhya. Do they cook their rice right there in the temple, do you think? Shave their heads like monks? You don't suppose she's gone looking for the King of Siam, do you?"

I could see her smile. And hear her sigh, "Will there never be an end to this searching?" What would she say if she knew what we had gone through looking for that other king, the King of Jordan.

Then, out of the blue, she was on the phone. Early March, the middle of the night. Some things never change. "Guess what, they've sprung me!" She started to sing, I recognized the first few bars of "Stranger in Paradise."

I was wide awake. "Oh, Jean. Oh, my God, is it really true?"

"Do you know what that's from, that song? A show called *Kismet*."

"Means fate, doesn't it?"

"Or destiny. In one of those languages in a part of the world we've been known to frequent."

"Could explain a few things." We laughed. Oh, how we laughed. "Where are you? I got a letter from The Countess. Something about Thailand."

"Countess no more. Deposed."

"Are we letting her keep her head? Oops … sorry, that slipped out."

"Didn't think of it that way but sure, she's not dangerous, not anymore, not to me."

"Glad to hear it. How are they, your parents?"

"Bound for all eternity, bad karma be damned. So good luck to them." Jealousy playing a hand here?

"So what is this business about Thailand?"

"Throwing them off the scent."

"*Jean!* Haven't we had enough of secrecy?" And deceit, I almost added.

"I'm thinking of becoming a Buddhist, seriously, but ask me again next month. No, look, the truth is I can't see anybody until I'm stronger, least of all them. I don't want them to know where I am for a while."

"Which is where, dare I ask?"

"Paris. Perfecting the language of love. As every Frenchman hastens to assure me. Though I never seem to be in a position, as it were, to use it. Afraid of the whole messy business."

"Still?"

"Still. And you?"

"Getting over it."

"Still? Then come here. I don't think we can stir up too much trouble—if we stay away from the Middle East. We're not dumb enough to pull that one again, are we?"

I had lost any appetite for travel. Yet it seemed right that having missed Europe we should at least see Paris together. I couldn't wait to be with her again. Besides, I could use the diversion. My grandmother had been ill. Although she rallied, the prognosis was not good, she might not have that heart attack left in her before the jig was up.

32

Paris. I flew at the end of March. Jean had a room in one of those small rues off the Boulevard St. Michel—*Boul Meeche* as we so smartly said—and was registered at the Sorbonne. We could have lunch there every day for a few francs, like our scams of old.

In the foyer of her building, an old woman in a tobacco-stained smock came out of a hole in the wall, muttering and pointing a bony finger at the stairs. *Quatrième étage*. Alarmed at how nervous I was, I climbed, heart racing, excitement like that of meeting a lover, like meeting Andreas. In Europe, so close to him. That stab of memory—the sound of his voice, each syllable plump in his mouth, soft as a kiss, how I wanted to hear words spoken like that but never did in the Greek restaurants I haunted for a time on Ninth Avenue.

She was on the landing. I couldn't see her clearly, washed as she was in light from the window behind her. I clung to the familiar figure, unwilling to let go. She grabbed her coat off the bed, same shabby old trench coat—I hadn't given mine up either—and we hurried out to a café near St. Séverin, the church with columns in the apse that look like a temple in Luxor. Sitting across from me she looked rested, at peace, no mark of what must have been a harrowing experience. And she had hair! Short and *très* chic. *Très* French. Eyes, the same piercing gaze. Same underlying sadness, too, but so beautiful. I could let go of that last terrible image of her.

I covered her hand with mine, for a few minutes able to speak only her name. *Jean, oh, Jean*. "I've thought so often about what this would be like … seeing your face, being together again." I bit my lip, pressing back the tears waiting to spring.

"Yes, me too."

"Listen, I … I don't know how to begin this. I mean we should talk about it, shouldn't we? We have so much to talk about. That place? They didn't … I mean, like your mother. Did they?"

"Fry me? No, nothing so dramatic as that. Drugs. Then a new one, which seemed to do the trick. Stuffed me full of vitamins, too, very keen on vitamins, the Swiss. Guess what? They made me gain weight!" She opened her coat, a flasher. "Even grew boobs. Sort of."

She had. Sort of.

"And exercise. Great believers in sound body, sound mind. The Greek ideal, you remember. Oops, sorry."

"It's okay. I'm not that tender about him." A lie.

"They embarrass you out of your excesses, bully you into behaving. Well, we know it isn't as simple as that. Forgive me, I can't really talk about it, Sirry. Not yet."

"But if we tried. To simplify, I mean. Do you comprehend it, what happened?"

"Some. Losing my mother, her illness, how awful it was to watch her go into her tailspins, watch her slip away, somewhere I couldn't follow. Identifying too much, way too much. Feeling helpless, blaming myself. I couldn't save her, I couldn't save them. Most of all wanting a place to belong, finding the doors closed …" Ticking off items on a checklist. But not quite.

"We learned well, didn't we? How to play the blame game. Too bad they don't give prizes, we'd be rich." I asked what the other patients were like. Had she made any friends?

"There were women whose husbands wanted to get rid of

them. Park them in a nuthouse while they romp around Europe with their mistresses. There were women who were unfaithful, because if you're unfaithful you're obviously off your rocker. What other explanation?"

"That's a little cynical, no?" Although I once read something similar in an article about patients in Payne Whitney.

"The world's a little cynical, no?"

My hand was shaking as I poured a packet of sugar into my coffee. "Are you angry with me, still? About Andreas? All of it?"

She looked out at the tree-lined square. "No. Yes. Sure, I wanted him too. You knew that. I didn't know how to handle it—those feelings all of a sudden. I was left out, not only the two of you, everybody. You knew that too. I didn't seem to catch on, how it was supposed to work, then I got caught up with Asif. When I heard how it ended between you, by that time it had become my dream too, strange as that sounds. I cried."

"You weren't alone."

"Bad?"

"Yes. The canvas wiped clean, nothing where all the bright colors had been. Nothing to guide me, what was right, what wrong, wanting to make sense of it. Finally, just wishing to be innocent again. No more hurt, that remorse. It was too much—not just him, everything we'd been through. Jesus Christ! When you think about it, what the hell were we supposed to *do* with it? Try dropping any of that into a conversation about the weather. Then I'm back with Sam, sitting on the curb at midnight in that little town as if nothing happened. Except it did happen. Andreas was gone. You were gone, I didn't know where."

At last the chance to say this to her, the one person who would understand. "I didn't trust my instincts. I'd lost the one man who could challenge me to be *alive*, who loved my sensuality. Men are threatened by that, you know, they don't even have to be

Catholic." I left out the part about suspecting the best of life was at an end, that all that remained was the memory of what I had (almost) become—with him. That being sensible meant you missed out and what came afterward was only a coda.

"I didn't believe in anything the way I once did. Certainly didn't believe in love—you can fool yourself but you can't lie, not about that. A delusion. Like Alexandria. Like characters in a play Andreas was writing."

"Whoa, now who's being cynical? He loved you, plain as the nose on your face."

"Did he?" I didn't want to acknowledge the suspicion that we needed her to complete the triangle, reminding me I'd won. Driven by desire, impulsive, I'd run roughshod over everyone.

"Jean, look, I … I should have stayed out of it. I should have let you have him."

"Dammit! Haven't you learned anything? Don't you see how arrogant … I didn't want your cast-offs! I don't now!"

"I don't mean it that way. I wanted so much and I didn't know what I needed to do—what I needed to *be*. I was too timid to make the leap." I stopped fighting the tears. "I failed the test. I hate admitting it."

"We both failed. If it makes you feel any better."

"You had courage."

"Courage! I was *nuts*. I don't know that it counts."

"You believed in him. Jean, you did. Don't get ironic on me again."

"A little grandiose, wasn't it? In retrospect."

What I had once thought. No longer. "You got involved in something meaningful."

"Got unmoored, you mean!"

We giggled at the pun, then laughed until our sides ached, raucous, and people in the café staring in disapproval.

"Our Moor was always quoting some ancient proverb or other, remember?" she said when we recovered. "One that I keep thinking about: *We learn wisdom from the blind for they don't take a step until they've tried the way*. Could be a good one for us to adopt."

"There's more than one way to be blind," I reminded her. "But what was going on with him? I've gone over and over it. Surely now we can say it out loud, tell the truth."

The all too familiar faraway look, the gaze, came over her.

"Jean, I read somewhere … one rumor keeps cropping up … King Hussein meeting with the Israelis. Covertly. Why, I don't know, seeking help with the Palestinian refugees? Did that have something to do with it?"

"The truth has nothing to do with what happened." What was that supposed to mean? She might as well have answered in Arabic. Another of their proverbs? Or was she simply saying what I had been trying to all along?

And then she said, "The scream you heard, at the checkpoint. They told me he was dead, showed a picture, someone sprawled in a pool of blood. Claimed it was Asif."

"Good God! No wonder you …"

"No, Sirrine, that wasn't it at all. You live with secrets long enough, you begin to believe almost anything. Or nothing. About Asif, I was pretty sure. So, no, that wasn't it. Besides, I was strong enough to deal with that. What I wasn't strong enough for—not then, probably not ever—was taking on The Countess. She wasn't like a mother, she was more like a lover. *Seductive*. Even with me. This was the trap. All the candy in the store and I gorged on it, greedy for it—for the attention. I confused it with love. The golden child whose mother couldn't live without her. It was perfect, we shut out everything else so it was just the two of us. We shut out my father. No room, no sympathy. What we did was cruel, we forced him into that corner where he stayed. The only way he knew to survive was drink.

"But when the chips were down, when I was in that place in Switzerland, *nothing*. Not a word, not for months. What had I done, that she would turn against me? It was all right for her to crack up but not the golden child. You see why I envied you? Your life wasn't all tangled up like mine, you had enough to hang on to. I never once hoped it would be different because I knew better. Every morning I got up in the world, I knew this was not a safe family to be in."

And went out and found something truly unsafe!

"I … I guess it was her illness," I said lamely. The Countess had seduced me too. I was anxious to absolve everyone. I thought of my own mother, had she felt shut out that way by my father and me? I followed Jean's gaze to the window, noticing how the wind had picked up, how it was pushing sheets of rain across the square.

"So where were we, back at that checkpoint, right?"

"Yeah," I said, thinking we should stay at this one longer, to try to understand. "But why didn't you tell me, that much at least? I mean what they threatened had been done to him. To Asif."

"I was afraid we wouldn't keep going, we'd lose our nerve."

She meant me, of course. I always knew she thought I would chicken out. I wasn't angry, not now. It was something I had been part of, however unwilling, or unwitting, that had lasting significance—redeeming significance. At least I hoped it did. And I was proud of it. I was proud of her. I would never again know anyone who would take such a risk, who would trust the word of one person and because of that leap of faith—*faith*, of all things—save lives? She believed she could change something. Optimism in that—probably what had pulled her through.

She lit a cigarette, fanning away smoke as she exhaled. I raised an eyebrow. Weren't we cured of our old addictions?

"C'mon, they had to let us keep some bad habits! Wouldn't want us climbing the walls over insignificant shit like this. Think about it." She dropped the lighter on the table. "I'm still in touch with him, Sirry. Have been for a while. He's going to London, an operation on his feet." She inhaled deeply. "That's not all that's wrong."

The delicacy with which she said it, the tone of voice … I knew it could only be about sex. Something psychological? Plenty of irony there—her fear, his fierce masculinity, caught in stalemate. *Tiger kissing a gazelle*. Once again the Phoenicians got it right.

"He told you this?"

"In so many words." We retreated into our own thoughts.

"What will you do now?" I asked finally.

"He wants me to come back to Beirut. Really nuts if I do that, right?" I had no answer, if it was indeed a question. "One of the doctors kept asking: 'Why did you go there, of all places?' How could I explain? That hothouse we were in, the nuns, Durrell, the book. That I needed to do something to exist. But that wasn't even the crazy part, was it? Because I did feel free in the desert in some weird way, not so cut off, so apart. Or maybe in that vast space we're all cut off and apart. All I know is that I would have gone to hell and back to get away from what I saw in the mirror."

She grinned. "Hey, wait a minute, maybe that's it! All the time looking for meaning and it's nothing more than life with the Bedouin and no mirrors!" I wasn't ready to concede the point, remembering too well what that had been like.

"Sirry, you have to admit, it was pretty amazing in the desert, those sunsets."

"Sunsets? Frankly, I don't even remember them. But sure,

sitting here in a cozy corner of Paris with our café crème, the best bread in the world, butter to inspire poetry. So why couldn't you hold on to it?"

"I don't know. Same reason you couldn't hold on to Andreas?"

"No, I told you why. What I haven't told you is how jealous I was, always. It wasn't the same thing, it wasn't any idyll of growing up with Granny and Sam I was after. I wanted whatever you had. And I never thought twice about whether I really wanted it, never got that far. Never thought twice about taking it away from you either." On this, I was determined to make a full confession.

"Jean, how could I ever tell what the hell was real? Competing, so determined to win, how could I ever be sure I had one legitimate feeling?"

"Aren't we being a little harsh?"

"Think of it like a vaccine. Repeat often enough, chances are good it'll prevent another outbreak."

"So what now?"

I told her that Sam was asking me to marry him. And accused her of sounding like somebody's Aunt Bertha when she said it sounded right. "You don't even know him."

"You talked about him enough times. It seems sensible."

"*Sensible!* I'm beginning to hate that word."

"Hey, don't knock it, it's a gift. Me, I'm different. It's okay, I accept it, so long as I don't have to get unhinged again."

"Oh, Jean." I brought her hand to my cheek, held it there, kissed it. "We didn't have a clue, did we?"

"No. But this is where we came in, isn't it?" She chucked me playfully under the chin. "Know what? We may have peaked a little too soon."

When we could stop laughing, I told her that I had

promised him I'd think about it. "That's all. I've done enough harm with my promises."

"C'mon, you've lost your touch! You can do better than that to complicate it!"

We talked like this for a while, went on to other things, my work, the rift with my father just beginning to heal, then back to Sam again. I told her that I knew it wouldn't be, I'd taken an irretrievable step away from him too.

"Do you regret … any of it?"

"No. I don't know … maybe not anymore. Except hurting Andreas, hurting you. I will always, always regret that."

"And you?"

"No. But we're only twenty-four. Let's check back in a few years."

The morning before I was flying home, we woke to find that spring had come, overnight. We could hear it. We could certainly see it, sun shining, pigeons basking on the windowsill where the milk was already turning sour. Spring was late, slashing rain every day I had been there, the kind of weather that made even Paris dismal and grey.

On the stairs, Jean hitched her arm in mine. "You know what? I think we should skip all this, if you don't mind, all this soul grinding. I vote we go out there and be normal for a change."

"Think they'll have us?"

We emerged from the cocoon of our winters, leaving dirty trench coats behind, walking with faces turned up, soaking in warmth. We walked all over Paris that day, through the Luxembourg Gardens and along St. Germain to Ile St. Louis, splurging on strawberry tarts, up through Place des Vosges and the Marais and on to the Tuileries, encouraging the mimes, across almost as far as the Bois de Boulogne, arms linked still. Happy again, friends again. This much had endured, would endure, as long as we were alive. On our way home we passed a jazz club featuring Memphis Slim, an American singing the blues. We'd treat ourselves, we decided. We'd get all gussied up, as Jean said and go hear him.

We walked along the Seine in the pink light of evening before turning into the narrow and by then darkened streets just off of it, to Le Chat Qui Pêche. The Cat Who Fishes. At the end of the last set, Memphis Slim got up from the piano and came over to us. He was a big man with a kind face, skin tawny and smooth like the Egyptians, like Andreas after a summer in the sun. Before any time at all, because he asked what we were doing there, where we'd been, we were pouring out the story of what had happened to us in Beirut and Amman and the desert.

He listened without a word. When we finished, he tilted back his chair, shaking his head. Then, in that deep, rumbling preacher voice of his, he said, "So you've been on the other side of the river. If my mama heard tell you crossed that River Jordan, she'd say you'd died and gone to heaven. Yes, she would."

His big hands covered ours. "Amen."

Amen.

Acknowledgments

So much gratitude to Nicole Parker King and Mick Wieland for getting this show on the road with style.

And to the indelible characters met along the way, some of whom wrote themselves into these pages.

Thank you to generous readers Paula Andros, Gerri Bowman, the late Richard de Combray, Stacey Farley, Sheila Geoghegan, Natascha Hildebrandt, Suellen Knight, Isabelle Laurenzi, Turi MacCombie, Marya Meyer, Jean Patnode, Annabelle Rinehart, Maryann Syrek and Joan Turner. Thank you also to Beverley Zabriskie, and especially to Peggy Healy who has constantly urged me on.

About the Author

Marcelline Thomson is a writer with wanderlust who explored realms unknown through books before traveling the world beyond her small Midwest town. Not a long leap, then, for a book to inspire an adventure. Thomson, who has lived in Bangkok, Beirut and London, settled down long enough to become a managing director of a major corporate and financial public relations firm in New York City. Recently she collaborated on two popular books, *Entertaining Friends: Easy Does It with 101 Rules of Thumb* and *Entertaining Houseguests: 101 Rules of Thumb for Host and Guest.* She has a B.A. from Manhattanville College and did graduate work in Middle East Area Studies at New York University. She lives with her husband, also a writer, in Manhattan and the Hudson Valley.

Made in United States
North Haven, CT
11 August 2022